A
WITCH
AND HER
MINOTAUR

A
WITCH
AND HER
MINOTAUR

Cover Design: Enchanted Ink Publishing
Editing: Enchanted Ink Publishing
Book Design and Typesetting: Enchanted Ink Publishing

The text type was set in Garamond Premier Pro

ISBN: 978-1-7326782-8-6 (Paperback)

Thank you for your support of the author's rights.

Instagram: @emberlywyndham

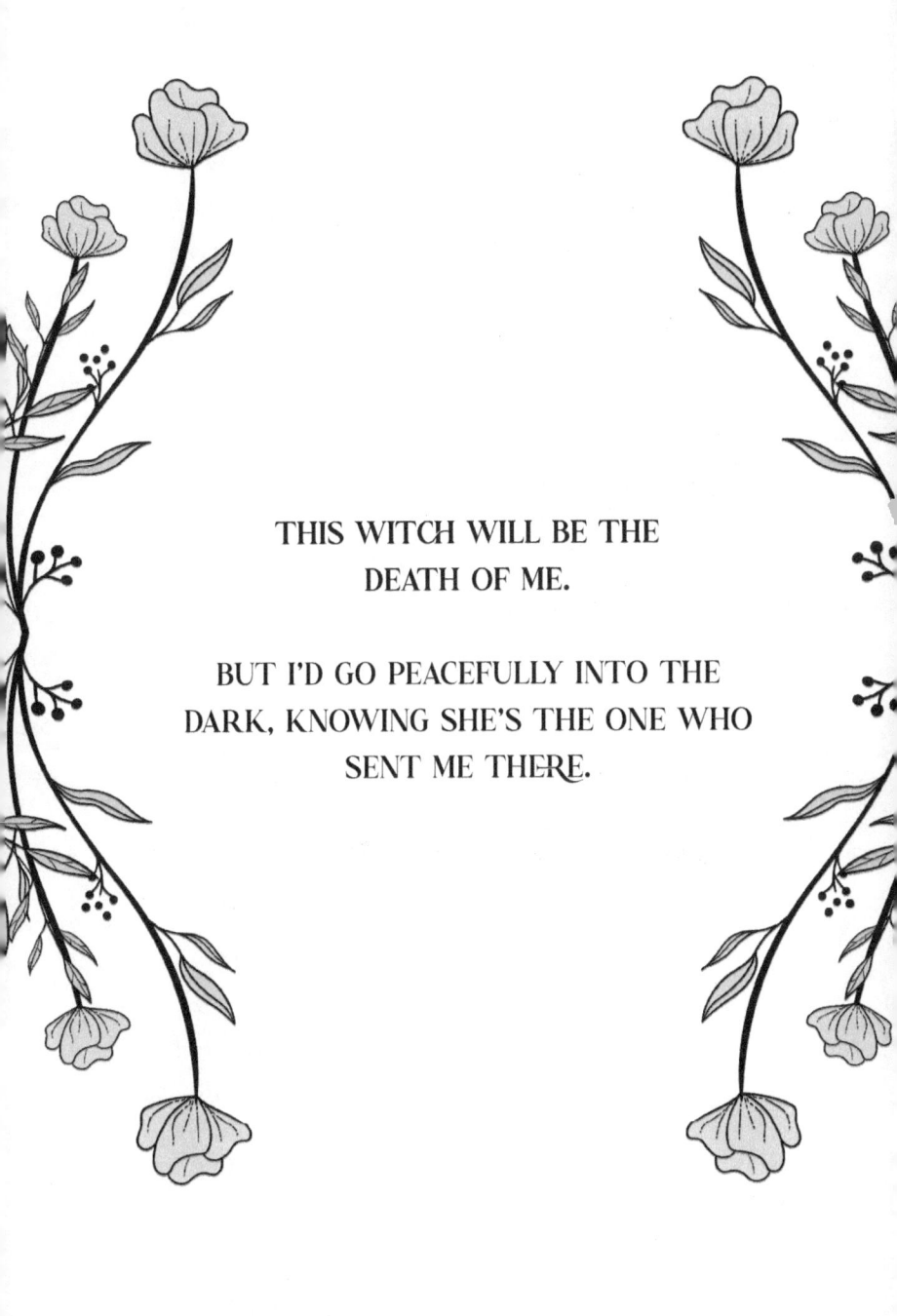

THIS WITCH WILL BE THE
DEATH OF ME.

BUT I'D GO PEACEFULLY INTO THE
DARK, KNOWING SHE'S THE ONE WHO
SENT ME THERE.

EMBERLY WYNDHAM

A
WITCH
AND HER
MINOTAUR

COVEN CREST ACADEMY

2

CHAPTER 1
LYRA

EARLY-AUTUMN SUNLIGHT BEATS DOWN ON THE glass greenhouse, turning the air an almost insufferable blend of sweltering and muggy. My forehead is damp with perspiration, and my hair sticks to the back of my neck, making me even more irritable as I try to painstakingly pluck weeds from a raised bed of midnight lotus flowers without damaging their extremely delicate petals and root systems.

I pinch a small—but formidable—weed between my forefinger and thumb and tug. Nothing happens.

Going to be difficult, huh?

I tug again. The weed holds fast.

My brow furrows, and a touch of heat goes through me as my irritation mounts.

For the life of me, I have no idea why I opted to take Exotic Flora as my elective this semester. I don't even like flowers and plants that much.

Oh, wait.

My eyes cut across the greenhouse to one of my roommates, Alina Ravenscroft.

The princess has her long blue hair braided back from her face, and she's intently studying a cluster of pink-veined flowers—I can't remember their name. Her knight and fated mate, Raelan Ashvale, stands outside the greenhouse. I glower at the back of his head as the breeze outside tousles his tunic. I wish I could open a window. I'm about to melt into a puddle in here.

The other students don't seem to be struggling quite as much as I am. Some are even wearing their academy-appointed robes still, seeming unbothered by the heat. My fire magic keeps me a comfortable temp even in the cold, but it also makes me overheat easily. And right now, I'm about to self-combust.

As if to punctuate my discomfort, a bead of sweat runs down my back.

So gross. All I want is a cold bath.

I tear my gaze away from Raelan and focus once more on my mortal enemy: the damn weed.

Yet again, I give it a tug. And yet again, it resists me with herculean strength.

With a scowl and a flare of irritation, I grab a garden trowel from the cart beside me, jab it into the soil, and pry the weed out of the bed.

And accidentally uproot an entire midnight lotus flower in the process.

The plant—beautiful and exotic and more delicate than a soap bubble—lies atop the garden soil, its petals already starting to lose their lustrous gleam as it withers before my very eyes.

I wasn't supposed to do that. Professor Fleur already warned me to be careful, and my grade in this class isn't looking good, even this early in the semester.

Maybe that's because I'm a fire witch. I don't have any business being in a garden, especially around baby-soft plants that die if you so much as look at them the wrong way.

"Ouch," says a student next to me. I don't know his name. I don't care to. "Murdered another one, huh? You're savage, Wilder."

He and his friend laugh.

The midnight lotus continues to wilt.

Another drop of sweat goes down my back.

I hate this.

And suddenly, my hands are smoking. The next thing I know, they've gone up in flames from my fingertips to my wrists, and the dying midnight lotus is already smoldering, caught too close to my sparks.

It happens almost before I can blink.

The fire leaps from one flower to the next, growing, smoking, chewing up each and every delicate petal in its path.

"Shit!" the boy next to me snaps, jumping back from the raised bed and lifting an arm to shield his face as if that'll protect him from the flames.

I reach out a hand, trying to calm the flames, to coax them into submission, but they don't listen to me. They *never* listen to me. I'm just their conduit.

All I succeed in doing is sending out another burst of fire, and the other students working around this raised bed yelp and jump away, their frightened expressions painted in red and orange from my flickering flames.

Now the whole bed of exotic plants is burning.

"Professor!" someone yells. I don't know who. It doesn't matter. It's not like our professor *wasn't* going to notice. I'm never that lucky.

All I can do is watch as the flames demolish every living thing in their path. And it's already too late when Alina sends a burst of frost dancing across my flames, smothering them in cold. She successfully puts out the fire—impressive, considering she struggles with her magic almost as much as I struggle with mine—but what's left behind can't be saved.

"Miss Wilder!" Professor Fleur whips around the end of the bed, a mixture of anger, horror, and grief twisting her delicate features. The other students step away from me, giving me a wide berth, like they're afraid to be associated with the impulsive fire witch who leaves nothing but ash in her path.

I get it. I don't want to be associated with me either.

Against my chest, tucked inside my white button-down, my spirit companion, Juniper, shifts, climbing up to peek over my collar to see what I've done.

At least she's still here with me. No matter how many times I mess up, she's still my friend. Her warm furry body gives me comfort, even if I'm still burning up from the sun and the stifling air and now my flames and the smoking remains of Professor Fleur's pretty little flowers.

The professor whirls around to face me. Her dark cheeks flare with a touch of red, and her pale green eyes go misty. These flowers are her babies; I get it. So I also get it when she seethes, "Kindly take yourself to the headmistress's office. *Now.*"

Over the professor's shoulder, Alina frowns, her forehead furrowed.

"Sorry," she mouths at me.

But this isn't her fault. It's mine. Like always.

I grab my academy robe—trimmed in yellow now that I'm a second-year—and stride from the greenhouse amidst stares and whispers from my fellow classmates. It makes my skin crawl, and I resist the urge to scrunch my shoulders up to my ears in shame, opting instead to lift my chin and stalk past them as if their words and sharp expressions don't leave wounds in their wake.

Shoving the door to the greenhouse open, I'm greeted by a chill breeze, and it immediately cools the sweat snaking down my back. Raelan looks down at me, one brow arched quizzically.

"Don't ask," I snap.

His expression doesn't change. "Okay, I won't."

Now that he and Alina are *together* together—as in she wears his shifter claiming mark like her most prized diamond necklace and told us that she's going to *marry* him once we graduate—Raelan has become a lot more talkative, and he's not nearly so cold and stoic. He's actually *fun* to be around . . . sometimes. But I don't feel like talking right now, even to him.

I start across the exterior gardens, and Raelan calls out, "You've got some dirt on your face."

With a grumble, I angrily reach up to scrub it away with the heel of my palm. At the same time, Juniper wriggles around and climbs up onto my shoulder, where she hides herself beneath my messy curls.

"Are you okay?" she asks. If anyone else were to hear her, they'd just hear little rat chirps and chattering. Witches can communicate with their own spirit companions, but not with anyone else's.

"I'm fine." My loafers strike the stone as I ascend the stairs to the side entrance into Coven Crest Academy. Another witch—a first-year, judging by her blue-trimmed robe—is just exiting the building and squeaks in surprise as I shoulder past her and into the cool hallways of the academy.

"You're not," Juniper says. She knows me too well to be so easily tricked.

But I'm not in the mood to talk about it.

Though I'm pretty sure Headmistress Moonhart isn't going to give me the option to say no.

THIS ISN'T MY FIRST TIME IN THE HEADMISTRESS'S office. It's not even my second. Last time I was in here, it was for very nearly burning the library down. That was a close call. My nerves still spike when I think of how close I came to destroying everything.

Headmistress Moonhart sits at her wide mahogany desk, a thin pair of spectacles perched upon her nose. She draws a quill across a piece of parchment, the scratch of the sharp tip meeting with the ticking of the clock standing atop the mantel and the low crackle of flames from the hearth. The big windows let in bright yellow-gold sunlight, and leaves twirl past the glass, caught in an autumn breeze. A thin strand of smoke twines from a lit stick of sage sitting on the desk.

Seated in a chair across the desk from the headmistress, I knot my fingers in my lap and try not to let my leg bounce like crazy. Juniper shifts inside the pocket of my robe, which I'm now wearing despite the warmth in the office. Thought it would better my chances if I at least tried to make myself look presentable, though I can feel how frizzy my curly hair is from the mugginess in the greenhouse. Nothing to be done about it now.

With a quick flourish, the headmistress signs her name on the parchment, then gives it a moment to dry before folding it up and sealing it with purple wax. She holds the letter up, and the great horned owl who was resting on a perch near the windows swoops over and snatches the letter from her fingers.

"Thank you, Barron." The headmistress twirls her fingers, and the door to her office opens with a brush of air magic.

Barron spreads his wings, and with the letter clutched in his beak, he soars from the room. Once he's gone, the headmistress closes the door with another brush of magic.

"So, Miss Wilder." She leans back in her chair and removes the spectacles from the bridge of her nose. "Care to tell me why you're here?"

"Not particularly," I whisper, choosing to stare at one of Barron's feathers sitting atop her desk rather than looking into her sharp blue eyes.

She lets out a small but unsurprised sigh. "I suggest you tell your side of the story before whichever professor sent you here arrives to tell me themselves." With an arch of her brow, she lifts her teacup and takes a delicate sip.

I picture Professor Fleur's teary eyes, the anger twisting her face when she saw that I'd decimated her precious midnight lotus flowers. She's going to have a whole lot to say when she gets here after class.

And I realize the headmistress has a point.

"I was in my Exotic Flora class . . ."

Headmistress Moonhart tips her head.

"And it was hot as hell—"

"Language, Miss Wilder."

"And the weeds were *refusing* to budge, and I accidentally uprooted an entire flower, and then . . ."

The heat curling through me. The flames. The smoke rising from the exotic little flowers as they succumbed to the fire.

"And then I accidentally . . . set fire to a flower. Well, an entire *bed* of midnight lotus flowers."

Headmistress Moonhart's eyes go wide, a furrow forming in her forehead. Then she shakes her head and lets out a breath. "Tala loves those flowers," she says softly, but I'm not sure she intends for me to respond.

"I didn't mean to, I swear. It just . . . *happened*."

Like all my accidents. Like setting fire to the bed curtains last year. Like almost burning the library down. Like the many instances of setting my books aflame only to hurriedly smother the flames and hope no one smells the smoke.

The headmistress sets her teacup down. "This isn't the first accident you've had this year." Her fingertips find her temple. "Goddess only knows how lucky we are that the library didn't go up in flames."

Why'd she have to go and bring that up? As if I'm not already thinking of the last time I was in here, the sharp scolding I received, the earful I got about all the irreplaceable ancient tomes and how priceless they are.

"At least flowers can be regrown," I grumble, still striving not to meet the headmistress's eyes.

"Yes, they can. But that's not the point. The *point*, Miss Wilder..."

She pauses until I finally meet her gaze.

"Is that your fire is erratic, not under your control. It's a danger to you and all the other students." Her eyes soften as she regards me. "And you recall what we discussed last time you were here?"

Again, how could I forget?

"Yes," I grumble. "Expulsion."

The word tastes rancid on my tongue. Papa would be so disappointed in me. I worked so hard to get here, and I'll never forget the day my acceptance letter arrived, the tears of joy and pride in my father's eyes, the little bit of wood dust caught in his beard from whatever project he'd been working on that day.

I can't get expelled, no matter what.

"Then you know it's imperative you get your magic under control," Headmistress Moonhart continues.

"I'm trying. I promise I'm trying." My fingers twine tighter in my lap. "But . . . it's not working."

I've tried meditating with Maeve in the mornings, have tried breathing exercises and visualization and cold baths and everything else that's been suggested to me. It still doesn't work. I'm too quick to temper, and my flames are even quicker. They have a mind of their own and enjoy listening to authority about as much as I do—which is to say, not at all.

The headmistress hums thoughtfully. She stands from her desk, and her long plum gown looks soft and silky as butter as she walks to the window and looks out at the autumn landscape. The sunlight turns her blue eyes an even paler shade.

I'm not sure what she's looking at, but her lips quirk up a bit, and she turns to regard me with a smile. "I think I know just the thing."

I try not to sink in my chair. I have I feeling I'm really not going to like this.

CHAPTER 2
CAIRN

THE KETTLE LETS OUT ITS GENTLE WHISTLE, coaxing me from the pages of my book—a compendium of fungi—and beckoning me to push up from my plush armchair and walk into the kitchen to pour my tea. This takes me a grand total of only a handful of wide steps—my hut on the outskirts of campus is rather small, especially for a man of my size.

I pull a large mug down from the top shelf, toss a sachet of lemon balm into it, and pour steaming-hot water over the top. The citrusy scent curls up in a rush of steam, sending my nostrils flaring with delight. With mug in hand, I return to my armchair and open my book to the chapter I just started: The Ghostlight Cap.

The most striking feature of the ghostlight cap is its natural bioluminescence, which emits a soft, pale blue glow in the dark—a captivating display that sets it apart from most other fungi. However, it also has another, less appealing trait: a strong—some may

say noxious—odor of ammonia. This pungent scent has cast doubt on the mushroom's edibility, making it more a subject of fascination than of foraging.

After enjoying my tea and finishing the chapter on the ghostlight cap, I rinse my cup in the kitchen basin and prepare to start my day. I shove my arms into the sleeves of a long-sleeve shirt, do up the buttons, and reach for the door handle. My favorite shirt and trousers vanished off the clothesline last autumn, and every time I think of them, I'm still sore.

One of the students probably. Always up to some mischief.

I huff out an annoyed breath at the thought, making my nostrils flutter.

Outside, the air is crisp—it is early morning, after all— but the day promises to be warm, with only a few wispy white clouds dotting the pale blue sky. A playful breeze sends colorful leaves skittering down from the trees overtop my hut and dancing around my hooves before carrying them off across the campus.

I need to rake the grounds today, get all the leaf matter picked up before an early snow can turn it to mush that the students will undoubtedly track all through the halls, turning the janitorial staff cross. But before beginning my day, I must tend to my personal garden.

All about the front of my hut, plants grow in mismatched pots. There are purple coneflowers, fireweed, yarrow, and plenty more. Bees buzz pleasantly around the colorful blooms, keeping me company as I water the pots before moving to the garden at the back of the hut.

At this time of year, when summer is slowly yielding to autumn, I've much to do: harvesting, composting, preparing beds for the winter and coming spring. But I always start my day by visiting my most treasured plant: the moonflowers.

They stand at the edge of my garden, where they exist on the boundary between the forest and civilization—much like I do, I suppose. They only bloom at night, under the light of the moon, and in the perfect conditions, they give off an otherworldly glow.

With the sun rising in the east, the white petals have already curled up, protecting themselves from the coming heat of day.

I kneel and work my fingers into the soil about the plants; it's still damp and will need nothing further from me today. But the same cannot be said for the other plants in the garden. There are tomatoes to harvest and can, potatoes to uncover from their deep-soiled hills, and garlic cloves to soon be planted. The spinach is still growing well, pleased by our cooler days and nights, and I can keep my carrots growing into the winter once I get my cold frames set up. But it's still early for that yet. And I've plenty to keep me busy.

I water the beds that need watering, leave those that are still sufficiently moist, and then give my garden a once-over, ensuring everything is as it should be. I've nothing left to toil over. So, with one last glance at the moonflowers, I dust the soil from my fingers, and then I get to work.

Raking Coven Crest's grounds is always a gargantuan task. Being surrounded by the Mistwood, which has its fair share of deciduous trees, the campus becomes buried in leaves during the autumn. And as the sole groundskeeper, it's my job to tidy them up.

Despite being big, it's simple, so far as jobs around here go: rake the leaves into piles, shovel them into a deep wheelbarrow, then make the trek to the compost piles in the big community garden. It's about time to turn the piles again, to introduce oxygen and encourage the breakdown of organic matter, but that's a job for another day. These leaves will keep me busy for some time yet—and through the rest of the season, as the leaves continue to fall.

I'm just returning from dumping a load of leaves when the headmistress's owl, Barron, swoops through the sky over my head. I glance up, meeting his yellow eyes. I know what the sight of the great horned owl means. And sure enough, about ten minutes later, the headmistress appears, moving down the cobbled walkway—which I meticulously maintain—at an unhurried pace. Barron drifts above her, having undoubtedly revealed to her where on the campus I could be found.

It's not that I dislike the headmistress, or anyone else on the grounds—on the contrary, they're all warm and genial with me—it's just that I prefer to work alone. And think alone. And *be* alone.

That can be hard to do on a campus full of students and faculty.

"Mr. Axton," the headmistress says as she steps off the cobbled footpath and crosses the grass to greet me. I've already got another pile of leaves ready to load into the wheelbarrow, but I pause in my raking to turn fully to face her.

She's not a small woman, and in fact, I believe she's considered tall for a human female, yet she still has to tip her head back just so to fully meet my eyes.

"Headmistress."

One of her silver-blue brows arches into a point. "Lysandra, please."

I soften a bit, shedding some of the formality with which I typically refer to her. "Lysandra. What can I do for you?"

"What makes you think I need something from you?"

Now it's my turn to arch a bushy brow. "Because that's the only reason you seek me out."

She puffs out a breath. "Well, I certainly used to chase you down and invite you all over the place. But I think you prefer that I not. Am I wrong?"

It's true—she used to invite me out for dinner and drinks with the other faculty members, and she even strong-armed me into joining her and some of the other professors at a music festival in Wysteria a couple years ago. But there were far too many people, the music was far too loud, and all I could think of the whole time was getting home to my hut and my moonflowers and my quiet.

Since then, I've politely turned down all her offers. So, no, she's not wrong.

"Point taken," I huff. Then I switch the rake to my other hand and ask again, "So, what is it?"

Lysandra gestures in the direction of my hut, the wide sleeve of her gown rippling with the movement. "Can we talk over a cup of tea?"

I DON'T NEED AN ASSISTANT," I SAY, VOICE BORDERing on a low grumble. "I'm perfectly fine working on my own." If I weren't sitting down, my thin tail would be lashing in irritation right now.

Lysandra sips the tea I brewed her—lavender with a dash of wildflower honey—then lowers the cup and levels a stare at me. "It's a disciplinary assignment," she says.

As if that makes it any better.

"Disciplinary? For what?"

The headmistress continues to tell me about a fire witch who's on the verge of expulsion, having already set fire to the greenhouse and having very nearly sent the library up in smoke. The more words that leave her mouth, the tighter my shoulders grow.

The *last* thing I need right now—or *ever*—is a volatile fire witch with a penchant for burning up exotic plants. I found Professor Fleur sobbing in the greenhouse yesterday, dark cheeks splotchy and eyes swollen, and I can only assume the fire witch in question is the same one who obliterated the precious midnight lotus flowers that the professor had worked so very hard to cultivate.

Seeing their scorched petals and stems in the compost later that day made my stomach twist. And now the headmistress is trying to put that very same fire witch on *my* plate. I'd rather eat rocks.

"So, this is discipline for her, or for me?" I rumble.

Lysandra twists her lips and cants her head at me. "Come now, Cairn. I know you're not one for working one-on-one with the students, but I think it could be good for her. And for you." She casts her gaze to one of my small windows, where more leaves are twirling down from the trees above, landing in a blanket across the ground. "There's always so much to do at this time of year. She'll be an extra pair of hands, if nothing else."

Tiny witch hands—with a problem controlling their fire. I'm quite sure I don't need such a pair of hands. Mine do perfectly well, thank you.

"And what is she supposed to get out of this . . . collaboration?"

Lysandra's pale blue eyes find me again. "She needs to ground herself, to learn how to control her magic. Hard work may be just what she needs. And plants can stabilize us. They're healing." She reaches out and places a hand gently on my knee, despite the mud and dirt still staining the fabric from my work this morning. "I'd hate to see her lose her place at Coven Crest because she can't get a handle on her emotions." Sympathy flickers in her gaze. "I'm not sure what else to do for her, Cairn. You may be her last hope."

Something squeezes in my chest. I wish it wouldn't. I'm much too softhearted for my own good.

Lysandra continues to stare at me with those big pleading eyes. How am I supposed to say no when she's looking at me like that?

17

I can't. And she knows it.

So, with a barely restrained groan, I yield. "Fine. I'll deal with the fire witch."

Lysandra's pout shifts into a big smile, and she squeezes my knee. "Thank you, Cairn. I promise you won't regret it."

And I promise I will.

TWENTY MINUTES LATER, AFTER LYSANDRA HAS FIN-ished her tea, she departs my hut with a smile and a wave, calling over her shoulder, "We're having dinner at Boar and Badger tomorrow night. You know you're always welcome."

With a frown, I close the door firmly. On the other side, I can hear her light laugh. Through the window, I catch a glimpse of Barron soaring across the blue sky.

Next time he comes looking for me, I've got half a mind to hide.

My tail flicks again in irritation. I have a feeling it's going to be doing that a lot in the days and weeks to come.

I carry the teacups into my kitchen and give them a quick scrub in the basin, then set them out to dry on a clean cotton towel. After wiping up the few droplets of water that spilled onto the countertop, I turn to regard my hut.

While admiring how clean and quiet and impeccably or-ganized it is, I get a terrible feeling in my gut—the feeling that this fire witch is going to ruin *everything*.

CHAPTER 3
LYRA

AT THE EDGES OF MY AWARENESS, I FEEL A featherlight touch on my cheeks. It's pleasant. Comforting. At least at first. But then it turns a tad cold. And a tad *wet*.

I crack one eye open. It's somewhat dim in our loft, with the drapes still drawn over the window.

And I'm being snowed on. Indoors. In my *bed*.

Snowflakes fall around me silently, drifting down to land on my cheeks and in my hair. On the pillow beside my head, Juniper twitches her whiskers but doesn't wake up.

"You awake yet?" Alina asks, voice still thick with sleep. She has the curtain around her bed pulled back and is staring at me through heavy eyes.

"No," I grumble.

In response, more snowflakes start to fall, and my irritation spikes.

"Stop it." I bat a few of Alina's magical snowflakes away. "What are you—"

"Your community service," Maeve says from her bed. Her curtains obscure her from view and distort her voice slightly. "You're going to"—she yawns audibly—"be late."

Shit.

My irritation spikes again as I recall that today is my first day of "community service," as Headmistress Moonhart so gently put it.

She should've just called it what it is: punishment.

I'm never up before the sun, so it feels sacrilegious to push my warm, cozy comforter aside and sit up in bed. The chill nips at my skin. I glare at the snowflakes still falling around me.

"Can you cut it out with the blizzard now?" I say.

Alina gives me a sleepy smile, then plops back down in bed. The snowstorm stops immediately.

"What is it?" Juniper asks from where she's still lying on my pillow.

I look down at her. She's now awake—but just barely—and stretching out her little paws.

"Community service." With a groan, I scrub my hands down my face, trying to wake myself up, then reach back and start untwining my hair from its braid.

"Oh, yeah." Juniper pads around on my pillow, then flops right back down in the warm spot where my head was a moment ago. "Forgot about that."

"Wait, you're not coming?" I ask, tone aghast. Is she going to make me go by *myself*?

In answer, she closes her eyes and wiggles her nose into the warm pillowcase.

Guess I'm alone for the punishment, then.

"I thought you were my spirit *companion*," I grumble down at her. She doesn't respond, but I swear she's smiling.

After *forcing* myself out of bed and into a comfortable pair of trousers and a sweater—Headmistress Moonhart at least had the decency to assign me to community service on Saturdays only—I plod down the stairs and find Poppy already sitting in front of the fire, reading a book and sipping a cup of tea. Her legs are tucked up under her, a knit blanket draped across her lap.

"Why are you up so early?" I ask around a yawn.

Poppy holds up her book and smiles. "I like to get some reading in before the world wakes up. More peaceful this way."

I shake my head at her while I pour a cup of strong black tea—I'm gonna need the caffeine. "I'll never understand you, Poppy Waverly."

With a shrug and a smile, Poppy goes back to reading her book. And I think I can already hear Juniper snoring.

Another flare of irritation goes through me. The teacup I'm holding grows warmer from my fire magic, and steam rises from the dark liquid.

Chill. It's fine.

I take a sip of tea, promptly burn myself, and realize that today is destined to be a *very* bad day.

THE ACADEMY GROUNDS ARE FOGGY AND DRIZZLY. When I tip my head back to look up at the dense gray clouds, my cheeks get misted on. This weather is going to turn my hair into an uncontrollable mess of frizzy curls.

Unlike the other students, who are probably warm in bed or curled up in front of their fires, I'm tromping through the wet toward the groundskeeper's hut. I have to pass through the big stone wall encircling the academy, and when I move under the barbican, the air gets even colder. My hands are buried deep in my trouser pockets, and the toes of my boots are already spattered in moisture and leaf matter. Thankfully, my fire magic keeps me warm despite the cold hanging heavy in the air.

Of course this guy lives on the edge of civilization, I think, still feeling half asleep and grumpy from having to get up so early for something I so dearly want *not* to do.

If only my magic would cooperate, I wouldn't be in this mess. But I don't know how to get it under control.

Maybe Mom could've taught me.

The thought sets me immediately on edge, and I banish it as quickly as it arose. There's no room for things like that in my head. I've already got enough going on without letting myself perseverate over what-ifs and if-onlys.

And besides, she doesn't deserve a thought from me. Not one.

Huffing out a breath that steams in the chill air, I continue down the winding cobblestone path, which meanders through an open field toward the Mistwood, and toward the dense tree line at the edge of the grounds.

I see and smell the woodsmoke before I see the hut. The smoke curls through the fog, thick and tinged with the light scent of sage. The trees in the Mistwood are dark with rain and moisture, their trunks creating a backdrop of shadow that's almost impossible to see through. And there, standing at the edge of the woods, is the groundskeeper's hut.

It's quaint, with a thatched roof and a large front door. Potted plants crowd the area in front of the hut, dripping with moisture, the flowers and exotic plants lending bright pops of color to the otherwise dreary autumn atmosphere. A few orange and red leaves cling to my boots as I approach the front door.

I can't believe Moonhart is punishing me like this . . .

With a furrow in my brow and a downward turn of my lips, I pull one hand from the pocket of my trousers and rap my knuckles against the door.

There's movement inside the hut, the thumping of steps across the floor.

Then the door to the hut swings open.

And I have to tip my head *back* to meet the groundskeeper's eyes.

I've seen him around the academy grounds, though I've not exchanged a word with him since the Samhain festival last year, when he was gruff and unfriendly at the mead table.

Even now, his dark brown eyes are narrowed, and his lips are pulled into a deeper frown than mine. His face is human in appearance, though his nose is a bit wider than is typical, and his septum is pierced through with a golden hoop that winks in the low gray light. He's got a scruffy dark beard and long dark hair, and his ears are slightly elongated and pointed. His most noticeable feature—apart from his hulking frame, swishing tail, and hooves—is his spiraling black horns. They're ridged and glossy, twisting up and out from either side of his head. Some minotaurs choose to adorn their horns with jewelry and delicate chains and other items, but his are bare. They catch some of the light from the fire burning in the hearth behind him, their surface twinkling like faceted onyx.

I cease my observance of him and refocus on his narrowed eyes. He says nothing, just stands there in the doorway, looking down at me like he's considering slamming the door in my face.

And honestly, that'd be just fine. I could report back to Headmistress Moonhart, and maybe she'd assign me community service with someone else, like the cook. I wouldn't mind hanging around in the kitchens, taste testing pastries and learning how to whip up the perfect spiced hot chocolate.

"I'm Lyra Wilder," I finally bring myself to say, since he seems uninterested in speaking first. "Headmistress Moonhart sent me—"

"You're late," he says, deep voice silencing mine with a heavy rumble.

I give him an approximation of an innocent smile. "Am I? I could've sworn I left on time."

Yeah, I'm late. I may have agreed—or been forced to agree—to this ridiculous community service, but I don't have to be *eager* about it. And besides, it doesn't look like he was busy or anything.

My gaze slides to one side of the hulking minotaur. He's too tall for me to see over his shoulder, but through the space under his arm where he's holding open the door, I can make out a quaint living space, a fire crackling in the hearth, and a hot cup of something steaming on a side table beside a well-worn book.

Yeah, looks like he was *real* busy. I let out a quiet scoff.

When he notices my curious gaze, he shifts in the doorway, blocking my view. His dark gaze appraises me from curls to mud-stained boots. "Those your work clothes?"

Glancing down at myself, I shrug. "Guess it depends on the work."

He huffs out a breath. It doesn't sound entertained. "Gloves?"

Now I cross my arms and arch a brow at him. "No one told me what I'm supposed to be doing, but you expect me to come prepared?"

His brows pull low over his dark eyes. Irritation flashes in them.

For a moment, I think he may want to put one of those sharp black horns right through me.

But then he steps back and says, "I'll get you a pair. Wait here."

Of course, he doesn't invite me in out of the damp. Instead, he just shuts the door, leaving me standing there on his drizzly doorstep.

Irritably, I blow a frizzy curl out of my eyes.

While I wait, I drift around his hut, curious about all the potted plants and flowers. Most are foreign to me, with stunning colorful blooms and petals that unfurl to catch the thin light of day. Around the side of the hut, there's a pastoral fence built of woven branches, and it looks like the groundskeeper—Mr. Axton, I think Headmistress

Moonhart said—is growing an abundance of food: tomatoes, assorted greens, onions, peas, beans, and more plants I don't have a hope in the world of identifying.

And to the back of the garden, along the forest line, there are pale flowers growing, with their petals all curled in, like they're trying to protect themselves from the cold. They draw my attention, and I've just taken a step forward when the door opens and closes at the front of the hut, and a gruff voice says, "Here."

Turning around, I find the minotaur offering me a pair of gloves. I arch a brow at him.

"They're the smallest pair I own," he huffs, flopping them toward me. "You want them or not?"

For some reason, I'm enjoying annoying him. Maybe it's because I have about a million better things to do than help this grumpy groundskeeper muck around in the mud all day.

I tip my head and purse my lips. "No thanks."

His eyes narrow. Annoyance level: rising.

Eyebrow arched, I ask, "So, what special brand of punishment do you have in store for me today?"

The minotaur tosses the extra pair of gloves onto a narrow table alongside the hut, already cluttered with pots and soil and gardening tools, and says gruffly, "Compost."

As far as I know, compost is supposed to be soft and fluffy and smell good.

This is not compost. This is slimy leaves and garden debris and muck. And it's *my* job to turn it. Because, apparently, compost likes to be turned. I didn't realize how high-maintenance rubbish piles could be.

I shed my cloak an hour ago, and I wipe sweat from my forehead before sinking the three-tined compost fork into the big pile and grunting with the effort it takes to turn it over. When Mr. Axton showed me how to do it, he made it look simple—of course, he's probably got about two hundred pounds of muscle on me, so for my scrawny arms and wrists, this is anything but easy.

With another grunt, I flip a glob of the unfinished compost, then pause to catch my breath. My hands sting, and with a wince, I peel them away from the handle of the compost fork to find blisters forming along my palms. They're angry red and tender to the touch. And now that I know they're there, they start to burn hotter. Funny how awareness does that.

Shit. My eyes narrow. *Should've worn those gloves after all . . .*

Movement to my left catches my attention.

It's Mr. Axton, bringing yet another wheelbarrow full of fallen leaves to dump onto the compost. There're numerous piles back here, and I'm only on the second one.

He doesn't even look over at me as he hefts the wheelbarrow up and dumps everything out. The tunic he's wearing is stained at the hem with mud, and he's a bit sweaty, like me, but somehow, it suits him—like he's meant to be part of the salt and the earth. Unlike me. I just burn everything down.

A flare of irritation goes through me. It's done that innumerable times today.

Why can't my magic just *listen*? Why can't I control it the way my peers can? It's gotten me into more messes than I can count, but this—I look down at myself, finding my pants and tunic smeared with compost and dirt and leaf litter—is certainly the worst of it.

And it's also the only thing standing between me and possible expulsion.

The thought of losing my place at the academy makes my stomach twist. I can't let that happen. Papa would be so disappointed, especially after how hard we *both* worked to get me into Coven Crest in the first place.

"Finished?" the minotaur asks.

It's only one word, yet it feels spoken slowly, and as he comes to stand beside me and I look up at him, I get the impression that he may have been a mountain in another life—ancient, stoic, towering above everyone else. But maybe lonely too. I've always felt like mountains are lonely, so high up in the sky, in the quiet and the cold.

I pull my focus back to his question.

"Not quite," I grumble.

His dark eyes narrow, and he crosses his broad arms. "Then why aren't you working?"

I want to tell him to kindly screw off, but my hands are burning even more now, and I'm not so sure I can finish this pile without utterly ruining my palms.

So, with a defeated sigh, I drop the compost fork to the ground and open my hands, holding them out toward him.

He assesses the bright red blisters with a furrowed brow.

I can hear the "I told you so" on his tongue, recall clearly the way he held the gloves out and I carelessly turned them away.

Go on, say it, I think bitterly.

With a huff, he draws himself up and says, "Come on."

Taking the handles of the wheelbarrow, he heads away from the compost piles and out of the garden. I hurriedly grab my cloak from where I tossed it across a garden table that wasn't in use, then scamper after him, having to move fast to keep up with his wide strides.

As we walk back across the academy grounds toward his hut, my gaze is drawn down to his hooves. I'm not sure how much of his lower half is human, as he wears baggy trousers that only just reveal his hooves as they press deep into the soft earth and grass, leaving moon-shaped prints behind. So far as I'm aware, minotaurs are all a little bit different, just like witches and humans and orcs and all the other creatures who call this place home.

I dismiss the curiosity as a few students pass us on the cobblestone path, looking like they're headed for the Mistwood and the long walk into Wysteria. I desperately wish I were at Poppy's mom's café instead, eating strawberry shortcake and teasing Alina about Raelan and how I was right about him all along. But instead, I'm stuck here, splattered in mud, with my palms covered in painful blisters. And I'm pretty sure my hair is one big halo of red frizz right now.

Ugh.

The students' eyes follow me, and I stare right back until they finally turn their gazes away.

Mr. Axton parks the wheelbarrow just outside his hut, then wipes his hooves on his doormat before walking in—and closing the door before I can follow in behind him.

Asshole.

Another spike of irritation goes through me, but it just makes my hands throb more fiercely. Blowing out a breath, I take a seat on the big bench outside the hut—big enough that the toes of my boots barely brush the ground. Perfect size for a minotaur, I suppose.

A couple minutes later, the door opens again, and Mr. Axton emerges with something held in his hand. Eyes slightly narrowed, like even this is an inconvenience to him, he holds something out to me.

I eye the squat little jar. "What is it?"

"Healing salve."

Sounds like heaven. But something stays my hand. Pride? Anger?

The minotaur looming over me arches a brow. "You want it or not?"

I meet his annoyed expression with one of my own. With a sigh, he starts to turn away. At the last moment, I lunge, intending to snatch the jar out of his hand. Instead, I accidentally knock it free, and it falls to the stone at his hooves, the little glass jar shattering on impact.

The breaking of the glass sounds ear-shattering against the stillness of the hut and the dried leaves rattling gently on the trees overhead. And the salve—which I can now tell smells of lavender and tea tree—sloops out onto the clover-packed stone beneath Mr. Axton's hooves.

"I'm sorry," I say immediately, starting to stoop to clean up the mess. "I didn't mean to."

But the minotaur holds out a hand, stopping me in my tracks. "We're done for the day." His hard brown gaze cuts toward the castle looming over the stone wall in the distance, then back to me. "You can go."

He doesn't want my help? Fine.

It's not like I want to be here anyway.

Whipping around, I snatch my cloak off the bench, then storm back toward the castle. But despite how high I hold my chin and how firmly I square my shoulders, one thought echoes in my mind.

I did it again. And I didn't even need my fire this time.

CHAPTER 4
CAIRN

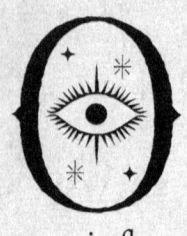NCE THE FIRE WITCH IS GONE, I GET BACK to work, ever more grateful for the quiet and the lack of her static energy. Even without speaking, I could feel her chaos, like she's dry kindling just waiting for a spark to go up in flames.

And flames are the last thing I need around here.

Since she didn't finish turning the compost piles, I tack that on to the end of my day, and by the time I return to my hut, the sun is already going down, sapping the warmth from the air and casting long dark shadows that reach across the academy's grounds, reminding me that once autumn arrives, winter is never too far behind.

Part of me is ready for the cold and the snow. I'll still have duties around here—helping keep fires lit, shoveling snow and ice from the walkways, repairing and sharpening tools for use in the spring—but many of my tasks will fall away at the same time that the last of the leaves spiral from the trees, and everything slows down in the winter-time, making it a time for rest and contemplation. The other part of me dreads the somber season, when the plants I love so much have either withered into husks or have gone dormant, waiting for the warm days of spring to arrive and wake them from their slumber.

Outside my hut, I scuff my hooves on the coarse door-mat, then brush the excess dirt off before stepping inside. Thanks to the witch not doing her part and me having to therefore work late, I didn't make it back in time to light the fire before the sun started to go down. Now my hut has a chill to the air, a bite of cold that sends an irritable twinge down my spine.

I'm a man of routine—there's a structure to my days, a pattern that I've come to find solace in. And yet somehow, Lyra Wilder is already snatching that solace away, throwing a fireball into my perfectly laid plans.

With a grumble, I tromp into the sitting room, drop to one knee, and sweep this morning's ashes from the hearth. Then I stack fresh logs in the belly of the fireplace, strike a match against the stone, and coax the flames to life.

And though I'm still irked by the witch and the ridiculous community service project this has become, I do wonder how much easier this would be if she were here to light the fire for me. Even after years of being around professors and students with magic running through their veins, it never ceases to impress me, to strike awe into my heart.

The logs catch, and the small ember steadily grows, already starting to put off a bit of heat.

Grunting, I push to my hooves, then stretch my arms overhead, trying to loosen up the kinks in my muscles from a full day of work. Now it's time to make something for dinner, take a much-needed hot bath, and then have my cup of tea while reading by the fire.

I'm determined to reclaim my evening, even if I'm a bit late getting to it because of the troublesome witch.

By the time I sink into my chair with a hot cup of green tea, the sun has already disappeared over the horizon, and my hut is cast in shadow. The fire has warmed the sitting room considerably, and I already took the time to light a few candles. Now warm firelight dances along the walls, and my frustrations with Headmistress Moonhart and Lyra Wilder have mostly drifted away—though I'm certain the hot bath I took earlier helped.

I pull my long hair up on top of my head and hastily tie it with a cord, then take a sip of my strong green tea. As I reach for my book, I accidentally brush a stack of paper to the floor. With a slight grumble, I set my teacup down and reach from my seated position to scoop the papers off the rug.

And the first one that catches my eye is from the Columbine Botanical Conservatory.

Or rather, a graduate of Coven Crest who works there now and reached out to me a few weeks back.

I hold the letter gently, careful not to crumple it or crease the edges. My brain tells me to throw the letter into the fire and let it burn, but my heart drives me to open the envelope and remove the letter tucked so neatly inside.

It opens with a whisper, and for perhaps the hundredth time, I read the words scrawled across the page.

Mr. Cairn Axton,

Hello, old friend! It's me, Milo. You know, that obnoxious kid who used to follow you around the gardens, asking a million questions about what you were doing and why. Well, wouldn't you know, I went on to get an internship somewhere I can be surrounded by plants all day: the Columbine Botanical Conservatory and Community Gardens (phew, that's a mouthful . . . quillful?). You ever been? It's beautiful. So many different species of plants and trees that I'd never heard of before coming here. You should really visit if you haven't already. I think you'd love it.

But I digress. I work here now, and word coming down the grape vine says one of our horticulturists is going to be looking for an assistant for this coming summer. We've got all these community gardens here, where people come to learn and grow food, and you know, every time I'm out there, I think of you for some reason. You still have those gardens back behind your hut? Ah, what am I saying? Of course you do.

And that's why I'm writing. Because I think you should apply for the job. And I'll put a good word in for you. Then I can irritate you like I did all those years ago, eh? Don't act like you wouldn't enjoy it.

All right, best be getting back to work. But think about it, Cairn. Coven Crest is a great place to be, but I think there's more for you out here, and I think you'd really love it here.

If you want to apply, just fill out the application I included and send it back to me, and I'll make sure it gets into the right hands. Don't wait too long though—they'll want to fill that position soon.

Oh, and tell the moonflowers hello for me.

Signing off with dirt-stained hands,
Milo Foster

I just about have the letter memorized at this point, know exactly how each of Milo's letters looks scratched into the parchment.

Yet I still haven't taken any action, haven't put even a drop of ink on the application Milo provided.

Because who would want *me* as a horticultural assistant? Apart from Coven Crest, I've never worked in gardens in any official capacity. And the Columbine Botanical Conservatory and Community Gardens is a well-known, reputable conservatory—of course I've been there. Many times. I've walked the gardens, sat on the stone benches beneath the trees, wondered what it would be like to take part in such an important project.

But at the end of the day, I'm just Cairn Axton, a nobody minotaur who'd rather whisper to moonflowers than speak to other people. I certainly don't have the qualifications for such a position, despite what Milo might think.

He was a good kid when he was here—though much too chatty for my liking. I did warm up to him eventually, and at some point his presence ceased to annoy me. I even kind of missed him once he graduated and moved on to bigger things. And now I know what those things are.

The botanical conservatory.

The possibility of getting a job there makes my skin pebble with excitement. But then I remind myself that I don't have the qualifications they'd most certainly be looking for, don't have the professional experience to snag such a job.

And besides, what would Coven Crest do without me? And what would *I* do without Coven Crest? I've been here for years, have built a quiet and predictable routine for myself. I know my duties like the back of my hand, and nothing ever changes—well, except for that fire witch.

A small bite of irritation goes through me.

Why would Lysandra assign the witch to me? She knows how much I value my peace and quiet, how important it is to me to stick to the schedules and routines I've built over the years.

It's almost like the headmistress is trying to punish me too.

Maybe I should apply for the job . . .

The thought feels as delicious as it does forbidden.

And before I can let myself dive too far down that minotaur-size rabbit hole, I gently fold the letter back up, slip it into the envelope next to the application, and place it back on the side table from which I knocked it.

Trying to put thoughts and dreams of the botanical gardens from my mind, I snatch up my book and my teacup and resume my reading, starting with a chapter on glomeromycota.

CHAPTER 5
LYRA

UCH!" I HISS, TRYING TO PULL MY HAND away from Maeve, but she holds fast, her storm-purple eyes cutting to me like a bolt of lightning. "That *hurts*."

"Well, it's going to continue to hurt if you don't let us help you," Maeve says. Her voice is crisp and matter-of-fact, leaving no room for my whimpering.

I'm cross-legged on one of the couches in our sitting area, Maeve on one side of me and Poppy on the other. They take turns dipping their fingertips into a small jar of salve that Alina made for me when I returned to the dormitory yesterday and showed them the angry blisters decorating my palms.

"These look so painful," Poppy says. She pushes her big round glasses up with a knuckle, a dainty furrow appearing in her brow. "Mr. Axton should've made sure you had the proper protective gear."

"Protective gear?" Maeve asks with an arched brow. "You mean gloves?" She chuckles to herself. "It's not like Lyra was tasked with wrangling a centaur or something."

Poppy's furrow deepens as she gently applies more salve to a particularly large and painful blister. "Even so . . . It's rather inconsiderate."

I could just *not* tell them that the minotaur did, in fact, offer me the proper protective gear, as Poppy so succinctly put it. But I've never been one for fibs—unless they're meant in good fun.

"Well . . ." I draw the word out slowly, and everyone in the room looks at me, including Alina and Raelan, who're cozied up together on the other couch in the sitting room. I'm not sure how it's possible, but those two are more inseparable now than they were last year.

"Well what?" Maeve asks. She's finished applying the salve and is reaching for a bandage now.

"Well . . . he *did* offer me gloves. I turned them down."

"Why?" Poppy asks.

I shrug one shoulder—the one Juniper isn't currently clinging to, hiding under my curls to keep warm. Early this afternoon, the sky turned a dark shade of gray and rain started to fall. The fire is burning, chasing the chill from our room, but with my fire magic, I put off plenty of heat, and Juniper likes to curl up and nap when it gets cold like this.

"I don't know," I say, and it's mostly true. "I guess I didn't want him to think I needed them, like I'm weak or something."

My mind replays yesterday afternoon, watching Mr. Axton push and dump the wheelbarrow with what appeared to be no effort, how he wielded the compost fork like a magic spell. I, on the other hand, struggled *all* day, and with such a simple task too. He gave me one thing to do, and I couldn't even complete it.

"Ow!" I snap when Maeve wraps the soft cotton bandage across my palm. "What are you, an orc?"

She rolls her eyes. "No, that'd be my stepbrother, remember?"

Oh, that's right. Aric, I think. The runeball player. I wish I were at a runeball game right now instead of here, with my palms blistered and everyone looking at me like I did something wrong.

"You've got too much pride, Lyra," Maeve says, though her fingers work at the bandage more carefully now, expertly wrapping the cotton until she can deftly tuck the end into itself to hold the material snug. When she's done, she flops an arm over the back of the couch and tips her head at me, her glossy dark purple hair catching the firelight. "Everyone knows minotaurs are built like mountains. It's not like he expected you to be indestructible."

"No," I scoff. "Just to cause destruction."

There's an extended moment of quiet as Poppy finishes with my other hand. My words hang there in the firelit dorm room, refusing to disperse. But they all know it's true. They've all seen what my fire can do—what *I* can do—when I'm not careful. It's what got me into this whole community service mess in the first place.

"And do you care what he thinks?" Alina asks. Her tone holds a twinge of playfulness, and I quickly cut my gaze to her.

41

Raelan has one arm draped across her shoulders, and he traces shapes onto her palm with his other hand. I wrinkle my nose at them.

"No," I snap. "Of course not. He barely speaks, he's cold as Norwyth, and I swear, every time he looks at me, I can *feel* how annoyed he is that he has to put up with me." A second later, I grumble beneath my breath, "That makes two of us."

Beside me, Poppy wipes her hands off on a plum-colored rag, then twists the lid onto the salve jar. "Maybe he's just lonely. He lives all by himself out there, and I barely see him around." She leans forward to grab her teacup from the low table, then tips her head to one side thoughtfully. "Maybe he just needs to warm up to you."

Raelan lets out a low laugh. We all look at him.

"Have something you'd like to add, dragon?" I cross my arms and cant my head.

When Alina told us the truth about what Raelan Ashvale is—one of the rare remaining dragon shifters—I somehow wasn't surprised. I knew all along he looked at her like she was a slice of apple pie he wanted to sink his teeth into.

"*Warm* up to you?" His lips pull up on one side. "You should be good at helping him with that. You know, uncontrolled flames and all."

"Ha, ha. The knight thinks he's funny now." The girls titter and smile as I uncross my legs and push to my feet. My movement wakes Juniper, and she shifts on my shoulder, her sharp little claws clinging to the fabric of my fluffy sweater. "I think I preferred when you were all stoic and grouchy," I add.

Raelan doesn't rise to my bait, just gives me another small smirk before tracing the shell of Alina's ear with his nose and whispering something to her that makes her cheeks go pink.

Those two make me want to be ill.

But in a good way. Because of course I'm happy for her. I held her more than once last year while she cried over him, but now that she bears his claiming mark, I've yet to see her shed a tear because of Raelan Ashvale.

"I'm going on a walk," I announce. "And thanks for the help," I call back to Maeve and Poppy. Then I shove my feet into a pair of plush boots—the kind I don't dare wear outside for fear of getting a speck of mud on them—and slip out of our dorm room and into the spiraling staircase outside our door.

As soon as I close the door behind me and breathe in a lungful of the chill castle air, I feel better, or at least less cooped up. I don't do well in tight spaces for long. Or maybe in any one place for long.

I start down the stairs, my soft-soled boots swishing across each stone step as I descend from the north tower. Another student in a wheelchair says hello as they float past, using air magic to hover up the spiraling corridor. The stained glass windows along the stairwell let in thin gray light, but it seems as though another storm is rolling in, if the darkening shadows are any indication.

Making it to the bottom of the stairs, I set off through the castle halls, letting my feet carry me wherever they want to go.

Despite it being the weekend, the castle is quiet. When the weather is nice, many students flock outside, wanting to soak up the sun and sprawl in the grass in the expansive courtyard, boots off and toes bare. But on rainy days like this—seems like it rains on most days during the autumn— many students retreat to their dorm rooms or take up spots near the big fires roaring in the library or dining hall. I only pass a few other students as I drift along. Two of them are still slightly damp, so they must've gotten caught in the first leg of the storm on their way back to the castle—from Wysteria, perhaps.

"Where are we going?" Juniper asks from her spot on my shoulder.

"You awake now?"

In response, she yawns.

"Don't know. Just walking."

"Well, can we make a detour to the dining hall?" She sniffs the air, her whiskers tickling my earlobe and making me giggle. "I smell cinnamon."

Per her request, I turn my feet in the direction of the dining hall. It's not quite time for dinner, even if the darkness from the storm is trying to trick me into thinking so. But throughout the day, students can swing by the dining hall and pick up snacks between classes or to tide them over until dinnertime. I must be one lucky witch, because I step into the candlelit room just as one of the cooks is setting out a fresh platter of steaming cinnamon-sugar muffins.

My mouth waters at the sight of them.

"Fresh out of the oven," he says. "Don't burn yourself."

Burn myself. That's funny. Fire never bites me—it just bites everyone and everything *around* me.

"Thanks." I snag the biggest muffin on the tray, then rip off a chunk and blow on it until it's cool. "Here." I lift the fluffy morsel up for Juniper, and she shifts her weight on my shoulder so she can take it with her front paws.

With her pleasantly nibbling in my ear, I take my own bite of the muffin, then resume my wandering.

The halls are darker now, and distant thunder rumbles low and deep.

And I suddenly know where I'm headed: my secret little alcove in the east wing, with the big window with the view of the Mistwood.

I head in that direction as rain starts to fall. It runs in thick rivulets down the windows I pass.

Suddenly, unbidden, voices start whispering in my head, echoing what I've been told recently.

You've got too much pride.

Your fire is erratic, not under your control.

As if in response to the reminder of how out of control I am, the blisters on my palms sting beneath the soft cotton bandages. My chest feels tight.

I know! I want to yell at them. I'm aware of my problems—have been for a long time. I don't need reminders.

Taking a bite of muffin, I chew aggressively, trying to shove the voices down.

But they refuse to leave. They're always there, lingering in the recesses of my mind, waiting to come out when I least want them to.

And now is definitely one of those moments.

They continue to whisper, taking on what I imagine is the voice of my mother. Not that I'd know what her voice actually sounds like. She left much too long ago for me to remember such a thing.

I turn down hallway after hallway, only passing a few students and faculty along the way—no one who wants to talk, thankfully, because I'm really not in the mood.

Finally, I make it to the narrow stairwell that leads up to where my nook is on the third floor.

"Another bite?" Juniper says.

I've already demolished half the muffin. Ripping another chunk of fluffy goodness off, I hand it up into her little paws and start climbing the stairs. The shadows feel deeper here, the air colder. But it feels good, like maybe it can help soften the fire burning just beneath my skin.

On my way up, the soft toe of my boot stubs on a step, and I let out a yelp and stumble forward. Juniper squeaks and drops her bite of muffin, grasping a lock of my curly hair with her paws.

"Shit!" That fire that I *hoped* might be calmed flares hot and bright. My blisters sting.

With a heavy sigh, I sink onto one of the stairs and lean my head against the smooth wooden banister running alongside the stairwell.

"You okay?" I reach for Juniper, and she lets me draw my fingers across her head and down her back.

"I'm fine. You?"

"Eh." I wiggle my toes in my boot and wince at the throb. "I'll be okay. Not broken."

With finesse, Juniper crawls down my sweater, then settles herself in my lap—where I'm holding the muffin. As she begins nibbling away, humming contentedly to herself,

I take note of the intricate vines etched along the side of the wooden banister. I'm certain I've climbed these stairs a hundred times, but I've never noticed this little detail before. The vines are hidden just beneath the lip of the handrail, so you have to really look to see them. But despite their being mostly hidden, someone took the time to put them there, and to do it *right*.

I lift a hand and skate my fingers across the beautiful carvings. And then a new voice joins the others in my mind. But this one is warm, loving.

Good woodwork is quiet, but it lasts. It matters.

Papa's voice is smooth and rumbly, soft with no hard edges. I call to mind the many times I sat with him in his woodshop, watching him measure and cut and sand with practiced grace. When the sun would stream through the little dusty window, the air would come alive with swirling sawdust, and it's always reminded me of magic. His own kind of magic—not like the fire magic that burns through my veins.

That's from *her*.

You don't have to be perfect, Papa told me the evening before I left for my second year here at Coven Crest. *Just show them who you are, what you're made of.* He smiled at me, eyes lined and tired, but still happy. And then he said, *I already know.*

I press my hand flat against the intricate carved vines. My throat feels like it wants to clog up with emotion.

Papa has worked hard my whole life. Raising me alone, he did everything he could to give me the best and most comfortable life possible. And when I told him I wanted to attend the academy, he started quietly working that much harder, saving up for my books and travel and everything else I need to be a student here.

Yet here I am, slumped in a lonely stairwell, on the verge of being expelled, of losing everything I've—*he's*—worked so hard for.

I picture the letter from him sitting in my nightstand beside my bed. I've not been able to bring myself to write back, to tell him about the fire in the greenhouse, the community service, the stoic minotaur who's been saddled with me.

I don't have the heart to tell him that I'm one erratic flame away from failing. It'd break me. And him.

He's always believed in me, I think, feeling tears well up along my eyelids, thick as the rain still running down the small high windows. *But what if he's wrong?*

CHAPTER 6
LYRA

ANOTHER WEEK PASSES, ANOTHER WEEK-end arrives, and I find myself waking early—though this time without Alina having to snow on my face. Not that she could've anyway; she stayed in Raelan's room last night, even though the headmistress communicated in no uncertain terms that such a thing is strictly forbidden. But I'm certainly not telling anyone.

I dress quietly, careful not to wake Poppy and Maeve. And this time, Juniper slips into the deep pocket of my old worn sweater, the one with the hole in the cuff, opting to join me for my community service instead of staying curled up in bed.

Breakfast consists of a day-old muffin and a cup of black tea, and then I'm pulling on my warm boots and slipping out of room NT33. The stairwell is silent save for the whisper of flames dancing in sconces along the walls.

"Did you eat enough?" Juniper asks in her soft sleepy voice.

I look down to find her head poking out of the pocket of my sweater, her paws gripping the edge of the fabric.

I shrug one shoulder. "Probably not."

She gives me her version of a stern glare. "You need to take better care of yourself."

"I know, I know." I yank up my wild curls and knot them on top of my head. "I just want to get this over with. I'll eat when I'm done."

"I don't approve." With a displeased twitch of her whiskers, she sinks back down into my pocket.

Rolling my eyes, I continue down the winding stairwell. I don't pass anyone on my way through the drafty castle, and Juniper is still my only company as I pass through the courtyard and into the morning fog, headed toward the groundskeeper's hut.

The days continue to grow colder as winter draws nearer. Midterms will be here before we know it, then Samhain. And soon after that, we'll have our winter exams, and the semester will be over.

A knot forms in my gut at the thought of the semester's end—and whether or not I'll still have a place here come spring.

I'm feeling grateful all I had was that stale muffin. My stomach is trying to dance right now, and if I'd eaten anything more, I might be sick.

When I arrive at Mr. Axton's hut, he's already outside working at the garden bench, and I get the opportunity to observe him as I finish meandering down the winding path through the valley. He's wearing the same worn-out trousers he had on last time I was here, but today his upper body is clad in a long-sleeved forest-green tunic, and something weird happens in my stomach when my gaze traces the round muscles in his shoulders and arms, the ease with which he flexes and moves.

His horns stand stoic atop his head, looking smooth and shiny as he tips his head this way and that. For the first time, I wonder what they might feel like if I were to run my fingertips across them. Are they smooth, the way they look? Or do they have a deceivingly rough texture?

I'm still pondering this when he looks up and meets my eyes. And immediately, his narrow, and a glimmer of suspicion shines in them.

"What?" I ask, hoping he didn't catch me staring as I come to stop a few paces from him.

His dark gaze continues to assess me. And after a too-long pause, he says, "I didn't expect you to be on time."

A flicker of irritation warms my insides. "You barely know me. Maybe you shouldn't come to conclusions quite so quickly."

His eyes remain narrowed. His mouth works as if he's deciding which words to spit out. But then he says simply, "Maybe."

And that's that.

He goes back to whatever he's working on, leaving me standing there in the early-morning fog still curling around my ankles and his hooves. After standing there a short while longer—being ignored by him all the while—I let out a sigh and move to stand beside him.

When I draw near, he turns his head slightly to look down at me, and I'm pretty sure I don't imagine how he shifts aside so my arm won't brush his.

Not a people person, clearly. Maybe I just learned a new way to annoy him. *Yay me.*

"What are you working on?" I ask, crossing my arms against the morning chill as I look down at the soil and tools spread across the garden bench.

"Transplanting sniffleblooms."

I arch a brow. "Sniffleblooms?"

With careful hands—which is impressive given how huge his fingers are—he delicately separates one of the young flowers from its siblings, then moves it into its own small square of soil. After adding a bit more dark brown earth, he packs it down and says, "If you agitate the blossoms, they'll release spores that'll make you sneeze pink for a week." His eyes meet mine, and he *almost* smiles. "Come to think of it, you can finish this up."

Next thing I know, he's pushing the tray toward me, and I'm fumbling for words. "W-wait, I don't know the first thing about—"

"Just go slow and be careful. Intentional." He points at the tray of soil squares. "One plant per square. Once they grow into these, we'll plant them outside."

"Why would anyone want to plant these?" I ask, feeling like I need to hold my breath. Things are going crazy enough as is; I don't need to be plagued with pink sneezes.

There's a hint of joy in Mr. Axton's voice as he say, "Keeps meddlesome students out of places where they don't belong."

And just like that, without any further instruction, he treads off, leaving me with the blossoms and their villainous pink petals. I glare down at the young flowers, really wishing I were back in bed.

"How long can you hold your breath?" Juniper asks from my pocket. I notice she's *not* sticking her head out this time. Smart.

I hold my breath as a light autumn breeze tickles my skin. Then I grumble, "Not long enough."

THE WORK IS SLOW. PAINSTAKING. TEDIOUS. THE FIRST couple of sniffleblooms take a damn lifetime to transplant, and a few times I hold my breath for so long that my head starts to feel woozy. But after the first three, miraculously, I'm actually getting the hang of it.

Slowly, I remove one flower from its companions, then ease its root system into a prepared square of soil and pack a bit more over the top, like Mr. Axton did. I hold my breath whenever a breeze comes to play, and there's something oddly calming about it—despite knowing one wrong move could leave me a sniffly pink mess for the next seven days.

Somehow, I get caught up in the work, so I'm surprised when I feel a tingle go down my back and glance up to find the minotaur watching me. He's holding a big basket full of fresh produce: thick heads of lettuce, soil-spotted potatoes, and a bunch of carrots with frilly green tops. His gaze feels heavy, like a big cloak draped over my shoulders, and I wrinkle my nose up at him.

"What? You waiting to see if I'm sneezing yet?"

It takes him a long while to respond—I'm starting to think these prolonged pauses are normal for him. When he finally speaks, it's accompanied by a subtle shrug from those massive shoulders of his. "Something like that."

I don't take my eyes off him—almost thinking he's trying to sabotage me and make me send the sneezy spores everywhere—until he passes behind me and then into his hut. The door closes, making my garden table wobble a bit. The sniffleblooms sway. Immediately, I hold my breath.

When I finally let it out and gasp in a lungful of the crisp autumn air, Juniper whispers from my pocket, "You think he did that on purpose?"

I shake my head and glare at the closed door. "Don't know."

But if he did, I think as I resume transplanting the pink flowers, *he's got another thing coming. I'll show him I'm not nearly so big a screwup as everyone thinks.*

CHAPTER 7

CAIRN

I GRAB MY THICK OVEN MITTS AND PULL THE CAKE tray from the oven, then set it on a heat mat to cool in the light breeze coming through the open window. It smells so good, I want to dive into it now, but it needs to cool before I frost it. And that'll take a while yet.

Removing my oven mitts, I realize I left the fire witch working on the sniffleblooms. I got so distracted getting the fresh produce put away and whipping up a carrot cake that I completely forgot she was out there working.

And now I feel a bit like an asshole. There's a reason I'm a groundskeeper and not a professor. I don't do well with babysitting.

Shit. She probably got bored and wandered off. Hopefully Lysandra doesn't see her and—

I yank open the door to my hut and come face-to-face— or rather, chest to face, seeing as how small she is—with the witch. Her messy red curls are knotted atop her head, her fingers are stained with soil, and the look on her face is more victorious than it has any reason to be.

"I'm done," she announces, more than a hint of pride coloring her tone.

My gaze slides to the garden bench alongside my hut, and sure enough, the delicate young flowers have all been transplanted into their own squares of soil, and they stand with their petals reaching for the autumn sunlight.

Suspicious, I shift my gaze to her again. And I watch her. And watch her some more.

A wrinkle forms in her brow, and she crosses her arms. "What are you looking at?"

My eyes narrow. "You're not sneezing."

The suspicion goes from her expression, and she smiles at me. No, *beams*. It lights up her whole face, crinkles her freckles into shapes like constellations in the summer sky.

And it makes my chest feel funny. Not in a good way.

"Nope. No sneezing for me."

An incredulous breath slips from me, and before I can stop it, I say, "Impressive."

"You didn't think I could do it?" She cants her head. The look in her vibrant crimson eyes tells me she likes to rise to challenges. Somehow, I'm not surprised.

"Truly?" I cross my arms. "No. I thought you'd sneeze all the way back to the castle."

"Well, joke's on you."

This time the sound that leaves me is a laugh. And it makes the witch arch a brow. "Joke's on me," I repeat, glancing once more at the tray of transplants. "Did you water them?"

"Nope." She reaches her arms overhead and stretches like her back is sore. "Figured I'd already done enough hard work for today."

"Huh. Figured."

The carrot cake I baked sends a delicious cinnamon-nutmeg scent swirling out of the hut from behind me, and the witch sniffs the air.

Immediately, her gaze tries to slide around me, but my frame blocks the doorway so fully that I imagine she can't see much.

"Hungry?" I ask.

She starts to shake her head, but then her stomach growls. Loudly.

And her cheeks turn a shade of red that reminds me of the chrysanthemums growing in my garden.

With a jut of my chin toward the back of the hut, I say, "Go sit down. I'll bring you a slice."

She starts to take a step back. "It's fine, I'll just—"

Suddenly, a rat appears from the pocket of her sweater, squeaking up a racket and startling me enough that I take a step back. It sounds like a lecture—and a firm one at that. The witch looks down at the rat, then back at me, then sighs. Her stomach growls again.

"All right. Fine." Her crimson eyes meet mine and narrow slightly. "But I hope you're a good cook."

I huff out another laugh. "Wash your hands in the basin. Can't have you getting everything dirty."

Her face contorts into an expression that tells me she's about to launch another sharp comment in my direction, but I slip into my hut and close the door before it can leave her lips. And when I hear her grumbling and stomping off on the other side of the door, for some reason, I smile.

Even though I probably shouldn't.

THE WITCH'S EYES WIDEN AS I SETTLE THE PLATTER OF freshly frosted carrot cake onto the bistro table in the garden, followed by two small plates—well, small to me, but they look like full-size dinner plates compared to her. I'm around students and faculty often, and yet I feel the small stature of this fire witch more clearly than I do with the others. Maybe because they don't sit at my table and eat off my plates.

"You made this?" she asks. Her gaze still hasn't left the cake.

It steams in the autumn air, and every breath I take is scented with spices and sugar against the earthy smell from the forest just behind us.

With a sigh, I pull out my chair and take a seat. The witch's rat friend pops out of her sweater pocket to look at me.

"Yes."

Her gaze slides slowly from the cake to me. She arches a brow. It's so pointy, it almost looks dangerous.

Something about it irks me, like a thorn piercing through my glove and right into my finger. "What?" I grumble.

"I don't believe you." She sniffs the air. "It smells . . . *good*."

"And you think I'm incapable of such a thing?"

This time when she tips her head, a stray red curl tumbles across her cheek. "Yup."

"Fine." I reach for her plate, meaning to take it and put it away. Seems she won't be needing it. But she snatches it up at the last moment, her thin pale fingers brushing mine.

And they're *warm*. Almost hot. Like she has a fever. Or like a fire burns just beneath her skin.

"You don't want it, give it back." I hold my hand out, trying to ignore the funny feeling the brief brush of our fingers caused in me. I tell myself it's just because I haven't touched anyone—or been touched—in so long.

"I didn't say I don't want it. Just that I don't think you made this."

"Right. The kitchen sprites did."

Her eyes widen. "I knew it."

A heavy sigh whooshes out of me. I'm too hungry for her nonsense.

Taking up the knife, I carefully slice myself a piece of carrot cake and move it onto my plate. And only when I've taken a bite and closed my eyes at how perfect I got the buttercream frosting does the witch finally cut her own slice and give it a try.

"Goddesses spare me," she says around a mouthful of cake and frosting. Her whole body slumps, like her bones went soft at one taste of my perfect recipe. She shovels another forkful into her mouth. "Juniper, you've got to try this."

I arch a brow as the rat climbs cheerfully out of the witch's sweater pocket and takes a seat at the edge of the plate, scooping little pawfuls of cake up, whiskers twitching.

Must be the witch's spirit companion, surely. There're all sorts of exotic animals around here. I'd know, since I'm the one who often has to clean up after them. That's one of my least favorite jobs—by far.

I'm only halfway through my slice when the witch sits back in her chair with a groan, the plate empty in front of her, save for the rat—Juniper?—licking up the crumbs. "That was way too good. I think I'm in a food coma already."

I smile just a bit—it's been a while since anyone tried my cooking. Always feels good to feed someone something they appreciate. Even if she is just a delinquent student.

She stretches her arms overhead, yawns, and then levels her crimson gaze on me.

And something in it makes the hair on the back of my neck stand on end—though whether in a good way or a bad way, I'm not yet sure.

"So . . . I don't see you around much."

I take another bite and shrug my shoulders. I'm around plenty; I just prefer to do my work out of sight. Means I have to talk to fewer people that way.

The witch leans forward, arms crossed on my bistro table. It makes me lean away from her, though I'm not quite sure why.

"You a recluse or something?"

The laugh that slips out of me is surprising. I don't laugh much, especially around the students. They're usually just a weed in the garden that is my day. But this fire witch has disturbed the soil, and she's making everything feel a bit . . . different.

"Something like that," I say. After taking my last bite of carrot cake and savoring the sweetness, I wipe my mouth with a linen napkin and level a stare at her. If she wants to talk so badly, maybe she can talk about herself. "What'd you do to land in community service?"

Her forehead crinkles, a sharpness appearing in her eyes. "Nothing."

"Nothing?"

She groans and crosses her arms. "I set the greenhouse on fire. On accident."

I know that part; Lysandra explained the matter when she sat down with me in my hut a few weeks ago. That wasn't exactly what I was getting at. But small talk isn't my forte.

With a tip of my head, I clarify, "Why?"

"Why what?"

My brow arches. She knows what.

The witch groans again. "I don't know, okay? I just . . ." She lifts her hands out in front of her, staring at them like they're a riddle she doesn't understand. "My magic is hard to control."

"Isn't it tied to your emotions?"

Her nose wrinkles. "What, you're an expert on fire magic now?"

Narrowing my eyes, I say, "I've been here for years, witch. I know how things work."

"It's *Lyra*," she snaps. Pushing up from her chair, she glowers down at me. "And I don't need magic tips from a minotaur."

I stand, and I can't help but to be slightly impressed when she doesn't so much as bat an eye as I tower over her. If I wanted to, I could swoop her up with one arm and chuck her over my shoulder without breaking a sweat.

Not that I want to. But still.

61

"It's *Cairn*," I grumble, infusing my words with the same amount of venom she injected into hers.

A flicker goes through her eyes, a softening that smooths the wrinkle in her forehead. But a breath later, the moment passes, and fire flickers to life in her gaze—and on her fingers.

"Keep those away from here. I'll not have you burning my home to the ground."

The witch, *Lyra*, looks down, and I can see the moment she realizes what's going on. Her cheeks turn a shade of pink, and she clenches her hands into fists, extinguishing the flames amidst little puffs of smoke.

"Come on, Juniper. We've done enough *groundskeeping* for the day."

I think that was meant to be an insult, but I couldn't care less.

"Don't burn anything on your way back," I say as I gather up our utensils and napkins.

"Very funny." She holds her hand out, and Juniper clambers into her palm. Seems dangerous to me, considering the flames that were just dancing across her fingers, but I say nothing. Then Lyra turns on a muddy heel and stomps—yes, *stomps*—away from my hut, her boots thumping along the path leading toward the castle.

Heat smolders in my chest as I watch her go, a mixture of irritation and something I can't quite get my thumb on yet. Without thinking on it, I snatch our dirty dishes off the bistro table and return to my hut, wondering if I shouldn't have shared my carrot cake with her after all.

CHAPTER 8
LYRA

THE STANDS ARE PACKED WITH STUDENTS and faculty, who're all cheering on the players as they sprint across the runeball field. There's a bite to the air, and a breeze sends my curls blowing into my eyes. In the distance, lining the academy's campus, trees rustle, sending red, orange, and yellow leaves twirling to the ground.

For a brief moment, I wonder if I'll be here next autumn to see the way the leaves change and cover the courtyard, or attend the fall runeball games with Alina and Maeve and Poppy. Or will I have already been expelled by then?

"Want some?" Alina holds her bag of cinnamon-sugar pecans out to me, pulling my thoughts out of an endless cycle of what-ifs. I eye the bag and the little toasted nuts, which're still steaming. Every time we come to a game, Raelan buys her a bag, and without fail, she always offers me some. Call it our runeball tradition.

"Thanks." I reach into the bag and take a handful. They're warm against my skin. Immediately, Juniper scurries out of my pocket, along my arm, and into my lap, where she grabs a pecan and begins delicately nibbling on it.

"You okay?" Alina tips her head. Her pale blue eyes blink curiously at me. Beside her, Raelan leans forward, also staring at me.

These two freak me out sometimes now with how in sync they are. Once the whole mate-claiming thing happened, everything changed.

"I'm fine," I say.

"You're not," Juniper says in my lap.

Alina's gaze goes to Juniper, then back to me. I know she doesn't believe me. But I also know that I don't want to talk about it. These are my problems to deal with.

"I'm fine, really. Just a bit worried about midterms."

That's not totally a lie. I *am* worried about midterms—but I'm also worried I might not even get to take them. Like the headmistress said, one more magical mishap and I could be gone from Coven Crest for good.

Alina's shoulders rise and fall with a sigh. "Me too. Poppy and I are going to study tomorrow. You want to join us?"

No, I *really* don't want to spend my Sunday studying after spending half my Saturday doing ridiculous community service. But it'd probably be good for me. And studying with Poppy always makes a difference. She's brilliant. Probably the most brilliant person I know.

"Sure. Sounds good."

The stands erupt with cheers and boos. I steal a pecan from Juniper—she hogs all of them, I swear—and turn my gaze to the game.

Maeve's stepbrother, Aric, is playing, and his team looks to be struggling to maintain control of the arcane sphere. The opposing team has impressive control of their magic, and it's making it difficult for Aric's team to take possession or score any points.

A witch with red hair—not unlike mine—blasts the arcane sphere through the fire rune, setting it alight. It glimmers orange and red, and there's concern on the faces of some of the players.

The fire-covered sphere is always tricky for them to handle, as dealing with fire takes so much caution and control.

My stomach turns as the fire witch dances through her opponents, using her fire magic to guide the sphere almost seamlessly across the field. She and a warlock pass it back and forth, and another cheer goes up when she sends it smashing through Aric's team's goalposts in a crackle of flames.

Beside me, Maeve sighs. "If they lose, Aric is going to be such a pain."

"Sore loser?" Poppy asks. She's bundled in a sweater and has her hair in two short braids. Her cheeks are pink from the bite in the air.

Maeve scoffs. "To the extreme. And we're supposed to hang out later. But I think he just wants help on his divination homework." She rolls her storm-purple eyes. "He's the third-year. Shouldn't he be the one helping me?"

"Maybe Poppy could help," Alina offers.

Poppy goes bright red. "I . . . I . . ."

Yeah, she's not great with strangers. Especially big orcish ones.

While Maeve laughs and slings an arm around Poppy's shoulders, I watch the fire witch down on the field. Her teammates are crowding around her, smiling and slapping her on the back. I don't know who she is, so she's probably an upperclassman. And looking at her, I get a sick feeling in my stomach.

Jealousy. Anger. Disappointment.

Why can she control her magic but I'm absolutely terrible at it? I bet she's never almost been expelled from the academy, and she most *certainly* wasn't ever tasked with community service alongside the stoic minotaur.

In my lap, Juniper puts her paw on my hand. When I look down, she's staring right up at me, little sugar crystals clinging to her whiskers.

"You're doing great," she says. "Don't get discouraged. You're going to figure this out—I don't doubt you one bit."

I offer her my finger, and she lets me stroke her head and under her chin.

"Thanks," I whisper to her.

I know she's trying to make me feel better, and my friends would all do the same if they understood how I'm feeling.

But no matter what anyone says, I know the truth.

I'm still a hazard. My magic is still out of control.

And I have no idea how I'm going to fix it.

CHAPTER 9
CAIRN

AS THE AUTUMN SUN SLIPS LOWER IN the sky and the air grows cold, I stack a few logs in the hearth and light a fire. Immediately, the warmth dances across my face and pulls a contented sigh out of me. There's something about a warm fire on a crisp fall evening that will always comfort my soul.

After lighting the fire, I put some vegetable stew on the stove to heat up, then fetch my basket of medical supplies and go sit on the plush old couch in my sitting room.

"Come on, let's see how it looks." I gesture to the red fox I've been nursing back to health, and he yawns before pushing up from the nest of blankets I made for him and hobbling toward me. I found him in the woods last week while I was gathering mushrooms for a big creamy soup, and he allowed me to bring him home.

Many animals sense the nonhuman parts of me, and it helps them to develop trust with me more quickly than they ever would with a human. It certainly comes in handy when wildlife needs a bit of tending to.

The fox lets me lift him onto the couch next to me, and he only growls a little bit as I unwrap the cotton bandage from his paw.

"Looking better," I say to him as I assess the wound on the pad of his paw. "Shouldn't be much longer now and you'll be good as new."

Using a poultice I mixed up earlier, I apply it to the wound, then take up a fresh roll of cotton and bandage the paw, being careful not to pull it too tight. The fox is incredibly patient with me, and when I'm done, I settle him back onto the floor.

"All finished. But don't bite at it, or we'll have to rewrap it."

He flicks his fluffy red tail at me, then retreats to his bed near the fire.

Even the wildest of creatures appreciate a soft place to rest their heads.

My stew is heated through now, and I wash my hands and put the medical supplies away before serving myself up a bowl—and grabbing a slice of carrot cake to have on the side. I carry the plates to the table and take a seat, but before I can dig in, I start to think of *her*.

The fire witch.

My eyes are drawn to the window near my front door, where I know the sniffleblooms are still sitting in their little squares of soil, waiting for the sun to rise and bathe them in warmth.

I expected the witch to leave here in a fit of sneezing and sniffles—it's happened to me on a number of occasions—but somehow, she was able to complete the task I'd assigned her without letting the delicate blossoms get to her.

She was so proud when she was finished, with that fiery look to her that told me she knew I'd given her a nearly impossible task but that she'd surpassed my expectations.

Suddenly, I find myself smiling, and my chest is getting a bit warm at the memory of her eyes, the focused furrow in her forehead as she worked, the twisty curl that fell across her cheek as she tipped her head at me.

And I realize with a jolt of dread what this warm feeling is.

I grip my spoon so tight I nearly bend the metal.

No, I scold myself. *I don't feel that way about her. I can't.*

I've spent years learning how to control everything in my life: my instincts, my anger, my emotions, my desires. After having my heart ripped out once already, I started keeping everyone at a distance, and I like it this way. It's comfortable. It's safe.

And the witch is anything but safe.

She's a spark waiting to combust, one fireball away from losing her place at the academy. I'd be an absolute fool to indulge in these feelings that have started to creep up on me, that have started to make me notice the color of her eyes when the sun hits them and the shape her freckles make when she smiles or scowls.

Nothing about this is okay. She's a student, a witch, nearly ten years my junior.

And I'll not indulge in such ridiculous and inappropriate feelings. I'll squash these emotions before they have another moment to take root.

With a decisive huff, I spoon another bite of soup into my mouth.

But somehow, it doesn't taste quite as good as it did a moment ago. It's blander, somehow.

And I try not to take that as a metaphor for my life.

I'm fine with my books and my cooking and my plants. I'm fine not having a woman to come home to at night or to hold in bed while snow falls and the air grows cold. And I'll not let one cranky fire witch change everything I've worked so hard to build. That's that.

CHAPTER 10
LYRA

IT RAINED LAST NIGHT—NO, *POURED*—AND THE grounds are absolutely soaked as I follow Cairn around, trying to keep up with his long-legged strides. I'm pushing around a wheelbarrow full to the brim with mulch. Cairn has one as well, and we've been mulching the flower beds around the academy. When I asked what the point was, Cairn said the mulch will help protect the plants from the bite of winter, keeping them warm and alive until the following spring.

"Put more here," he instructs, pointing to the spot where he wants me to dump the mulch. With a grunt, I heft the wheelbarrow up and dump the remaining mulch onto the ground—though I miss the spot he indicated by about a foot, and his huff and arched brow communicate his frustration.

"Do we need more?" I ask, glancing at his empty wheelbarrow sitting nearby.

He pauses moving the mulch from where I dumped it to where he needs it and gazes into the distance. Tipping his head—and those big curled horns—he says, "A bit. One more wheelbarrow should do."

"All right." I shove my hair out of my face with the back of my hand, then take up the wheelbarrow and start pushing it back toward the garden, where the mulch pile is. Wet leaves and shallow puddles dot my path, and I try to weave around them as best I can.

It's late morning now, and the other students are up and about. Many are outside, soaking up the sun. Some sip warm drinks from mugs, while others already have their books cracked open and are studying for our upcoming midterms. I *really* don't want to think about that. I've been worried for days and days, and every time I picture having to display my magic in my Elemental Magic 201 class, I get a sick knot in my stomach.

Two warlocks are messing around, using air magic to stir up the colorful leaves and send them flying around their witch companions. The girls laugh and bat the leaves away as I pass by, trying not to catch their attention.

It's not that I'm embarrassed about helping Cairn or having to do community service; it's the whispers, the looks, the knowledge that I'm a fire witch who can't control her magic, who's hanging on to her enrollment here by the tips of her fingers.

What will Papa say if I get expelled? I wonder.

And *that* thought sends me on a rapid downward spiral. He's spent my whole life bending over backward, doing everything he can for me. As a single parent, he had it twice as hard, and I know my childhood wasn't easy on him. I can't count the number of times I set things on fire during temper tantrums. He used to have to keep a bucket of water in the house just to douse the flames.

Useless, I think. *I've always been useless.*

The next thing I know, leaves are spiraling around me, impeding my view as I push the wheelbarrow through the wet mud and grass. The wind tears at my hair and clothes, and the dry leaf matter strikes my face, stinging my skin.

"Hey!" I snap, gearing up to give the warlocks an earful. "Why don't you—"

My boot hits a slick spot of deep mud, and before I can right myself, I go down. Hard.

I try to catch myself, but it's futile. As soon as my hands hit the mud, they slide out from under me, and next thing I know, my face is *literally* in the muck.

And my wrist is on fire. I landed on it at an awkward angle, and heat pounds through it with every beat of my galloping heart.

Along with the rage.

An angry roar bursts out of me as I push myself out of the mud with my good wrist.

"What the *fuck*!" I scream, and fire pulses from my hands, heat tearing across my skin as I glare toward the two warlocks who were messing around with the leaves.

They stare back at me with wide, terrified eyes.

"I'm going to *roast you*!" I scream at them. But when I try to get to my feet, I slip again, and I'm right back in the mud.

The warlocks and the witches who're with them take off, getting away from me as quickly as they can, though not without some giggles as they glance back at me.

My skin burns with anger and embarrassment. I look down at myself and find my sweater, trousers, and boots completely slicked with mud. It's in my hair and in my mouth, gritty against my tongue.

Suddenly, I want to give up. I don't want to do this anymore, don't want to struggle and battle just to be here when everything I do feels worthless.

My vision starts to blur with tears. Stupid, traitorous tears. I'm already covered in mud and leaves; I don't need the other students to see me crying on top of it all. I'd much rather be mad than sad.

Just as a tear drips down my mud-coated cheek, footsteps approach from behind me. They're slow and heavy, and they stop next to me as a horned shadow falls over my shoulders.

"Are you all right?" Cairn kneels beside me, unconcerned about the knee of his trousers getting muddy.

"I'm fine." I don't look at him. It's too humiliating.

With a grunt, I try to push to my feet, but my wrist is *definitely* not okay, and it sears with pain, making me gasp and clutch it to my chest.

I'm so glad Juniper wasn't in my pocket when I fell. She would've been squashed. She definitely made a good choice deciding to sleep in this morning.

"You're hurt," Cairn says.

Using one clean spot on my sweater, I wipe my eyes, then turn to look up at him.

And I find his dark eyes narrowed with concern, his lips pulled into a deep frown. He doesn't avert his gaze from me, doesn't smirk or laugh at how pitiful I am.

"It's my wrist. I landed on it when I fell. But I'll be fine."

"You probably sprained it." He reaches for it, but I pull it away.

"I'll be okay."

With a heavy sigh that only a minotaur is capable of, he pushes up and reaches down to take me by the elbow, tail swishing behind him. "Come on. I'll wrap it for you."

"I don't—"

Ignoring my complaint, Cairn cups my elbow and helps me to my feet. But even once I'm on my feet, his hand remains there, warming me through my knit sweater. I meet his eyes. A moment passes as we hold each other's gaze. Then he pulls his hand away.

"Let's go."

He grabs the wheelbarrow and starts back toward his hut. I glance over my shoulder and find a few of the lingering students watching me. But when they meet my glare, they turn quickly away, acting like they weren't just blatantly staring at me.

Or maybe they were staring at him. At his broad shoulders and curling horns. At the nose hoop he wears, which glints when the autumn sunlight catches it.

I wouldn't blame them. Sometimes I find myself staring at him too.

"Lyra," he calls out to me, already halfway across the courtyard by now.

My name sounds warm even as he says it with a hint of irritation in his tone. And it finally gets my muddy boots moving, carrying me back toward his home at the edge of the woods.

CHAPTER 11
CAIRN

I'M STILL NOT SURE IF I'VE MADE A BAD CHOICE. It feels like I'm treading dangerous water, knowing sea creatures are lurking just beneath my hooves. But for some idiotic reason, I refuse to get out of the ocean.

Lyra sits on my couch, her wrist held close to her chest, crimson eyes sweeping across my furniture and bookshelf and the herbs that are hanging upside down to dry.

I shouldn't have brought her in here. It would've been better to sit her in the garden, like when we ate carrot cake together, and tend to her wrist outside. But it felt inconsiderate, somehow. So now she's here, in my home, where very few ever are.

Basket full of the supplies I need, I walk into the sitting room to join her, my hooves thumping across the hardwood floor. Her gaze flicks to me as I slowly sink onto the couch beside her, being careful to keep my tail away from her and maintain distance between us—though it's somewhat difficult, seeing as I take up most of the couch on my own.

"You really don't have to," she says, but the fire has gone out of her voice. She doesn't mean it.

"Let me see it." I set the basket on the floor by my hooves, then hold out a hand.

Lyra hesitates. She assesses my hand as if determining whether or not it's safe. Then, slowly, seeming to have made her decision, she settles her wrist into my grip.

"It's warm," I say immediately.

She shrugs. "I'm always warm. Fire magic."

I don't look up at her. It seems dangerous to do so. "I know. But this feels like inflammation. It's already swelling."

"Oh . . ."

"I don't have ice, but I can wrap it. That'll help support it and reduce swelling."

She tips her head at me, but I still don't meet her eyes. "How do you know all this?"

With a shrug, I reach into the basket and pull out a roll of cotton. Seems I'm using a lot of this lately. I'll need to get more next time I go shopping in Wysteria.

"When you're on your own," I say quietly, "you have to learn how to care for yourself."

Taking the roll of cotton, I start to slowly wrap it around Lyra's wrist, noting how bird-thin it is, like one pinch of my fingers could crush it.

I'm careful, tender. And I try to ignore the heat in my stomach at the feel of her skin against mine.

For one whole week, I almost didn't think of her. I thought I'd gotten it through my head that there can't be— isn't—anything here. I'm just doing what anyone else would do—helping someone who needs it.

"Do you like it?" she asks.

My mind having wandered, I can't recall what she's referring to. I glance at her. And it's a mistake, because her vibrant red eyes are so close to mine that I can see the thin bands of gold around her pupils, can almost imagine myself falling into the galaxy that is her gaze.

I clear my throat and quickly finish wrapping her wrist, tucking the end of the cotton into itself so it doesn't come unwound. "Do I like what?"

Her lips quirk up on one side. "Being alone."

"Oh." I reach up and scratch my beard—anything to distract my hands and my mind. She's perched right here on my couch, her muddy boots are sitting outside my door, and this is starting to feel much too intimate. Inappropriate. Maybe even dangerous. "Uh, yes."

The hesitation was a mistake. Lyra picked up on it, if the arch of her brow is any indication. "Really?"

"Yes, really." I stand and grab my basket of medical supplies, fingers flexing around the handle.

"Hmm." She regards her wrapped wrist, then looks around my hut again. "I don't."

It seems like she wants to keep talking, so I linger. "Why?"

The quirk of her lips falls away. A ghost of pain flickers across her face as she shrugs. "I get lonely."

"Don't you like your own company?" I ask.

Her laugh is lacking in humor. "Not particularly."

Words rise onto my tongue, and they spill out before I have the good sense to swallow them down. "Well, I do."

She lifts her eyes to mine. The power in her fiery gaze has my chest squeezing.

How is it that a tiny fire witch has me feeling so vulnerable? It's been years since I felt so exposed, so . . . laid bare. And all she's doing is looking at me.

"I find that hard to believe," she says at long last.

Part of me wants to push back, to tell her that despite her whining and random flares of fire, she's actually fun to be around. In a weird way, of course. But this time my brain catches up before I can make yet another mistake, and I shrug instead of speaking.

There's the sound of claws clicking across my scuffed wooden floor, and the red fox appears from my bedroom, where he ran off to when I opened the door and he smelled Lyra. When he sees her, he freezes.

Her brows rise, her lips opening in surprise. "Who's this?" she asks. Moving slowly, she gets off the couch and sinks to the floor—though she's careful not to use her wrapped wrist.

"I found him in the woods a while back. Had a paw injury. I've been nursing him back to health. He's almost ready to go home."

The fox regards Lyra with a cautious stare. She holds her fingers out, unhurried, letting him choose whether or not to approach. And slowly, he does. He inches forward, one paw still wrapped in a bandage, and sniffs her hand. Then he allows her to scratch him beneath the chin before whirling around and vanishing back into my bedroom once more.

Lyra sits back with a smile. And I wish she wouldn't make that face around me. I think I prefer her scowls and eye rolls; her smiles are much too perilous.

"Wow. That was so cool. I've never met a fox before." She tips her head thoughtfully. "Well, that's not totally true. One of my roommates, Alina, has a snow fox companion, Yuki. I've never met a *wild* fox though."

I lean against the wide doorway leading from the sitting room into the kitchen. "There are plenty around here. But they'll only show themselves if they trust you."

Her face falls, and she gets slowly to her feet. "Makes sense. I don't think anyone trusts me."

I roll my thoughts around for a moment, weighing them, then say softly, "That's not true."

"Oh?" Her brow arches again. She goes to cross her arms, then winces at her wrist and lowers her arms back to her sides. "Are you saying *you* trust me?"

A smile tugs on my mouth. I try not to let it out, but I fail. "You *did* transplant those sniffleblooms without a single sneeze. That's worth something in my book."

She laughs again, but this time, it sounds joyful. She's so hot and cold, flickering between smiling and frowning, like a fire dancing, sending light and shadow twirling together in a mesmerizing display. "Well, that makes one person. And Juniper, I guess. She counts too."

I remain there in the doorway, leaning against the wood, regarding the small fire witch standing in my sitting room, sweater and trousers smeared with mud. And she regards me right back. What does she see when she looks at me? A reclusive groundskeeper? A faculty member? A minotaur who's much too old for her?

Somewhere deep in my chest, an ember of yearning flares to life.

A yearning for her to see deeper than that, past my cold exterior and into the truth of who I truly am.

But that yearning is forbidden. And I shove it down as quickly as it arises.

Problem is, I'm not so sure it'll acquiesce to being buried.

CHAPTER 12
LYRA

THE STAIRS UP TO ROOM NT33 ARE LONG and spiraling. I'm pretty sure I'm leaving a trail of mud behind me as I climb each step, but I don't want to turn and look. I just want to go take a long hot bath and wash away all the gunk from the day.

My wrist is still sore from falling and spraining it, but more than the pain, I feel Cairn's hand as he lifted me off the ground, then the tenderness with which he wrapped the cotton bandage around my wrist, his fingers warm and gentle. I still have a slight tingle where he touched me, and it's making my brow furrow, making me wonder why my stomach flipped and flopped in a not-wholly-unpleasant way while I stood in his sitting room and watched him lean in the doorway, his horns twisting so high they nearly brushed the ceiling.

One of our exchanges comes back to me, making my throat warm.

Don't you like your own company? he asked me.

And when I told him I don't, his response was, *Well, I do.*

He didn't elaborate, but when I looked up and met his eyes, they regarded me unflinchingly, sturdy as a big old oak tree.

He likes my company . . .

Before I can stop it, a smile is rising to my mouth, lifting the corners of my lips.

Do I like his company too?

My body responds before my brain can, getting warm and tingly at the idea of seeing him again, hearing that deep voice, perhaps even feeling the warmth from his big, strong hands.

Shit. I've always liked men with big hands.

I'm so lost in thought that I almost walk right past our dorm room; if not for Raelan standing in the hallway, the colorful light from the stained glass window glowing down over his short dark hair, I probably would've just kept on going.

He arches a brow at me. "You okay?"

With some effort, I banish the smile from my lips. "Fine."

Quickly assessing me, mud and all, he says, "Looks like you had an interesting morning."

I blow out a strong puff of air, sending one of my curls dancing. "You've got no idea."

He smiles, just a little bit, and I turn to walk into our dorm room.

The air is warm with a hint of sage from Maeve's morn-ing incense meditation, and the girls are all sprawled about the sitting room: Poppy reading from a book on sentient flora, Alina copying runes into a notebook with a feather quill, and Maeve lounging on the couch, one leg over the back, letting Isis curl about her arm.

When I close the door behind me, they all glance in my direction.

"She lives," Maeve says dryly. Her eyes narrow a bit as I pull off my muddy boots and deposit them beside the door. "Does the academy offer mud baths that I'm unaware of? Because that would be amazing."

I roll my eyes. "I slipped and fell. Made quite a scene."

Poppy pushes her glasses up the bridge of her nose. "Are you all right?"

"Mostly. Just wounded my pride." I hold up my arm. "And sprained my wrist."

Alina puts her quill down and turns in her chair to regard me. Concern furrows her smooth brow. "Who wrapped it for you?"

It's a simple question, one that shouldn't take any effort to answer. Yet I find myself growing warm, like there's a can-dle flickering just inside my rib cage. And I have to make an effort to shrug nonchalantly, avoiding eye contact as I say, "The minotaur."

A moment of quiet passes. I can see the girls glancing at one another in my periphery as I pull my muddy sweater off over my head. I'll need to do laundry earlier this week than I typically do.

"That was . . . nice of him," Poppy says. Her voice lilts a bit, as if trying to entice me into saying more.

But I refuse. Instead, I force a scoff. "It was the least he could do. It's his fault I fell in the first place."

There's a whisper of little paws on wooden floorboards, and when I look up, Juniper is peering down at me from our loft.

"You got hurt?" she asks, her voice a quiet squeak.

"Barely," I tell her. Then, before the girls—or Juniper—can interrogate me further, I announce, "I'm going to take a bath. Then anyone want to get lunch?"

"Me!" Maeve sits up on the couch as Isis slithers around her shoulders and twines about her neck.

That still creeps me out.

"I could eat," Alina agrees. "How about you, Pops?"

Poppy smiles. "I've got an even better idea."

We all exchange looks, then say at the same time, "The Wandering Cup!"

Just like that, I'm able to slip away, having escaped being asked more questions about the minotaur than I want to answer. But as I gather what I'll need for my bath, I find myself looking out the window in the loft, over the spires of the castle and down to what I can see of the campus below.

And I find myself thinking of him, wondering what he does in the quiet when no one is around. It makes the candle behind my ribs burn ever brighter.

CHAPTER 13
LYRA

THE AUTUMN SUNLIGHT WARMS MY FACE AS I stand in the courtyard with all the other students in my Elemental Magic 201 class. With midterms fast approaching, we're spending our classroom time outdoors, practicing for our elemental magic exam. Students are sprinkled about the courtyard, all practicing their magic a safe distance from one another.

Maeve is in this class with me—I had Introduction to Elemental Magic with Alina last year—but she's on the other side of the courtyard, a few warlocks gathered around her as she creates a dark purple storm cloud and makes it rain. The guys all smile and laugh and try to move closer to her, as if she's interested in any of them. Maeve could probably have her pick of the warlocks in Coven Crest, but she mostly seems bored by them. I just roll my eyes.

All around me, flames whisper, wind sends skirts and robes billowing, vines rise from the earth, and droplets of water shimmer in the air. And I stand in the center of it all, palms outstretched, brows pinched in frustration.

This class is *supposed* to be easy for me. I'm an elemental witch, a fire witch. The other elemental witches and warlocks seem to excel in this class, but I certainly don't.

Air and earth magic aren't so bad to learn, and while my water magic could still use some practice, it's my fire magic that's making me so nervous for midterms. Because it's my fire that's uncontrollable, that flares at the smallest provocation, that makes me dangerous to the other students and any flammable thing within my reach. And it's my fire magic that's on the brink of getting me expelled.

I clench my teeth and flex my fingers. Thankfully, my sprained wrist is very nearly healed, and I'm no longer wearing the bandage Cairn gave me. Though that hasn't stopped me from keeping it close—in the nightstand beside my bed, to be precise. I tell myself it's just because I want to give it back to him next time I see him, but part of me whispers that it's more than that. But I can't think about that right now.

Hands held out, I take a breath and call to my fire magic. This didn't used to make me nervous, but as of late, the flames that used to be my friends now give me a tingle of fear whenever I summon them. A small arc of fire leaps from my fingertips, then flares too bright, too hot. The flames crackle and spark brighter. I wince and draw back instinctively, and the fire sputters out with a hiss.

"Too forceful again, Miss Wilder," Professor Stone says from off to my right, arms crossed, watching with the weary patience of someone who's seen too many singed sleeves and flaming textbooks—at least a few of which were because of me. He narrows his brown eyes. "You're trying to bend it to your will. Fire doesn't like to be bent. It doesn't like to follow rules. Guide it. Invite it instead of forcing it."

Guide it. Easy for him to say. He's an earth warlock, not a fire witch, and earth isn't nearly so finnicky. I close my hands, curling my fingers tightly. I need to do well, need to prove to Headmistress Moonhart that I deserve my place here at the academy, that I can control myself and get my flames in check before I accidentally set the castle and all its inhabitants on fire.

I take a breath. Pressure coils inside my chest like a clenched fist squeezing my heart. I know that fire responds to emotion; of all the elemental magics, it's the most volatile, arguably the most difficult to control. Powerful but erratic. A sword with two sharp edges.

"Be intentional," Professor Stone says. And his words cause a memory to flash in my mind.

Just go slow and be careful, Cairn said in regard to the sniffleblooms. *Intentional.*

Go slow. Be careful.

I listened to his instructions, was as delicate as possible while transplanting the vicious little blooms. And I did it. Not once did I breathe in their sneeze dust.

A little tingle goes through me when I hear Cairn's deep voice say, *Impressive.*

I did something *right*. I saw it in his eyes, heard it in the tone of his voice.

And I can do this right too. I *have* to. If I want to stay at Coven Crest, I have no other choice but to get my magic under control. Somehow . . .

I take a deep breath and flex my fingers, holding my palms out again. This time, I don't push. Instead, I let my flames rise like a flower slowly blossoming in the spring, calling them with warmth instead of force. The fire sparks to life on my fingertips, flickering delicately, steadily—a stream of gold that curls around my fingers like the pillowy kiss of a satin ribbon. No flare. No bite of intense heat. No backlash.

Professor Stone steps forward, arms still crossed and eyes narrowed—though this time in surprise rather than judgment. "Much better," he says slowly, as if raising his voice will cause the fire to lash out and singe him. "That's progress, Miss Wilder."

Something small and fierce flutters in my chest. I can't help myself—I smile. Not just from relief, but with pride. Maybe I belong here after all.

And maybe Cairn—with his gentle ways and quiet insights—is more than an annoying community service project, more than a reclusive minotaur. Maybe he can teach me how to control myself, my emotions.

Maybe, in some small way, he's exactly what I need.

CHAPTER 14
CAIRN

BY SOME STROKE OF GOOD LUCK, IT'S NOT RAINing on my shopping day. I'd anticipated needing to make the long trek into Wysteria in a gray drizzle, but instead, the sun is shining, birds sing as they drift through the breeze, and the air smells of autumn—one of my favorite smells, perhaps second only to the smell of the garden after a summer rain.

I pull a small wooden cart behind me as I walk. It's empty now, but by the time I'm on my return trip home, it'll be loaded down with everything I'll need for the next few weeks. I try to stock up as much as possible to avoid having to make the long walk, and though Wysteria is nice so far as big cities go, it's much too busy and chaotic for my liking, so I limit my trips there as much as possible.

My hooves feel nice sinking into the dirt and leaves as I walk the meandering path through the Mistwood, enjoying the quiet and the dappled light slipping through the trees overhead. Probably won't be long now before the snow starts to fall, making this trip a hell of a lot harder than it is now. So for the time being, I enjoy it, and I keep a smile on my face all the way to Wysteria.

I'M FINALLY ON MY LAST STOP OF THE DAY: THE Brass Mirror. It's one of the only clothing shops in Wysteria that carries clothing in my size. Typically when I'm here, other nonhuman shoppers are here as well: other minotaurs, orcs, and shifters. But today, it's quiet, and it gives me a brief reprieve from the bustling street outside.

"Be right with you!" a man calls from the back.

I've been coming here for years, so I know the familiar voice well. "Just me, Winston."

"Cairn?" the shopkeeper calls back. "That you?"

"Yup."

Without needing him to show me around, I roam through the racks and shelves of clothing. Some of my trousers are starting to get worn and rip, and I could use some more long-sleeved tunics before winter arrives.

I pick up two new pairs of trousers—specially sized for minotaurs—then add a couple tunics to the pile in my arms: one in forest green and one in burnt orange. By the time I make it to the front counter, Winston is just coming out from the back room.

As one may expect of a clothing connoisseur, he's impeccably dressed—gleaming golden hoops in his ears, a snug vest with polished buttons, trim trousers, and boots that look like they've never touched a dusty cobblestone in their life. When he sees me, he holds out his arms, and I huff as he wraps me in a crushing hug. He may look willowy, but vampires are surprisingly strong.

"Cairn, it's been too long. Why don't you come in more?"

He releases me from the hug and moves behind the counter as I put the trousers and tunics on the tabletop. "Maybe you should sell lower-quality goods," I say with a shrug. "Then I'd have to shop more often."

Winston narrows his golden eyes and says with a hiss, "Lower quality? Preposterous. Only the best for my customers."

I shrug again. "Can't have it both ways."

"Well, if only you'd come and be social sometimes." He flashes me a sharp glance. "You know, have a meal and a drink, share a few laughs. Be *personable*."

I have to actively strive not to grimace, but Winston knows me better than that.

"I know, I know." He holds up his hands, which are bejeweled with rings. "You prefer fungi over friendly banter." His marble-smooth brow furrows. "Though I'll never understand why."

He quickly tallies up the cost of my trousers and tunics, and I pass him the eldertokens I owe. With expert hands, he refolds the articles of clothing, then ties the bundle with a strand of twine and knots it with a bow.

Just as he slides the bundle over, a display of gloves catches my eye. Like everything in the Brass Mirror, they're well made, and a handwritten sign over the shelf reads *Enchanted Gloves*. I arch an eyebrow.

"What's with the gloves?"

Winston glances over. "Oh, they're on consignment. A witch friend of mine made them. They're enchanted to last forever." He flashes me a fanged smile. "Or *nearly* forever. And they're fireproof too. Perfect for gardening, baking, what have you."

"Fireproof?"

Unbidden, Lyra Wilder jumps into my head, her curls all tangled and frizzy, her brow furrowed in concentration. I recall the blisters that marred her palms on our first day working together, the much-too-big gloves I offered her. But these gloves . . . They look perfect for her.

I reach out and pick up a pair. The fabric is soft and pliable, not heavy like some gardening gloves. And if Lyra's going to be working with me for the rest of the year, she'll surely need *something*.

Trying not to overthink it, I place the gloves on the counter.

Winston leans forward, regarding them with a quizzical arch to his shapely eyebrow. "I hate to say it, dear friend, but . . ." He holds up the gloves, gaze shifting from them to me. "I don't think these come in your size."

With a huff, I reach into my pocket and pull out my eldertokens. "Not for me."

Now his quizzical expression turns curious. "No? Sounds like there's a story to be told."

I shake my head, though I'm careful not to catch my horns on the chandelier hanging over Winston's front counter. "No story. Just need the gloves."

Despite Winston's pouting, I don't tell him anything about Lyra. There's nothing to tell.

She's just a student whose time with me is numbered. We'll finish the year, and then it'll be like nothing ever happened.

But at the very least, I can make sure her hands are protected. And there's no more story to be told.

CART LADEN WITH EVERYTHING I PURCHASED TODAY—bags of grain and flour, clothes, more medical supplies, some interesting new seeds I've never tried before—I start down the cobblestone street away from the Brass Mirror. I got everything that was on my list, and I can finally start the long walk back to Coven Crest.

But just as I settle in to my pace, passing the big glittering bronze statue of a stag standing in the center of the city square, someone calls my name.

At first, I consider pretending I didn't hear him. I'm really not in the mood to do any more socializing; all I want is to get home and pour myself a hot cup of dandelion-root coffee.

But then he calls to me again.

"Cairn! Hey! Cairn!"

This time, the voice sounds familiar.

I slow my pace and turn to look over my shoulder.

And sure enough, there he is: Milo Foster, the kid who used to follow me around the gardens. The one who works at the botanical conservatory now.

The one who sent me the letter and the application to said conservatory.

I'm surprised enough that I stop dead in the road, and the people walking behind me have to grumble and veer around. Milo jogs over, and though he's a bit older now than when last I saw him, with a bit of scruff where he once was baby smooth, he's still the same kid I knew.

"I thought that was you," he says, propping his hands on his narrow hips. "I'd know that I-can't-stand-people scowl anywhere."

I blink in surprise—I don't recall him being so forward—and Milo laughs.

"Sorry, bad joke." His glasses catch the sunlight as he tips his head and smiles. Then his expression sobers. "Wait, you remember me, don't you? Milo Foster?"

I blink slowly, saying nothing.

Now his expression turns downright glum. "What? Come on! How could you forge—"

With a chuckle, I smack him on the shoulder, and he stumbles so hard his glasses slide down the bridge of his nose. "Come on, Foster. Of course I remember you."

Milo lets out a relieved sigh as he pushes the glasses back up the bridge of his nose. "Your humor is still dry as ever. You really had me fooled for a second there."

"You make it too easy." I flick my tail and cross my arms over my chest.

"Yeah, yeah." He waves me off and uses his other hand to push his mop of unruly brown hair out of his face. Then his brown eyes light up. "Hey, let me buy you a drink."

That would mean having to postpone my walk home. It would also mean having to be around other people for longer than I already have been today. Sounds terrible.

I open my mouth to tell him no, but he holds up a hand to stop me.

"Come on, no turning it down. They've got pumpkin ale at Boar and Badger. You'll love it." He sets off across the square, the same bouncy, lanky stride I'm so familiar with.

My nostrils flutter as I let out a heavy sigh and glance back at my cart. Then I follow him.

CHAPTER 15
LYRA

WHEN I GET BACK TO THE DORM AFTER A particularly grueling mathematics class—seriously, when will I *ever* need to know that stuff?—the air smells of sugar and spice. Immediately, Juniper pops her head out of my robe pocket and says, "I smell frosting."

"Lyra!" Alina calls as I peel my loafers off and drop them on the mat beside the door. "Layla brought cupcakes!"

"Oh, sweet goddess," Juniper whispers, whiskers twitching. "Her red velvet cupcakes are the best."

I laugh and reach down to stroke a finger over her head.

"Poppy, your mom came by?" I call out as I pad into the sitting room in my stockings.

"Yup!" She's pouring a cup of tea and looks over at me. "She claimed she made too many cupcakes and needed someone to give them to, but I think she just wanted an excuse to come visit." Her lips pull up in a smile. "Go on, there are a few left over. Juniper, you can have one too."

"*Part* of one," I correct, looking down at Juniper as I take a seat on the couch next to Alina. "Too much sugar and you'll be up all night."

"You," Juniper says as she scurries out of my pocket and into my lap, nose scenting the air, "can speak for yourself. I'm much older than you in rat years."

I arch a brow at her. "But I'm the one you keep up when you're on a nighttime sugar high."

Juniper pretends not to hear me—or maybe she really is just too focused on the cupcakes to process what I said.

There are a few flavors still available: a chocolate-vanilla swirl, what looks like a chocolate cupcake marbled with caramel, and Juniper's favorite, a red velvet.

"How about we split it?" I offer.

Juniper nods once. "Deal."

I cut the red-velvet cupcake into two halves (mine is *slightly* larger), then settle back on the couch to enjoy it. Juniper readjusts herself in my lap and takes a pawful of the dessert, getting crumbs all over her whiskers.

"Where's Maeve?" I ask as Poppy takes a seat on the other couch, teacup cradled in her hands.

"Went on a run with Aric, I think," Alina says from beside me. Yuki is curled up in her lap, and she has her nose stuck in a book.

I grimace. "A *run*?"

There are few things more painful than forced exercise. The fact that Maeve chooses to willingly exert herself like that is insane to me.

As if to prove my point, I take another bite of my cupcake.

"So, are those for her?" I point to the last remaining cupcakes sitting on the low table.

Poppy shakes her head. "No, she already had one. And so did Raelan."

Oh, right. I thought he smelled oddly sweet when I passed him in the stairwell.

As I take another bite, I recall the carrot cake Cairn made, the buttercream frosting so smooth and the perfectly fluffy cake beneath it. I'm pretty sure he has a sweet tooth, not unlike Juniper. And he *did* help me when I sprained my wrist. Maybe I could take him a cupcake as a thank-you gift.

Does he like chocolate? I wonder, staring at the two cupcakes.

"What is it?" Poppy asks, eyeing me over her teacup.

I reach up and snag a curl, then twist it around my finger. "Do you mind if I take those?" I ask.

Beside me, Alina lowers her book enough to gaze at me over the pages. "Take them where?"

Of course she's going to give me a hard time about it. Must be payback for how often I nettled her about Raelan last year.

In the most nonchalant tone I can manage, I say, "I want to take one to Cairn. To thank him for helping me with my wrist."

Alina and Poppy exchange a glance. And despite how they try to hide it, they *both* smile.

THE SUN IS ALREADY GOING DOWN AS I LEAVE THE castle and start making my way through the courtyard and toward Cairn's hut at the edge of the trees. I pass under the barbican, feeling the cold air pebble my skin despite my cloak, then step through to the other side, where the Mistwood towers high over my head, casting long shadows in the falling light.

And there, standing across the valley at the edge of the tree line, is Cairn's thatched hut. Smoke puffs slowly from the chimney, curling into the cool leaf-scented air before disappearing into the pine trees above.

As I approach, the door to the hut opens, and Cairn steps out. There's a cart parked just outside his door, loaded down with wooden boxes and what look like bags of grain and flour. He hefts one of the huge sacks easily over his shoulder, then starts to turn. But he must catch sight of me in his peripherals, because he stops suddenly, head swiveling in my direction, wide horns catching the evening light.

When he meets my gaze, a full-body shiver goes through me, and I tell myself it's just from the chill in the air and not the depths of his dark brown eyes.

I close the distance between us, holding the covered platter of cupcakes in my hands. Cairn doesn't move as I approach, just watches me curiously, that huge sack still slung over his shoulder. It probably weighs nearly what I do.

"Hi," I say as I come to a stop a few paces from his door.

He stares at me, brow furrowed. Then, slowly, he says, "What day is it?"

Tipping my head, I say, "Wednesday."

My community service is only on Saturdays, and I've never visited him on any other day of the week. Maybe that's why he's confused.

He reaches up to scratch his scruffy beard, and I get the overwhelming desire to know what that beard would feel like beneath my palms, running through my fingers.

Uh-oh.

"So . . . why are you here?" he asks.

Clearing my throat, I hold out my hands, and his gaze slides to the platter held aloft. "I brought you a little something to say thank you for helping me with my wrist the other day."

Cairn's eyes meet mine again. As I recall how careful and gentle his hands were when he wrapped my wrist, my cheeks start to tingle with warmth.

Quickly, I turn my face and body toward the cart, trying to banish the rush of heat. "D-do you want some help unloading this?"

A long moment of silence passes. It's long enough that I actually glance over at him.

He still looks confused.

I sigh. "Here, I'll put these down, and then I'll help."

Instead of waiting for his okay, I brush past him—and try to ignore the even bigger rush of heat his proximity causes in me—and step into the little hut. The fire is crackling, and it smells like woodsmoke and mountain sage. A few bags are already sitting on the floor in the kitchen, and there's a wooden box atop the table. As Cairn steps through the doorway behind me, I set the cupcake platter on the kitchen table. We sidestep each other—this space feels significantly smaller with him standing in it—and I hurry outside to the cart. There's a sack of flour sitting at the edge, and I look at it with determination.

I can get that.

Grabbing hold of the edge of the bag, I grit my teeth and heft it up and onto my shoulder. And immediately, the weight tips me off-balance, and I stumble back, already preparing myself to hit the ground.

Stupid, stupid, stup—

Strong hands grasp my waist, steadying me. They're big enough that they could probably encircle my entire waist. Such big hands . . .

Heat rushes through my veins as I tip my head back and find Cairn looming over me.

Okay, maybe not so stupid . . .

Cairn huffs out a breath, and with what looks like no effort, he lifts the bag of flour from my shoulder and transfers it to his own. "Why don't you get that instead?" He points to a small wooden crate loaded with what look like gardening supplies.

"S-sure," I say, trying (and probably failing) to banish the blush from my cheeks.

Taking hold of the crate, I lift it (definitely more my size) and carry it into the hut. While Cairn sets the huge sack of flour down, I put the crate onto the table.

We work in companionable silence, unloading everything from the cart. Once it's empty, Cairn leaves me standing by the front door while he pulls the cart around the back side of the hut. And I'm still standing there, wondering what the heck I'm even doing here, when he returns.

His shirt sleeves are rolled up, revealing the taut muscles in his forearms, and his chest looks even bigger as he crosses his arms and regards me with an arched brow. His tail whips behind him, though I can't tell what the sharp flicks of it mean.

"Why are you really here?" His voice is deep and cautious.

I draw myself up. "Already told you." Gesturing toward the hut, I say, "I brought cupcakes."

"You came all the way here to bring me cupcakes?"

I can't tell if he sounds annoyed or amused. Maybe a bit of both.

"Well, I *assumed* you like chocolate, but if not . . ." I shrug. "I could take them back. Raelan will probably eat them."

"Raelan?" His tone sounds slightly sharper, and his brown eyes narrow.

For some ridiculous (and probably immature) reason, I opt not to clarify. He doesn't need to know Raelan is Alina's mate and fiancé.

"I guess I'll go, then." I turn and start into the hut. "I'll just grab the cupcakes and—"

"Wait."

A smile wants to curl across my mouth, but by some miracle, I'm able to keep a straight face as I look back at him.

With an unnecessarily heavy sigh, he drops his arms and says, "I like chocolate."

This time, I do smile.

"WHO MADE THESE?" CAIRN ASKS. WE'RE SEATED AT the bistro table in the garden, the cupcake platter between us. He started with the chocolate-caramel cupcake, and I think he's melting into his chair right now as he takes another bite.

"My roommate's mom. You ever been to the Wandering Cup? In Wysteria?"

Cairn shakes his head and takes another bite.

"It's a little café. Poppy's mom owns it. She brought some cupcakes today, and we had leftovers. So I snagged you some."

He finishes the cupcake and dabs his lips with a cotton napkin, then clears his throat. His eyes flick up to meet mine. "Well . . . thank you."

"Mm-hmm." Instead of looking away, like I usually do, I hold his gaze. One second, two, three. A tingle goes through me. And by the way his eyes narrow slightly and his gaze flicks down to my mouth, I wonder if he's feeling what I'm feeling right now.

And I shouldn't be feeling this way. I know that. He's a faculty member, and I'm already on the verge of being expelled. But I can't help being drawn to him. He's so different, so unlike anyone else I've ever known. And I want to know more.

Like what his beard feels like. What his lips taste like. What his—

Cairn breaks eye contact, looking at something over my shoulder.

I turn and find the red fox he's been tending to standing just outside the open door. The fox sniffs the air, ears perking up. Then it turns and regards us with a steady gaze.

"I-I must have left the door open," I say, starting to panic as I push to my feet. "I'm sorry. I'll—"

"It's okay." Cairn stands slowly. A smile tugs on the corner of his lips. "I think it's time he went home."

My focus slides back to the fox, even as Cairn walks around the bistro table to stand beside me.

"Are you sure?" I whisper, as if my voice might scare the fox away.

Above me, Cairn nods. "I've been leaving the door open, letting him decide. And it seems he's ready to go."

On quiet hooves, Cairn walks out of the garden and approaches the fox. He kneels and holds a hand out, and the fox must understand his intentions, for it offers its paw, waiting patiently as Cairn unwraps the cotton bandage and double-checks the wound.

"Looks healed," he says, though I think he's talking to the fox and not to me. "You're fine now, my friend."

The fox tests its weight on its paw, not limping in the least as it twirls in one circle, then another. Then it leaps up onto Cairn's knee and licks his chin.

And Cairn laughs. It's such a deep and beautiful sound, like a song of the mountains. It makes my chest squeeze.

"You're welcome," he says to the fox.

And just like that, the fox lopes across the grass and toward the tree line, a smudge of crimson against the darkening night. At the edge of the woods, it pauses for a moment to look back, as if to say thank you one more time, and then it vanishes into the trees, disappearing into the shadows like a specter on Samhain.

Cairn watches it go, then stares at the place where it disappeared for a few long, quiet moments. I observe his profile: the twirl of his glossy horns, the firm set of his brow, the nose ring he wears as it catches the last of the autumn sunlight.

And I know, can no longer deny, that I want this man.

I want him *badly*.

He pushes up from the grass, and I swallow as he turns to face me. Our eyes meet. My mouth goes dry.

Does he feel the same? No, of course not. How could he? I'm a fire hazard, an extra duty he has to see to in his day. But the look in his eyes makes me wonder, tempts me to hope.

Cairn glances away, then back. He shifts his hooves in the crinkly autumn grass.

And if I'm not completely imagining things, I think he looks almost . . . nervous.

Of my fire? Or of me?

The thought makes more of that hope shimmer to life in my chest.

"The moonflowers will bloom soon," he says, breaking eye contact again to glance at his garden. "As soon as the moon rises."

Tipping my face to the sky, I can just barely see a few tiny stars twinkling into view as the sun finally sinks over the distant horizon.

"I've never seen a blooming moonflower before," I remark, lowering my head to regard him again. Beneath my ribs, my heart pounds harder. "But . . . I'd like to."

Cairn flexes his fingers into fists at his sides, then releases them slowly. With a quiet voice, he says, "You could stay a while longer, if you'd like. To see them."

Veins threatening to burst, I give him what I hope is a subtle smile. "Sure. I'd like that."

CHAPTER 16
CAIRN

I DON'T KNOW WHAT THE HELL I WAS THINKING when I invited her to stay.

Well, I *do*, but it's dangerous. Foolish.

And I hope I don't end up regretting it.

Now the witch is sitting beside me in the garden. I went into my hut and brought out a blanket, and we're seated upon it, staring at the moonflowers at the forest's edge, waiting for them to unfurl.

She's sitting close enough to touch, but I'm very careful to *not* touch her. I can feel the heat she puts off from here, and combined with her close proximity, my head is starting to spin.

I've not felt like this in a long time. Not since I was a young man falling in love for the first time, then getting my heart broken when she decided I wasn't what she wanted.

Since then, I've kept to myself, have kept my head down. Plants are so much easier than people, and they never lie or manipulate or mislead. They wilt when they need water or sunlight or soil amendments. They bloom when they're good and ready. They communicate without needing to say a word. And I like that about them. They're predictable, safe.

Unlike witches. Especially fire witches. Especially *this* fire witch.

My gaze slides to her.

She has her knees pulled into her chest, her arms draped around them. Her hair is down today, chaotic curls falling all around her shoulders and down her back. She's not grumbling or scowling or setting fire to anything, and in the darkening night, I almost think she looks luminescent, like a fire burns just beneath her pale freckled skin.

I think of the gloves hidden away in one of the crates she helped me bring in. Should I give them to her now? Would that be strange? Too much?

Am I misreading this whole thing? Maybe she really did just want to bring me cupcakes and watch the moonflowers bloom. That's innocent enough.

But women have never made sense to me, and Lyra Wilder is no exception. I can't read her well, don't know what her glances or lingering looks mean.

I'm a lost cause.

And I'm trying desperately to figure out what to do when Lyra lets out a small gasp.

"Look!" She points, and I follow her finger to the moon-flowers, which are slowly starting to uncurl their creamy white petals.

And from deep inside their stalks, they begin to glow.

But despite their beauty, I find my gaze being pulled back to Lyra. She's leaning forward now, crimson eyes wide, mouth lifting into a slow-spreading smile.

She's what's beautiful, I think.

And I'm so screwed. Because I'm pretty sure I'm falling for her. For a *student*.

Fuck me . . .

"They're glowing," she says. "I didn't know they glowed . . ." She pushes to her feet and glances down at me. "Is it okay if I . . . ?"

"Sure."

I remain seated on the blanket as Lyra moves toward the flowers. As she draws near, their glow catches her face, turning her skin a shimmering shade of silver. Her smile fades slowly, until she's staring at the moonflowers with a focused expression, as if they're a mystery she's trying to solve.

Meanwhile, I think she's the mystery *I'm* trying to solve.

Why her? There are other faculty members here who've shown an interest in me, who've invited me to dinner or drinks, who've tried to get to know me. And I've turned them all down. I've never been interested in disrupting my calm, predictable life for the chance at something with someone.

But Lyra arrived here like a firestorm. She came into my life without any permission from me, and slowly, week by week, she started to warm something inside me that has been long frozen. And now I'm starting to burn for her.

"Cairn," she says, drawing me out of my musings.

My name isn't particularly interesting or exotic, but the way she says it, it's like a word I've never heard before. And I want to hear her say it again and again. I want to listen to all the words she says, all the shapes her lips and tongue make.

The thought makes my cock jump.

So, so screwed.

"What?" I say, tearing my eyes away from her and looking down into my lap, where my steadily growing hard-on is already starting to press against the fabric of my trousers.

"Thank you."

The inflection in her voice makes me look up. She takes a few steps toward me, then pauses. The sleeves of her sweater are clutched in her hands, and her eyes are slightly narrowed as she looks down at me.

If I didn't know any better, I'd think she was about to cry.

"For what?" I ask.

One of her shoulders lifts in a shrug. "I don't know. My wrist, the fox, putting up with me . . ." A little laugh slips out of her. "You're a good person."

A good person wouldn't allow themselves to feel this way about someone so *clearly* not right for them. I could lose my job. My home. She could get expelled. None of that is good. It's very, very bad.

And maybe I should put a stop to it right now, before it goes too—

Next thing I know, Lyra is kneeling beside me, the glow from the moonflowers illuminating half her face. Her proximity makes me hold my breath. Her heat washes over me.

What is she—

Before I can pull away or push her back, she leans forward and crushes her lips against mine, almost losing her balance in the process.

111

It's rough, chaotic—not so unlike the witch herself.

And it's also magic. Because the moment I taste her, I know there's no going back, no slowing this down, no telling her I don't feel this way about her.

Her spell weaves around me, and my hands move of their own accord, gripping her by the waist and lifting her smoothly into my lap where I'm still seated on the blanket in the dry grass.

A little voice in the back of my mind tells me to be careful, that someone could see us. But they'd have to be way out here on the edge of the woods, and with the night growing darker still, they'd need to draw close to make out who we are, who the hitched breaths belong to.

Lyra's weight settles atop me, and my cock strains for her. Then her hands are on either side of my face, and she pushes her fingers through my scruffy facial hair.

I should trim it. It's grown way too long.

She breaks our kiss, and breathlessly, she whispers, "I love your beard."

Okay, in that case, maybe I won't be trimming it.

When my hard-on jumps again, Lyra's eyes widen. She definitely felt it. Then she arches a brow, and her mouth quirks up on one side. I've only a moment to consider what's going through her mind before she reaches between her legs and trails her fingers along my cock. With only the fabric of my trousers separating us, the touch makes me groan.

"Fuck," I grunt out.

I want this. I want *her*.

An image flashes through my mind of Lyra on her back in my bed, legs spread, pussy stretching around my cock.

No.

This can't happen—for many reasons.

She's too young, too *small*. I'd hurt her, I'm sure of it. And not to mention I could lose my job and she could be expelled. And I can't let that happen to her. She's been working so hard—I saw it when she transplanted those sniffleblooms, then again when she fell in the mud and had to rein in her temper before it flared and burned the campus down.

Being with me like this could ruin her.

And it's my responsibility to make sure that doesn't happen.

So even though it's physically painful to resist her, especially when she's sitting on me like this, I lean away, preventing her from capturing my mouth with hers.

"We have to stop," I whisper, voice husky with hunger.

Her lips—swollen and red from kissing me—pull into a pout. "Why?"

"You know why." I take her by the waist and move her onto the blanket beside me, then try (and fail) to arrange myself in my trousers. But there's no room, nowhere for my cock to go, so it just sits there, hard and throbbing, as I prevent myself from doing what I so badly want to do to her.

"No, I don't." Lyra crosses her arms and glowers at me.

"Because," I grumble, "if someone sees you with me, you could get expelled. And . . ." I let out a slow sigh and scoot away from her. "And I don't want that to happen."

The glower softens, and Lyra's tense shoulders droop. "No one's going to see us out here," she says, but I can tell by the tone of her voice that she's uncertain.

113

Good. She should focus on her studies, not on me. I'm just a minotaur groundskeeper, a man who likes flowers and herbs and staying away from people. I'm no good for her. And she's no good for me.

With a grunt, I push to my hooves, then turn away from her and cross my arms, wishing my hard-on would go away and stop tempting me.

"They might," I say gruffly, not allowing myself to look at her. "It's too dangerous."

Lyra's clothing rustles as she rises to her feet, and I feel her approach from behind, but I don't turn to look at her. "We could . . . go inside."

That same image pops into my mind: her legs spread, bottom lip caught between her teeth, chest rising and falling with panted breaths.

I shake my head hard and flick my tail. "No. That's . . . not a good idea."

"But you want to." A hard edge has entered her voice. "Don't you?"

"What I want is irrelevant."

"Just admit it." She eases around me, and I tense at the feel of her hand on my arm. The moonlight catches her crimson eyes as she gazes up at me. "Tell me the truth."

Staring down at her, I consider my options. I could tell her no, that this was a mistake and I've no interest in her. But I've never liked lying, and the fact that my dick is still creating a tight bulge in my trousers says more words than I need to.

A sigh whooshes out of me, and I scrub one hand down my face. "Yes, I want to." My gaze meets hers again, and I'm unwavering. "But we're not going to. And that's final."

I'm not sure what I expect her to do. Pout, maybe, or narrow her eyes and set me on fire.

Instead, her lips pull up into a sideways smile. And that's more terrifying than her chaotic fire magic.

What's she thinking right now?

"Okay, Mr. Axton." She steps away from me, and I suddenly don't like when she says my name like that. It reminds me of our imbalanced power dynamic, our age difference, the fact that I definitely shouldn't be feeling the way about her that I am. And I think that's exactly why she used it. To nettle me. Provoke me. Taunt me.

My nostrils flutter with a hard exhale.

Meddlesome witch.

"Well, enjoy that last cupcake," she says, taking another few steps away. "And I'll see you soon." Pushing her vibrant red curls over her shoulder, she tips her head and says, "Try not to think of me while I'm gone."

My lips pull into a deep scowl.

Then she's waving goodbye and setting off through the moonlight, walking back toward the castle, leaving me standing in the dark with my cock still throbbing for her.

CHAPTER 17

CAIRN

As soon as Lyra disappears back into the castle courtyard, I storm inside and immediately relieve myself, stroking my hard cock until I release all the pressure that built up inside me. Only then can I stop seeing Lyra's flushed cheeks and feeling her mouth on mine, her weight atop my lap and the heat between her legs. Only then can I even *try* to think clearly again.

For an hour, all I do is clean, scrubbing tables that are already spotless and sweeping floors just to sweep them again. I look toward the little bed where the red fox spent so much time, and a wave of melancholy floods me when I realize he's no longer here. It's better this way, better that he healed and has gone back home, but I'm going to miss him.

And now I don't have anyone to talk to about everything whirling through my head.

Jerking off may have released my pent-up sexual frustration, but now my mind is swimming and swirling—not just with Lyra and how wrong and dangerous these feelings are, but with everything Milo said to me this afternoon after he convinced me to sit down and have a drink with him at Boar and Badger.

He attempted small talk for a while, going on about the weather and what not, but I've never been particularly good at chitchat, and he gave up as soon as our frothy pumpkin ales arrived. At first, I thought it was a good thing. Until the next words came out of his mouth.

So, have you filled out your application to the conservatory yet?

My shoulders tense up as his voice echoes through my mind.

You haven't? he said when I told him no. *Why not? It's a perfect fit!*

I told him the truth: I don't have the qualifications to work in such a place, have only ever been a groundskeeper at Coven Crest. He waved me off, acting like it was a nonissue, encouraging me to fill out the application before they find and hire someone else.

Just to get him to stop badgering me, I told him I would apply. He was too easily convinced.

I toss the rag I was using to wipe down the kitchen table into the sink. Then, as if my hooves have a mind of their own, they carry me into the sitting room, where I grab the envelope with Columbine Conservatory's crest stamped on the front. Then I return to the kitchen and take a seat at the perfectly clean table.

And I stare at the envelope. Then stare a little longer.

The cupcake platter Lyra brought for me still sits in the

center of the table, the metal gleaming a bit in the low light cast from my many candles and the fire in the hearth. Lifting the lid off the platter, I hurriedly snatch up the last cupcake and bite into it—it's a chocolate-vanilla swirl, and the flavors make my taste buds dance.

Just the distraction I need.

With the sugar further muddling my already-messy brain, I finally force myself to pull Milo's letter—and the still-blank application—from the envelope. The pieces of parchment sit there on the table, so small and insignificant and yet potentially holding a different future for me, one I've scarcely allowed myself to imagine.

Working with a horticulturalist, helping grow food for the people who need it, burying my hands in the dirt and never having to clean up after students again.

Thinking about it makes something go both warm and tight inside my chest. And it makes me think of Lyra, the kiss, the fire that burns in her eyes.

What would she do? I wonder. Then I laugh to myself, because I know what she'd do.

She'd fill out the application, probably mark it in blood, and then would march it straight to the conservatory and demand someone read over it at that very instant.

And I realize how much I admire her fire, her fearlessness.

Maybe I can try to learn from her, take a page from the book of Lyra.

Maybe I can be brave.

After wiping the last few remaining crumbs from my lips—I inhaled that cupcake in about twenty-five seconds flat—I retrieve my quill and inkwell, trying to ignore the resistance mounting inside me.

A voice tells me, *You're not good enough. They'll never hire you. Be grateful for what you have instead of trying to reach for more.*

That voice has always kept me looking down, focusing on the dirt beneath my hooves rather than the stars stretching across the never-ending sky. And I love the dirt. Of course I do. But maybe ... maybe it's time to tip my head back and look at the stars. And it might be a little red-haired witch who's giving me the confidence to do just that.

CHAPTER 18
LYRA

IT'S BEEN A GRUELING WEEK. MIDTERMS ARE HERE, and everyone drags from one class to the next, bags beneath their eyes from staying up late studying, hair in messy buns and robes slightly rumpled.

And it's time for my Elemental Magic 201 midterm—the one I've been most dreading. The book portion of the midterm wasn't a problem; it's the practical exam I'm worried about. Each student has to demonstrate to Professor Stone their proficiency in air, water, earth, and fire magic, and I'm nearly sick to my stomach as I wait for my turn, leg bouncing erratically beneath my desk.

Juniper wanted to come today, but I was too nervous to let her tag along, so I don't have her to console me or to tell me to stop biting my nails.

But the thought of her voice is enough to get me to lower my hand. I cross my arms over my stomach, gaze darting to the door, where Professor Stone's third-year student assistant, Nella, appears every ten minutes or so to fetch the next student and escort them to the practice room for the exam.

I jump when the door opens, and Nella steps into the doorway. She holds a clipboard and what looks like a quill enchanted to never run out of ink—I should definitely get one of those. Scrunching her forehead, she works down the list, then says, "Maeve Vandermere."

I'm not sure if I'm relieved or frustrated. Both, I guess. I'm terrified, but I want to get this over with so I can run back to my dorm and flop into my bed and sleep for an eternity—or at least until Samhain. I'm definitely not missing the festival this year.

Maeve stands and moves gracefully toward the door, all eyes on her as she pushes her glossy hair over her shoulder. Before stepping into the hallway behind Nella, she tosses a glance at me and winks one purple eye.

Then the door closes, and I'm left to spiral into more worrisome thoughts.

If I fail, will that be it? Will Headmistress Moonhart expel me? And even worse, what if I totally fuck up and set something on fire? What if I set Professor *Stone* on fire?

With a groan, I lean forward and rest my forehead on my desk.

Goddess, I just want this to be over.

Four students later, Nella steps into the room and calls another name.

"Lyra Wilder."

For a moment, I don't move, just stare at her like she's here to escort me to my own fiery doom.

"Lyra?" She tips her head and arches a brow curiously. "Is that you?"

"Y-yes," I say, then push to my feet too fast, causing my chair to tip back and fall to the floor with a clatter. The other students titter with laughter, but I don't care. It's not like they understand how much is riding on this moment for me.

And I get an even heavier sinking feeling when I realize these are just midterms—and I have to make it through another two and a half years here without accidentally setting fire to all the irreplaceable tomes in the library or burning down the exotic greenhouse plants . . . again.

Grabbing my bag, I slip the strap over my shoulder, then right the fallen chair and follow Nella into the hallway.

"Are you okay?" she asks as we set off down the hallway together. "You look a little pale."

"I'm fine." I swallow hard and flex my fingers into fists at my sides.

"Nervous?" Her voice is light and friendly, like she's never been worried about a midterm in her life.

I let out a scoff. "That would be an understatement."

"You're going to do just fine," she says comfortingly. As we approach the door to the elemental magic practice room, she says, "It helps me to face away from the professor as I perform my magic—then I can pretend I'm alone, just practicing like it's any regular day." Her shoulders lift in a shrug. "Maybe that'll help you too."

Doubt it.

"Maybe," I say, stare locked on the door. "Thanks for the tip."

Nella flashes me a bright smile. "Anytime. Good luck!"

She opens the door and gestures me through, and I take a deep breath before stepping over the threshold.

Professor Stone stands at the front of the room, a book open in his hands. The sight of it makes me queasy.

It's his gradebook, the book that determines whether I pass or fail.

I wish I could enchant it to give me passing marks.

"Miss Wilder," he says as Nella closes the door behind me, leaving me to my fate. "Set your bag down by the door, then come stand in the center of the room."

I do as I'm told, but my feet feel leaden as I walk to where the professor indicated. The room is completely bare, apart from golden runes that glow on the walls, ceiling, and floor. The runes make the practice room resistant to elemental magic, so it's safe for students to use their magic without fear of burning something down or sending a typhoon gushing through the hallway.

"This is your elemental midterm," Professor Stone says. He closes his gradebook with a thump, then regards me through slightly narrowed eyes. "You will demonstrate appropriate control over all four elements—air, earth, water, and fire, in that order. Each manifestation must be precise, deliberate, and contained. Remember, power is nothing without discipline."

I swallow hard and flex my fingers.

Fire last. I'm not sure if that's a blessing or a curse.

Professor Stone nods once. "You may begin when you're ready."

Despite being a fire witch, I've always found air and earth to be the easiest of the four elements to control. They're not as finnicky as water and fire, more open to suggestion and manipulation.

All right, air.

I extend my hands, stretching my fingers wide. With a little bit of coaxing, I'm able to summon a gentle breeze and shape it into a spiral. The air movement makes Professor Stone's long black robe flap around his calves, and his messy brown hair ripples like he's underwater. His face displays no emotion.

With a flick of my wrist, I funnel the wind into a small controlled vortex that dances at my feet before dispersing with a whisper.

I look to Professor Stone, and he gives a subtle nod.

Okay, one element down, three to go.

I can do this, I tell myself. *It's not so hard.*

Earth's next.

Kneeling, I place both palms flat on the floor, imagining that the stone beneath my feet is moving, breathing. A slight vibration tingles through my palms, and I catch it, hold on like it's a kite being tugged along by a summer wind. Standing from the floor, I pull on that subtle vibration, and with a crack, a narrow column of stone rises before me. I narrow my eyes, focusing my magic, picturing what I want to do before I try to do it. My fingers twitch as I move them through the air, imagining myself a painter, a creator. The sharp edges of the stone column begin to smooth out, and the stone groans as it changes shape—until the previously blocky column now somewhat resembles an oak tree.

It's not my *best* creation, but Professor Stone raises his brows a little bit, and I think that's his version of being impressed.

The stone crumbles into dust with one clap of my hands. *Two more.*

Water. The second-hardest element to master. And master it I have not. But this midterm isn't about mastery; I don't have to be perfect, just good enough to pass.

I lift my hands, trying to focus on the moisture hanging in the cool air. At first, nothing happens. No water condenses out of the air. A little ember of panic flares to life in my chest. Then I inhale and steady my breathing. *Focus*, I think.

Again, I attempt to pull moisture from the air. This time, a little bubble of water starts to form, individual droplets combining to create one rippling sphere of clear water. It wobbles when I move one hand too fast, but I'm able to steady it and keep it from splashing to my feet. With focus and a furrowed brow, I gently coax it into a narrow ribbon, which twirls and twines through the air before I banish it in a shimmer of mist.

Three down. Fire's last.

Is it just me, or did the room just get a bit too warm?

I tug at the collar of my academy-issued sweater, trying to cool the back of my neck, but it's no use. Professor Stone is watching me with a wary expression, maybe getting ready should he need to shield himself from an erratic fireball or something. Wouldn't be the first time . . .

I take a breath. Then another one. But it does nothing to slow the thundering of my heart.

My fingers tremble slightly as I lift my hands out in front of me, preparing to call on my magic.

But the fire comes too fast, before I've truly had a chance to ground myself. Suddenly, my palms are encased in flame. Whips of fire lash up and out, painting my face with heat and bursts of bright light. One of my curls gets too close to a flame, and the scent of burning hair twines around me before I yank my head out of the way.

On the other side of the flames, I see a subtle movement from Professor Stone, one of his hands reaching out, preparing to quench my flames should I be unable to get them under control.

No, I tell myself. *I can do this. I have to do this!*

My pulse pounds in my ears. I shift my hands, facing them toward each other, trying to contain the blaze. It fights me, hissing and writhing and spitting embers that catch on my sleeves, leaving tiny burn holes in the material. I can feel the fire's desire to break free, to consume everything in its path.

Like the midnight lotus flowers. Like so many other times before.

My throat goes dry.

Not this time. This time, I'll contain it.

I grit my teeth and widen my stance, rooting my feet to the floor. I imagine standing in Cairn's garden, pushing my roots into the earth, holding myself firm and strong, like the moonflowers.

Breathe.

I take a breath, then let it out slow. The fire dims, but just slightly.

Intention. Intention. Intention.

Cairn's voice echoes in my mind, each utterance a balm on my frayed nerves. And every time I hear him, I rein my flames in a little more.

They buck and hiss, fighting my control, trying to take it back from me. But I start funneling them inward, folding the fire over on itself, flame by flame, breath by breath. When I'm done, what remains is one gold-red orb of flickering fire, held aloft in the cage of my firelit fingers. It continues to dance, moving this way and that, but it no longer rages against me. For once, it's almost . . . calm.

Likewise, the racing of my heart has slowed, and I can finally catch my breath.

My mouth threatens to pull into a smile. I cradle the orb of fire in my palms, then toss it toward the ceiling. Professor Stone flinches back as there's a small thump, like the far-off detonation of a firework.

Sparks rain down over me, harmless this time, and sizzle to ash that I brush from my shoulders and shake from my curls.

I meet the professor's eyes. He regards me for a long moment. Then he gives me a firm nod, and I think he's *almost* smiling at me.

"Well done, Miss Wilder. You should be proud." He raises his gradebook and opens it, then scribbles something down that I wish I could see from here.

I'm still standing there, fingertips tingling, when he looks up and says, "You may leave."

He doesn't have to tell me twice.

I grab my bag from the floor, use the burnt sleeve of my sweater to mop the sweat from my brow, and pull the door open. Immediately, cool air rushes in to greet me, kissing the heat from my skin.

Nella is leaning against the opposite wall, and she straightens up. "How'd it go?" she asks.

And I give her a big smile. Because I'm pretty sure I just passed my midterm.

CHAPTER 19
CAIRN

I'M RAKING MORE LEAVES IN THE COURTYARD—the trees around here must be spelled to drop leaves constantly all autumn long, much to my chagrin—when a sudden pounding of feet startles me out of my thoughts of the conservatory and what it might be like to work there. And next thing I know, a small body is crashing into me, arms coming around me, though they don't get far on account of how tiny they are and how big I am.

The arms are warm, though, despite their size.

Startled, I twist my head around to glance over my shoulder.

And my eyes widen when I see a full head of curly red hair.

Lyra.

She smells like paper and ink—with a little bit of ash on the edges. Like a fire witch who just finished her midterms.

Immediately, I glance around the courtyard, and sure enough, a few students have noticed Lyra's display and are looking at us curiously.

Gently, I remove myself from her arms and take a wide step away from her. Holding the rake between us so she can't tackle me again, I say lowly, "Miss Wilder. Is there something you need?"

My tone seems to confuse her, if the furrow that forms in her brow is any indication. "What?"

Clearing my throat, I glance pointedly toward the students seated on the grass in the courtyard, their robes spread out under them and their faces bathed in autumn sunlight.

Lyra glances at them—much too obviously, in my opinion—then looks back at me and offers an innocent smile. "Oh, sorry. I was so excited, I didn't even realize they were there." She clutches her yellow-lined robe in her hands, nearly vibrating where she stands.

"Excited about what?" I ask.

"My midterms," she says. "I passed!" She lets out a squeal and dances on the spot, her curls bouncing around her shoulders. "Or, well, I'm pretty sure I did. No, I'm *certain* I did. I can feel it."

Despite knowing there are eyes on us, I can't keep from offering her a big, proud smile. "You passed," I say, somewhat quietly. My grin doesn't falter. "I knew you could do it."

My arms long to reach out and pull her into a hug, to crush her to my chest while I bury my face in her chaotic mess of curls and whisper to her how proud I am of her.

But we're in public, and I can do no such thing.

Instead, I grip the handle of the rake, clutching it in my fingers, using it as a distraction so I don't try to reach out and touch her.

"I'm glad someone did, because I really had my doubts." Lyra pushes her hair back out of her face with one hand and props the other on her hip, robe hanging in the crook of her arm. "I was really nervous for my elemental magic exam, but I did it! And I didn't even set Professor Stone's hair on fire."

An image pops into my mind of the stern professor with his hair singed on the ends, a burnt smell trailing him everywhere he goes, and I let out a laugh. "What changed?" I ask her, feeling some of the tension uncoil from my shoulders as the students across the courtyard lose interest in us and resume their own conversations.

Lyra's lip quirk up on one side. They're so pretty and pink, I want to run my thumb across them, followed by my tongue.

A pressure starts to build in my low abdomen, and I immediately banish the dangerous thought.

"The sniffleblooms," she says matter-of-factly.

Now it's my turn to arch my brow in confusion. "Huh?"

She laughs, and by the goddess, it's a beautiful sound. "You—*they*—taught me to take my time, to go slow and to be intentional. When I called on my fire magic, I heard your voice in my head, telling me what I needed to do." Her freckled cheeks take on a pinkish hue. "And it helped. A lot." Her eyes meet mine, flaming red in the autumn sunlight. "So . . . thank you. I know I've said it before, but seriously. I'm not sure I could've done that without you."

My heart swells, emotion making my throat squeeze tight. I have to clear my throat before I can speak again. "That was all you, Lyra." I keep my voice down so no one will hear me using her name so informally. "I didn't do anything. It was *you*."

She flushes brighter red and makes a move toward me as if to hug me again. I take a wide step back and give her a pointed look, tail flicking behind me.

"Oh, sorry." Her laugh dances around us again. "Okay, well, uh . . . I guess I'll get going. I have to tell Juniper and my roommates the good news. But you were the first on my list."

First on her list?

Again, my throat wants to close up. What is this witch doing to me?

"But I'll see you at the Samhain festival, won't I?" She tips her head and regards me with what I interpret as a flirty smile.

Glancing away and trying not to let my own cheeks flush red, I say, "You will. I work the mead table every year."

"Great. I'll help you, then."

Now my gaze snaps back to hers. "Well, no, that's really not—"

"Okay, bye, Mr. Axton!" Lyra raises her voice a bit, as if to ensure the other students hear her using my surname, as she's expected to. "Thanks again!"

She starts off across the courtyard at a jog, messy curls

bouncing as she goes, and I'm barely able to tear my eyes away from her.

And I'd be lying if I said I'm not exponentially more excited for the Samhain festival now.

I'm in so much trouble . . .

CHAPTER 20
LYRA

IT'S A DRIZZLY MORNING, AND RAIN STREAKS down the dorm room window as I sit at the desk and stare at my father's letter. His handwriting is familiar—scratchy, with letters of varying shapes—and it makes my heart feel both warm and tight. He wrote to me weeks ago, but I've been too ashamed to write back, worried that I was moments away from expulsion and that I'd only have bad news for him. But now that I've passed my midterms, some of that weight has lifted off my chest. I'm not in the clear—not by a long shot—and I've still got the rest of the year to get through, but at least I can tell him that I passed my midterms and school is going well.

Juniper sits on the desk beside the inkwell, staring out the window as rain runs down the glass. She's been nettling me to write back to Papa, and I imagine she's relieved that I'm finally doing it.

She and my dad have always gotten along. I actually had a sneaking suspicion that he was going to miss her more than he'd miss me when we left for Coven Crest late this summer. And I was perfectly okay with that.

Taking up my quill, I dip the tip into the ink, then draw it slowly across the page.

I'M FEELING LIGHT AS A FEATHER. I PASSED MY EXAMS, I finally wrote my father back to tell him my good news, and—potentially most exciting of all—I'm going to see Cairn tonight.

Like the last Samhain festival, I dress in all black, though this year, I opt for something a bit more risqué—though I tell myself it's *not* because I want Cairn to see me in it.

The black dress reaches to just above my ankles, and it has slits up either side, all the way to my hips, where laces pulled taut reveal flashes of my pale skin beneath. The material is stretched tight across my breasts and wraps up and around my neck, where I've clasped a golden necklace. My shoulders and arms are bare, and Alina helps me dust them with a bit of glittering gold powder. I'd probably be cold tonight if not for my fire magic. Thankfully, it'll keep me from needing to cover myself up in a sweater.

When Alina's done making me sparkle, she puts the fluffy makeup brush back into my bag and crosses her arms, leveling me with a stern gaze. "Okay, what's the occasion? And don't tell me Samhain. This is on a whole other level, even for you."

I've not told the girls about Cairn. I'm not sure anything will come out of it—even if that thought makes my stomach twist uncomfortably. When I'm sure there's something to tell, my roommates will be the first to know. Well, after Juniper. *She* knows everything, including the details about my first kiss with Cairn while the moonflowers bloomed.

"Do I need to have a reason for wanting to get dressed up?" I ask Alina while I reach around her to grab a stick of kohl from my bag. She moves to stand over my shoulder as I lean toward the mirror and smudge the black makeup across my eyelids.

"No, but it's you. And I feel like you're not telling me something." Her lips pull into a frown, her forehead creasing.

With a smile, I turn to face her. "If there's something to tell you, I promise I will. But for now . . ." I shrug and flash her a smile.

Her blue eyes widen. "So there *is* something going on!"

"What's going on?" Poppy calls from the lower floor, where she and Maeve are waiting for us so we can all four go to the festival together.

"Lyra is keeping secrets from us," Alina says as she starts down the stairs, leaving me to finish my makeup on my own.

On the end of my bed, Juniper says, "You're not going to tell them?"

I double-check my reflection in the mirror, pleased with the way the dark kohl makes my red eyes pop, then turn to face Juniper. "Not yet. For now"—I glance over my shoulder and lower my voice—"it's between you and me. So don't tell Yuki or Isis either."

Juniper twitches her whiskers with amusement. "Your secret is safe with me."

136

Smiling, I kneel down and press a kiss to the top of her warm brown head. "Thank you." As I straighten up, I tip my head at her. "You sure you don't wanna come tonight? I can carry a bag for you."

Juniper shakes her head. "No. Just promise to bring me back a caramel apple."

My lips pull up into a smile. "I'll bring you that and so much more. I promise."

She squeaks in approval, and then I give her a scratch beneath the chin before grabbing my platform boots and heading down the stairs to join up with the others.

And deep in my chest, my heart pounds just a little bit faster with the knowledge that I'm going to see Cairn.

CHAPTER 21

CAIRN

I MANAGE THE MEAD BOOTH EVERY YEAR, AND I'M typically annoyed about it. The bonfire is too bright, the music is too loud, and mingling with drunk students and professors is very low on the list of things I enjoy doing in my free time.

This year is different though. Because this year, my gaze keeps tracing the crowd for a head of bouncy red curls, and my ears strain to hear her voice, her laugh. I know I shouldn't allow myself these desires, but lately, I seem to be losing control over my fantasies. Between Lyra Wilder and the job at the conservatory, I feel like I'm spinning around and around beneath a starry sky, losing my balance and tumbling in the dark, unsure where I'm going to land.

But for some reason, I can't quite bring myself to stop. Even if I really, *really* should.

"Hello?" the witch in front of me says.

I snap to attention and try not to glare at her—but I'm not so sure I'm successful, because she flinches back a bit from my gaze.

"How many?" I ask.

"Two. How much will that be?"

I tell her the cost while filling two mugs with honeyed mead, then slip the coins she gives me into the coin purse around my waist—where I keep the money just in case a drunk warlock thinks he wants to be clever.

The witch scurries away, mugs sloshing as she goes, and over her head, I finally see what I've been looking for all night.

Her.

And oh, wow. *Wow.*

Tonight, she looks dangerous—like she might eat men whole and then string their teeth onto a necklace to display for all the world to see.

Her hair is wild, untamed. The smoky makeup she wears makes her crimson eyes more vibrant, like candles burn behind each iris. And that dress, pulled tight and laced at her hips . . .

Am I going to faint?

I'm definitely feeling lightheaded, and I know for certain it's not from the one mug of mead I've been nursing all night.

With some difficulty, I pull my gaze away from her, but my head still feels muddled as I pour and serve and take the eldertokens that're offered to me. The next time I glance up, searching for the fire witch, she's nowhere to be seen.

My stomach sinks.

Foolish, I tell myself. *It's better this way.*

Hopefully she avoids me all night, sticking with her roommates and students her own age. With the way she looks tonight, I'm not sure I can trust myself around her.

So, yes, this is for the—

"Hi, Mr. Axton."

That voice . . .

I look up from the palmful of coins I was counting, and there she is, close enough I can see the tiny golden necklace she wears around her throat—close enough I could take her into my arms, throw her over my shoulder, and carry her far away from here.

Though I strive not to, I can't keep myself from looking at her body. Wrapped in that tight black dress, her every curve is visible, and the hints of skin peeking through the laces along her hips tempt me to reach out and touch her, pluck the laces with my fingers until they fall away.

She braces her hands on the booth and leans forward, tipping her head, looking sharp and catlike. "Happy Samhain."

Clearing my throat, I stand up straighter and command my dick to *not* get hard. Whether or not it'll listen is another story. "Happy Samhain, Miss Wilder."

Her smile is coy, knowing. She dressed like this on purpose, certainly. And now here she is, draping herself over the booth, knowing full well what it's doing to me.

"What can I get you?" I ask. There are other students in line behind her; I can't allow myself to let on about how badly I want her.

"I'll take five," she says. She hands me a few eldertokens, and if I'm not mistaken, she lets her fingertips graze my palm slowly, her touch like fire against my skin.

I pull away and focus *very* hard on the honeyed mead and not on the fire witch standing right behind me. After filling five mugs, I slide them toward her. Another witch appears at her side, a tall dark-haired man behind her. He looks too old to be a student here, with eyes too sharp and with too much experience. But it's none of my business who they are. Lyra isn't even any of my business—despite me wanting her to be.

"Thank you!" she says, taking two mugs and letting the others grab the rest. After taking a few steps away, she turns back around and says, "I'll see you around later, won't I?"

Another student is already stepping up to the table, trying to tell me how many mugs they need. But my eyes are on Lyra. And though I shouldn't, I give her a small nod. Because of course I want to see her later. How could I not?

She gives me another one of those tempting smiles, then moves off into the crowd, hips swaying as she goes.

CHAPTER 22
LYRA

POPPY YAWNS, THE LIGHT FROM THE BONFIRE reflecting in the round frames of her glasses. "I'm exhausted," she says. "I think I'm gonna turn in for the night."

Alina and Raelan are already gone, though I'm pretty sure wherever they are, they're definitely not sleeping. So it's just me, Poppy, and Maeve still standing by the writhing fire, watching as festivalgoers dance around the flames to the tune played by a troupe of musicians standing on an elevated platform nearby.

"Same." Maeve lifts her mead mug and swallows down the rest of it. "You coming, Ly?"

I've been waiting for this all night, an opportunity to slip away. Finally, it's here.

I shake my head. "No. I'm gonna stay a while longer."

My roommates give me quizzical looks.

"You sure?" Maeve asks. "The festival's almost over. And

besides"—she tips her head back, eyes regarding the cloudy night sky—"it's about to rain."

I can't see anything in the clouds, but being a storm witch, Maeve can probably feel the rain moving in.

Trying to be nonchalant, I shrug and say, "It's the fire. I just wanna stay a while longer, watch the flames."

Poppy and Maeve exchange looks, then seem to accept my reasoning as fair. I'm a fire witch—of *course* I'd want to spend more time with the fire.

Or with Cairn, but they don't need to know that.

"Okay." Poppy squeezes my hand. "We'll see you back at the room, then?"

I nod once. "Yeah." Then I remember I promised to bring Juniper some treats, and the booths are quickly closing. "Actually, will you do me a favor?"

They nod.

Hurriedly, I move booth to booth, purchasing Juniper a caramel apple, a slice of warm pumpkin bread, and a crinkly bag full of cinnamon-spiced nuts. Poppy and Maeve take them from me.

"Thank you," I say. "Just want to make sure she gets them in case I'm late."

"She might like us more than you now," Maeve warns with a flick of her silky hair over her shoulder.

I let out a laugh. "That's a risk I'm willing to take."

"Okay, see you soon," Poppy says.

The two of them move away from me, the flickering candles that float midair lighting their way as they go.

Finally alone.

Crossing one arm over my chest and sipping from my mug of mead, I turn back toward the flames, staring into them as they move against the chill of the autumn night. And only when I'm certain my roommates have made it back to the castle do I cast my gaze toward the other side of the flames, where Cairn has been manning the mead booth all night. It was almost impossible to keep my eyes off him, to resist the urge to keep glancing his way. My roommates are perceptive, and they would've noticed right away.

I swallow down the rest of my mead, liking the way it makes my skin tingle and my head sway. It takes the edge off, just a bit, and makes me perhaps a bit more reckless than I should be. But it's nighttime, and most of the festivalgoers are one or more mugs of mead in. They dance and laugh and sway together before the fire, not paying any attention to me as I head toward Cairn's booth, my boots crunching softly through the dried grass.

There's one witch at the booth when I get there, but she quickly takes her mug and moves away, and then Cairn looks up and meets my eyes.

A wave of heat goes through me, warming the spot between my thighs.

I remember seeing Cairn here last year, remember thinking he was rude and brash and being annoyed by his gruff nature. But looking at him now, with his long hair knotted atop his head and his horns gleaming in the firelight, all I can think about is his warm voice, the way he so tenderly cared for that injured red fox, the feel of him beneath me as I sat in his lap on the blanket under the stars.

He was hard that night, his cock pressing against me through his trousers, but he wouldn't let me go any further, and I've been thinking about it ever since, wondering what he'd feel like inside me.

And if the way he's looking at me right now is any indication, I'm pretty sure he's been thinking about it too.

Slowly, I walk toward him, liking the way his gaze follows the movement of my thighs, which slip through the slits in my dress and shine silver and orange in the pale moonlight and dancing flames. When I make it around the booth and step up beside him, his throat bobs with an obvious hard swallow. My lips quirk up in response.

"Hi," I say.

He draws himself up, fingers curling into fists at his sides. His nose ring winks in the firelight as he moves his head. "Miss Wilder. Do you need something?"

He's using his formal faculty voice. And I understand—there are still festivalgoers around us, students and professors and people visiting from Wysteria. But I can't help pushing him, just a bit.

"No." I prop a hip against the booth, knowing it exposes one of my legs completely, the slit in the dress revealing my skin from ankle to hip. Cairn's gaze flashes down, and he swallows hard again, then turns away, looking at anything but me. "I'm here to help *you*," I clarify.

His nostrils flutter when he snorts. "I don't need any help. You should go enjoy the festival."

Tipping my head, I regard him—his wide shoulders, broad chest, strong frame. I definitely don't want to be anywhere else right now. Except maybe somewhere alone . . . with him.

"I already am." I stare at him until his dark eyes slide toward mine. "So, how can I help?"

He looks like he's about to send me on my way, to tell me to get off his booth and go irritate someone else. But then he sighs and gives a subtle shake of his head, and I know I've won—at least at *this* game. But I'm still many levels from where I'm hoping to get with him tonight.

Sniffing the air, he says, "There's a storm coming in. If you really want to make yourself useful, you can help me start packing up."

"Okay!" I push off the booth and prop my hands on my hips, tossing him a grin. "Where do I start?"

With another sigh—he seems to do that a lot around me, though I'm starting to find it endearing—he points to a few big bins full of dirty empty mugs. "Get those loaded up in the cart; I'll need to take them to the castle kitchen tomorrow for cleaning. And I'll start putting the kegs away."

"Will do."

We work together, not speaking, just moving around each other, like we do when we're working on the grounds, whether raking or weeding or preparing the gardens for the cold to come. And we have impeccable timing.

Cairn is just putting the last of the kegs onto the cart when the first few raindrops start to fall. They're fat and they're cold, and I gasp when one hits my forehead before trickling down my nose.

As the sky opens up and a deluge of frigid autumn rain starts to fall, Cairn grabs the cart handles and says, "Run!"

146

A squeal of delight bursts out of me as Cairn takes off at a jog, me and the cart trundling along behind him. While many of the festivalgoers run for cover, some remain dancing around the fire, like the rain only heightens their experience.

The festival is held in the castle courtyard, so Cairn and I have to run all the way under the barbican and down the path to his hut at the edge of the woods. I'm glad I wore boots tonight—something appropriate for running through misty fields and over slick cobblestones while rain falls.

I keep laughing as I run, invigorated, and soon, Cairn is laughing too. He has such a wonderful laugh, deep and rumbly. I wish he'd laugh like this more often. Maybe I can help him with that. The idea of it warms my chest.

By the time we finally get to his hut, I'm soaked through, my dress clinging to me like a second skin, wet curls hanging limp and sticking to my face, neck, and shoulders. I shiver a little bit, but not from the cold. If I weren't a fire witch, I'd probably be freezing right about now.

"Get inside!" Cairn calls to me over a roll of thunder.

I only hesitate for a moment, wondering if he knows what he just did, what he just *invited* me to do. We're in an autumn rainstorm at night, and he just invited me into his home.

Not that I'm complaining. I'm very much *not* complaining.

I yank the wooden door open while Cairn grabs a big canvas tarp to toss over the cart. The last thing I see before stepping inside is him unfurling it, his arms flexing beneath the long sleeves of his forest-green tunic, dark eyes narrowed against the frigid raindrops.

Inside his hut, the sound of the rain is dampened by the thatched roof. It's dark, and the air is cold. I peel off my soggy wet boots and leave them on a mat beside the door. Now in bare feet, I cast my gaze around the darkened space. The furniture appears like hulking shadows lit only by the scant bit of moonlight that manages to sneak through the thick rain clouds hovering outside.

Having been here once before, I know my way around—kind of—and am able to find my way into the sitting room and to the hearth.

I discover that Cairn has already stacked logs in the fire, so all I have to do is call a little flame into my palm (carefully, of course) and blow it into the kindling tucked into the logs. Thankfully, the fire responds to my coaxing—without trying to burn anything down. Immediately, the sparks catch, and the fire soon bathes my face in light and warmth. I sit back on my heels, smiling to myself, even laughing a little at the memory of running through the rain, chasing after Cairn as he left hoofprints in the soft earth.

I think I'll remember that for many years to come.

A moment later, the door opens and closes, and then Cairn appears in the wide doorway to the sitting room. I stand and meet his eyes.

His long hair has come loose from the knot it's usually tied up in, and damp curls fall around his cheeks and chin. The tunic he's wearing is sopping wet, the lovely forest-green color turned almost black with rainwater.

Plop. Plop.

Water drips off of him, landing in a puddle near his hooves. He seems to notice it at the same moment I do and quickly says, "I'll grab towels."

I nod once, and when he's gone, I take a deep breath. My heart thumps rapidly, a mixture of nerves and excitement curling through me.

Cairn returns a few moments later, now dressed in a dry long-sleeved tunic and trousers, and he reaches out to hand me the towel, keeping his body far from mine, like perhaps he's nervous to come too close.

But that's exactly what I want.

Take it slow, I tell myself as I accept the towel with a gracious smile. *Don't want to scare him off.*

The thought makes me smile to myself. It's a bit funny, considering he's a minotaur yet I'm the one who has to be careful not to push him too far too fast.

Gentle giant, indeed.

Using the towel, I scrunch my curls until they're no longer dripping, then dry off my arms and legs. My dress is getting uncomfortable now, still wet and sticking to me. I need to get this thing off—either by his hands or by mine.

"Do you have something more . . . comfortable I could put on?" I ask.

Cairn is in the process of scrubbing his face and beard dry, but he stops and looks at me over the edge of the fluffy towel.

I gesture to my dress and arch a brow.

He hesitates for so long that I wonder if he's forgotten how to speak.

So, I say softly, "Maybe a sweater? I just need to get dry."

Finally, he nods. "My room's there." He gestures with his head, his horns casting shadows on the walls. "Pick anything you like."

"Perfect, thanks."

As I walk past him, he steps out of my way—so far out of my way that I can tell for sure now he's trying to avoid being too close to me, yet I feel his eyes on my back as I walk down the short hallway to his bedroom. And when I turn around to close the door, he's too slow to glance away before I catch him staring.

Cairn's bedroom is simple and minimal, while also being spacious enough for him to navigate around comfortably. A huge bed takes up one wall, and the candles burning atop his nightstand gently illuminate the armoire standing near the window. I pull open the drawers one at a time, allowing my fingers to drift over the fabrics, imagining all the while what it would feel like to touch Cairn's naked skin, to know what he looks like from the neck down—seeing as he's always in tunics and trousers, I don't even know where the human part of him ends and the bull begins.

How big is he? I wonder as I pull a soft lightweight knit sweater from one of the drawers. It smells like him—like earth and flour with a hint of sweetness.

Stripping out of my dress, I let it flop into a wet heap upon the floor. Naked now, I glance back toward the closed door. Should I walk out there like this? Show him what I want him to do to me? The idea is tempting, for sure, but I don't think he'd go for it. I can already hear his voice in my mind, telling me we shouldn't, we can't.

But we can. And we *should*.

Abandoning the idea, I slip my arms into the sleeves of the sweater and pull it on over my head. It falls past my knees, and the sleeves very nearly drown me—I have to roll them up again and again, resulting in funny bulging cuffs, just to gain free access to my hands.

I look down at my legs. The sweater is longer than most of my dresses, so I opt to forego trying to find something for my lower half. It would probably be a fruitless endeavor anyway.

After scooping my wet dress up, I open another door off his bedroom and discover a washroom with a big wooden tub. A shelving unit nearby holds a large bar of soap, and the sink has a single toothbrush.

He's so organized, it makes me want to cause a bit of chaos. But I'm pretty sure I do enough of that as is, so I instead opt to just drape my wet dress over the side of the tub, leaving it to drip dry.

Then I go to find my minotaur.

CHAPTER 23
CAIRN

"HOW DO I LOOK?"

I turn at the sound of Lyra's voice.

And the image of her in my old sweater, her pale freckled legs bare from ankle to mid-thigh, makes my heart skip a few beats. Her curls are still damp and hang around her face in dark red ringlets. Feet bare, she takes a few steps toward me, and I can't decide whether I should scoop her into my arms or open the door and gallop outside into the still-falling rain in an effort to cool the heat building in my chest.

I don't do either. Instead, I stand frozen in the kitchen, holding a tea kettle in one hand and two teacups in the other.

When I don't say anything, Lyra plants her hands on her hips and tilts her head. A smile pulls on her mouth. "That good, huh?"

Snapping back to reality, I clear my throat and set the cups on the wooden table, then fetch a trivet to put the kettle on so it doesn't burn the tabletop.

"Would you," I start as Lyra sinks into a chair at the table, "like a cup of tea?"

"Please." She crosses her arms on the table and smiles up at me, looking more innocent than I know her to be.

Her eyes throw little flames of warmth at my back while I turn to peruse my tea selection. "Lavender, lemon balm, or green?" I ask her without turning around.

"Hmm . . ." Her fingers drum out a soft rhythm on the tabletop, mixing with the sound of the rain thumping against the thatched roof. "I think lavender."

I agree. After adding lavender leaves to two sachets, I grab my jar of wildflower honey and a silver spoon to go with it. Then I have nothing left to distract myself with, and I steel myself before turning and joining her at the table.

She watches with childlike excitement as I add honey to each cup, then pour hot water and toss in the sachets. Immediately, the calming sweet scent of lavender curls around us, and I breathe it in deeply.

Unfortunately, it does nothing to ease the frenzied pounding of my heart.

Apart from Headmistress Moonhart, I don't recall a woman ever having joined me in my hut. And Lyra is already making herself at home, pulling one knee into her chest and blowing softly on her steaming tea as she holds the cup in both hands. Always in such a hurry . . .

"Careful," I say, feeling oddly protective of her. "It's hot."

One of her brows arches in the corner. "I don't mind some heat."

Oh, goddess.

I tear my eyes away and will myself not to imagine what's under that sweater—if anything at all. Her dress almost killed me tonight, but I think the sweater and bare legs might be even more dangerous.

Not good.

"So," Lyra says as I stare at a point on the kitchen wall, "tell me about you, Cairn Axton."

She says my name slowly, drawing it out intentionally. I flex my jaw and take a slow breath, trying to keep my horns on straight.

"Me? There's not much to tell." I lift one shoulder in a shrug. "What do you want to know?"

"How'd you end up here?" In my periphery, she gestures around my hut with one hand. "Did you always want to be a groundskeeper?"

A gruff laugh slips out of me. "No."

I didn't know what I wanted, exactly. But like most things in life, the job presented itself to me unexpectedly—and right when I needed it.

After taking a sip of tea, I ask Lyra, "And you? Why are you here?"

"Well," she says, "there was this rainstorm, and I had to run for cover, and—"

I tip my head and cast her an unimpressed look, and she cracks a smile.

"At Coven Crest?" she asks.

I nod.

Now the playful smile slips from her lips. She sets her teacup on the table and looks down into her tea, the steam curling up around her pretty freckled cheeks.

"My mom attended Coven Crest," she says softly. "I don't know her, really—she left when I was little—but I know she was a powerful fire witch, and I want to be one too." Her shoulders, drowning in my sweater, rise and fall with a shrug. "So, here I am. Not sure it's done me much good though." Her crimson eyes flick to mine, but the smile she attempts doesn't quite reach them.

My heart squeezes. Perhaps for the first time, Lyra is letting me see something that resides somewhere deep. She's being vulnerable. And it makes me hurt for her.

"I'm sorry," I say softly.

Lyra blinks. "For what?"

"Your mother . . ." I clear my throat. "A parent shouldn't abandon their children."

"Oh, that." She shrugs again, like she's trying to let it roll off her shoulders, but I can see the weight that hangs there, even if she tries to disguise it. "It was a long time ago. And I have Papa. Though I know I wasn't easy on him coming up." A bit of a sparkle returns to her eyes. "Actually, I'm pretty sure I was a terror. Still am."

She laughs, and the sound makes me smile.

"That," I say softly, "I can confirm."

"Oh, please. I've been mostly on time, I haven't set anything on fire—"

"Yet," I cut in, setting my teacup down on the table.

"—and most of all, I put up with *you*."

My eyes narrow. "What's that supposed to mean?"

"It means," Lyra says, pushing to her feet, "that you can be insufferable at times. Grumpy, cold, prickly . . ."

I'd argue with her, tell her she doesn't know what she's

talking about, but she's stepping toward me on bare feet, and my throat squeezes closed as she slips her legs around my hips and sinks onto my lap, arms coming up to drape around my neck.

Her face is so close now, I can see the different shades of red in her crimson eyes, can see the firelight dancing in her midnight pupils.

"Lyra—" I start.

She puts one hand on my cheek and leans her forehead against mine. Her skin is hot to the touch. I catch my breath.

"It's okay," she whispers. "You don't have to pretend like you don't want this." Her hand drifts down my cheek and neck to rest on my chest, right over my heart. I know she can feel how fast it's beating. "Whatever you say, I know you want me too."

Her eyes burn into mine. No matter what words my mouth forms, my body doesn't lie, and it's already reacting to her.

"You know why I can't," I whisper, trying to turn my face away from hers. But she catches my cheek in her hand and forces me to look at her.

"I know why you *won't*," she corrects. "But we're alone. No one has to know." Her gaze slips down to my mouth, and her thumb brushes delicately over my lips, making my cock twitch. "It'll be our little secret."

"If someone finds out—"

"I won't let that happen," she says. Her eyes flash with determination. "I know what that would mean for you. I know what's on the line." She pushes her fingers through my beard, then leans in again, so close I can feel her breath on my lips. "But I want you so bad. Please, Cairn. I'll beg if I have to. I'll do whatever you want."

I squeeze my eyes closed, trying to ground myself, but no matter what I do, I can't stop my cock from hardening. She's sitting right on it, and it strains to reach her through my soft trousers.

"I'm too old for you," I whisper, eyes still closed. I'm trying to remember all the reasons why I shouldn't do this, but they flash by like streaks of lightning, gone before I can pinpoint their exact location.

Lyra lets out a laugh. "According to who?"

"Society," I grumble.

She leans in closer, breath tickling my ear. "Fuck society."

Her sharp words send a bolt of surprise through me, followed closely by desire.

I keep waiting for her to kiss me, to make this decision easy, but she doesn't. And when I finally open my eyes, she's staring right at me, watching, waiting.

This is my choice to make; she's already made hers.

I see myself reflected in her firelit eyes, and I see how scared I am: scared of losing my job, scared of doing something I shouldn't, scared of what others might think, scared of letting myself think I can have this—have *her*.

Fuck society, I think. I've never liked it anyway, so why let it control me? Why let it steal from me the joy and pleasure that's currently seated in my lap, staring at me with hungry eyes and a pouty mouth?

"Fuck society," I whisper. And I think I've made my choice.

Lyra doesn't even have the chance to smile before I grip the back of her head in my hand and crush her mouth to mine.

CHAPTER 24
LYRA

INALLY. *FINALLY.*

Cairn's mouth is on mine, hot and hungry and tinged with the taste of lavender and honey. His hand is in my hair, fingers tangling in the damp curls, and his other hand comes up to grip my hip. Everywhere he touches me, little flames lick at my skin, burning me from the inside out.

But I love it. I want more. I want everything.

My fingers find the hem of Cairn's tunic, and he breaks our kiss for a moment to look into my eyes. I hold his gaze as I start to lift the soft material, and he doesn't resist me. Instead, he holds up his arms, allowing me to wiggle the tunic over each one. He has to help me maneuver it over his horns, but then the fabric falls to the floor, and he's sitting shirtless before me. I lean back a bit where I'm seated in his lap, letting my eyes take him in.

His chest is broad and strong, toned from all the manual labor he does. My fingers skate over his brown skin, causing his skin to pebble and nipples to harden—just like mine are doing under the soft material of Cairn's sweater.

I'm not wearing any underwear, and I'm pretty sure I'm leaving a wet patch where I'm sitting in his lap.

As if he can read my mind, he glances down at where my legs are spread around him, but the sweater is long and hides me from his view.

With a grunt, Cairn grips my ass cheeks with his hands—they're so big they cup me completely—and stands from the chair, hooves tapping against the floorboards as he turns to set me on the table.

I look at where I was seated on him, and like expected, I left a wet spot on the fabric—right where his cock is straining to break free. Cairn braces his hands on the table on either side of me, and his mouth finds my jaw, then my throat. I tip my head back, closing my eyes as he kisses and nibbles and licks me from earlobe to collarbone, leaving heat everywhere he touches.

I reach forward, letting my fingers find the hard bulge between his legs, and he draws a sharp breath. Slowly, I stroke him through the fabric, already realizing he's *much* bigger than any cock I've taken before. I expected it, of course—he *is* a minotaur—but now my curiosity is piqued. I want to see him, want to feel his weight in my hands.

With a new hunger spurring me on, I grab the cord holding his trousers and tug it free. He ceases sucking my earlobe but doesn't make any move to stop me. So I wrap my fingers around his waistband and ease the fabric down—until I guide it over his erect cock and finally see what he's been hiding from me.

Releasing the fabric, I let it fall, eyes widening as I take in the length and girth of the shaft bobbing in front of me.

He's . . . *huge*. It'd take both my hands to wrap around him, and I'm already wondering if my mouth can even come close to opening wide enough to get his tip past my lips. Veins raging with blood snake up and down the length, and his head is bright reddish pink and already glistening with moisture.

Looking past his cock, I find two bulging balls, hanging like weights between his strong thighs. Curiosity getting the better of me, I lean forward and cup them in my palms. As I heft their weight, Cairn trembles and lets out a groan. The sound alone makes me get wetter. I hope he doesn't mind cleaning the table later.

I let my eyes trail over the rest of him, drinking in his naked form.

His top half is human—apart from his horns, of course— though his chest is broader and stronger than those of most human males. He's still human form at the waist, apart from the tail flicking behind him. His thighs lead to human knees, and then his legs slowly transition into hocks, which lead down to his fetlocks and hooves. His warm brown skin is covered in a short-haired coat from his knees down.

I've wondered for so long what his body looks like, and I finally have my answers.

After giving his balls one more squeeze, I move my hands to his shaft, gripping it at the base. His body goes tight, muscles in his neck bunching as I begin guiding my palms up and down his length. There's so *much* of him, it takes moving my entire arms to stroke him. And when I circle his bright red tip with my thumb, smoothing the moisture over his hot skin, he drops his head back and moans.

"Cairn," I whisper as I continue stroking him, gaze moving from his face to his cock as it twitches in my palms.

He says nothing.

I lick my lips. "I want you to fuck me."

This gets his attention. I look up at him, hands still wrapped around his shaft, and he narrows his eyes at me, forehead furrowing. Almost with a hint of pain in his voice, he says, "I can't."

My hands still, and the furrow in his brow deepens, frustration flashing in his dark eyes.

"Why?" I ask.

His hips push forward just a bit, as if begging me to keep going. Instead, I drop my hands to the tabletop and lean away, focusing on his face.

"Because," he grunts out, muscles in his jaw feathering. "I won't fit inside you. You'd tear."

That probably shouldn't turn me on even more, but it does. The idea of him filling me until I can't take any more, of stretching me to my absolute limits, has me spreading my thighs on the table, pulling up the hem of his sweater so he can see the moisture gathering between my legs.

His gaze flicks down, and immediately, his cock pulses, bobbing in front of me, more glistening moisture gathering at the tip.

"Please?" I say. "Can't we just try?"

He's so entranced by my pussy that he doesn't respond at first. His tongue darts out to wet his lips, and he finally drags his eyes back to mine. "No. You'd get hurt."

My lips pull into a pout. "Then what can we do?" I reach out with one hand and trace my fingertips over his heavy balls, teasing him and liking the way the muscles in his neck strain at the contact.

He swallows hard, chest rising and falling with heavy breaths. "We'd have to . . . prepare you," he finally says.

"Prepare me?" I arch a brow and squeeze one of his balls, then lean away again, leaving him looking even more frustrated and breathless. I decide I like seeing him this way, on the verge, brought to his edge and then left to tremble for me. "How do we do that?"

His tongue wets his lips again. Whatever he's thinking, I'm pretty sure it's making him even harder. "You'd need to be . . . stretched."

My brows rise.

Goddess, that sounds like fun.

With a little tip to my lips, I lean back on my elbows and bring my feet flat on the table, legs spread so Cairn can see between my thighs.

"Okay," I say. "So, stretch me."

CHAPTER 25
CAIRN

THIS WITCH WILL BE THE DEATH OF ME. AT this moment, I know this to be an irrefutable fact.

But I also know that I'd go peacefully into the dark, knowing she's the one who sent me there. Though I'd really like to fuck her first.

"So, stretch me," she says. And I about cum right there, all over her as she reclines on my kitchen table, the sweater she's wearing pulled up just far enough that I can see her pussy, pink and already slick with wetness.

"It's not that easy," I say, but I'm losing this battle. She's already got me naked in my kitchen, with a raging hard-on that's begging to be touched.

"Cairn," she says, voice low and edged with irritation. "I *really* want you to fuck me. Do you want that too?"

I narrow my eyes and flex my fingers into fists. Slowly, I say, "Yes."

"And it order to do so, you have to prepare me. *Stretch* me. Is that right?"

Goddess, the way she says that makes my dick jump.

"Yes," I say again.

With the firelight dancing in her crimson eyes, she pulls the sweater up a little farther, revealing her hips and low belly. "Then I want you to do it."

My heart wants to burst out of my rib cage and gallop around the room. I'm not supposed to even *think* of her this way, yet somehow, she's got me stepping forward and taking hold of her thighs, sliding her to the edge of my kitchen table.

Witchcraft. It's got to be witchcraft. They teach charms classes here, and potions classes. Maybe she spiked those cupcakes she gave me. Maybe this is all a spell.

And maybe I should just stop overthinking it and touch her.

"It won't be comfortable," I whisper, trailing my fingers down the inside of her thigh.

Her skin pebbles beneath my touch, her eyelids fluttering closed.

"Speak for yourself," she mumbles.

"I'm serious, Lyra. For you to be able to take me, we're going to have to work at this." To prove how serious I am, I line the head of my cock up at her wet opening and push, just a little.

Her eyes flash open, and she looks down between her thighs. My head isn't even close to being able to fit inside her; *that's* how much work we have ahead of us.

"Well," she says softly, lying back on the table and looking up at me with smoldering eyes. "You'd better get started, then." As if to prove how serious she is, she spreads her legs a bit wider for me, letting her knees fall open, giving me full access to her wet pink pussy.

And finally, I can resist her no longer.

Spell or not, she's caught me in her web, and I'll do whatever she wants.

Slowly, I guide my fingers from her inner thigh to the top of her mound, where her bright red hair has been trimmed short. Using the pad of my thumb, I sweep across her clit, and she jerks her hips in response.

"Try to relax," I tell her. "Don't tighten up."

Her eyes meet mine, and she gives me a little nod.

I press the pad of my thumb to her clit again, rubbing it, deep and slow. It throbs, growing larger as a flush creeps up her neck and into her freckled cheeks. Then I move my fingers lower, slipping through her wet folds. And when I find her slick entrance, I push one finger inside.

She moans.

I push my finger in deeper, then pull it back out, working her until she softens. Then I add another. My fingers are thick, and a tiny gasp escapes her as I ease the second one in and begin fucking her with both. My other hand finds her clit, and I rub it, making her wetter, making my fingers slide easier.

"Is that," she pants, "it?"

A chuckle slips out of me. "We've barely gotten started, witch."

Eyes meeting mine, she says, "Then do it already."

"Always in such a rush." I break eye contact and focus on her pussy again. "Relax," I remind her. "This might hurt."

I pull my fingers out of her and replace them with both my thumbs. Then I begin pulling my thumbs apart, stretching her pussy to its limits, making her gasp before I let off for a few seconds, then stretch her again. I stare at her as I work, cock throbbing each time her pussy opens before me, just begging me to push inside.

When I've finished stretching her side to side, I readjust my thumbs, pushing them a bit deeper, making her whimper beautifully as I work to stretch her up and down.

Her pussy continues to leak with moisture, and her chest rises and falls beneath my sweater, her breathing coming in rapid pants. Eventually, I look up from between her thighs and ask, "Are you . . . enjoying this?"

She doesn't respond in words, only little mumbles and moans.

Maybe that's enough for her first time. And maybe now I just want to watch her cum.

I remove my thumbs and replace them with two fingers. As I push them in and out of her, my other hand finds her clit again. It's swollen, enlarged to the point that one brush from my fingertips sends her writhing on the table. So I touch it more gently, putting gentle pressure on it. Beneath the pad of my finger, I can feel it throb, can feel each beat of her heart.

"More," she whispers.

I arch a brow, surprised and impressed. Okay, I'll give her more.

I add one more finger, and it's a tight fit, almost impossible to get all three fingers inside her.

She starts moaning then, the sound building as I sink my fingers inside her and rub her clit with a featherlight touch. Her back arches off the table, knees shaking. Inside her, I curl my fingers, massaging her slick insides.

And with a gasp, she cums for me.

It's wet and beautiful and so much better than I anticipated. She soaks my hand, her pussy walls clenching my fingers as her clit throbs beneath my touch. Pink lips open, she pants and moans, freckles crinkling as she squeezes her eyes closed.

With every thrust of my fingers inside her, I have to tell myself that I *can't* fuck her yet, no matter how badly I need to at this very moment. She'd get hurt, and I couldn't live with myself if I hurt her. And her pleasure is more important than mine. I can jerk off later—with the sound of her moans and the memory of her pussy around my fingers, it certainly wouldn't take much.

But the witch surprises me, as she so often does.

When she's done cumming, she pushes herself into a seated position on the table. Her hair, still slightly damp from the rain, sticks to her cheeks, which sparkle with light perspiration. She's breathing hard, trying to catch her breath. And she gives me a small coy smile before taking my cock in both her hands and starting to stroke it again.

"You don't have to," I tell her. But she just smiles more.

And then she leans forward to lick the precum from my tip. And I'm as good as a dead man.

CHAPTER 26
LYRA

PUSSY LEAKING ALL OVER CAIRN'S TABLE, I lean forward and drag my tongue across his glistening head. Immediately, his cock throbs in my hands, and if he was about to say something else, to tell me to stop or that it's time for me to go back to the castle or that we really shouldn't be doing this, the words die on his tongue.

I stroke him slowly at first, alternating between swiping my thumbs and my tongue over his tip. The veins in his shaft are engorged with blood, and it looks so good that I drag my tongue along those as well, making him gasp for breath. I wish I could take all of him into my mouth, but when I try, I can only just barely get his head between my lips. With both hands still stroking him, I suck on him gently, swiping my tongue along the thick tissue on the underside of his tip.

Then Cairn's hands are in my damp hair. He twists the curls into his fingers, and I can feel his desire to pump my head, to force himself deeper into my mouth, but he doesn't. He just grips me, hands and knees shaking, his head tipped up toward the ceiling. When I glance up from between his thighs, I find the veins in his neck bulging, his every muscle coiled tight.

In my hands, his cock gets harder. He's almost there.

My tongue finds his tip again, and he's leaking so much precum that I have to keep lapping it away, making him groan with each pass of my tongue over his head. Wrapping my lips around his dick, I suck and lick and keep pumping my hands.

And finally, with a rumbling moan, he cums.

And it's shocking, to say the least.

I try to catch it in my mouth, but I'm quickly overwhelmed, and I have to sit back, watching as ropes of cum spurt from his cock, covering my borrowed sweater and dripping onto my bare thighs. His hands are still in my hair, but after he drains everything he has onto my body, he softens his hold. When he looks down and meets my eyes, I make a very obvious show of swallowing the cum I've been holding in my mouth.

He growls, more beast than man.

And then both of us look at the sticky mess I—and the table—have become.

We'll both require a good cleaning.

"Are you okay?" Cairn asks at long last. His cock is still hard but slowly losing its demanding firmness. His chest rises and falls as he breathes heavily, his nose ring catching the light from the fire in the sitting room.

"I'm more than okay," I whisper. "That was . . ." Words evade me, so I just laugh.

This makes Cairn crack a small smile. "It was," he agrees. One of his hands finds my face and cups my cheek. His thumb strokes my skin. "Your freckles are beautiful," he says softly.

My lips pull up in a smile. "I didn't used to think so."

"But you do now?" His thumb continues to brush along my skin, as if he's trying to remember every constellation on my face.

"I'm learning to," I whisper.

His brown cheeks are flushed, and there's a sheen of sweat on his forehead and shoulders. But his heavy breathing is slowing, and we both seem to have caught our breath.

"Come on," he says. "Let's get you cleaned up."

Instead of standing up, I hold my arms out to him and tip my head. "Carry me?"

His dark eyes flash with surprise, and then a smile curls across his bearded mouth. "Really?"

I continue to hold my arms out.

With a roll of his eyes, he stoops to wrap one arm under my knees and the other around my back. I let out a little squeal when he scoops me off the table. I feel weightless in his arms, as if I'm floating on clouds.

Curling myself into his firm warm chest, I allow myself to feel safe and secure and like nothing in my outside world is going wrong. And for a moment, Cairn helps me believe it might be true.

THE TUB IN CAIRN'S WASHROOM IS HUGE—I SUPPOSE it has to be to fit a minotaur. But to me, it feels more like a swimming pool than a basic wooden bathtub.

Cairn brought water in from the well outside, and I used my fire magic to heat it until it was steaming like a hot spring. Now we lounge in the warm water together, Cairn leaning against one side with his legs stretched out, me leaning back against him, my head resting comfortably against his chest.

Tipping my head up as I lean back against him, I admire his horns and the way they catch the light from the candles I lit on the shelf beside the tub.

Cairn takes the bar of soap and works it along my body slowly. I close my eyes and breathe deep as he massages it into my shoulders, my breasts, down my abdomen to the place between my legs. When he touches me there, a pulse of desire goes through me, but my pussy is already sore from him fingering and stretching me.

"Cairn," I say as he moves the soap to my thigh.

"Hmm?"

I watch the soap bubbles floating atop the water, catching the light from the candles and gleaming with little rainbows of color. "How long will it take?"

He continues to work the soap into my thigh, then behind my knee, leaving no spot unscrubbed. "How long will what take?"

A smile pulls on my mouth. The bathwater sloshes as I sit up and turn to face him. "Stretching me." I glance down into the soapy water, where his cock is just barely visible through the soap bubbles, still impressively wide and long even when it's soft. "How long until you can fuck me?"

His jaw feathers, and through the water, I can see his cock twitch, just a little.

"I don't know," he finally says, but he's not meeting my eyes. "I've only . . ." Something like embarrassment creeps across his face, turning his cheeks a slightly darker shade of red than the hot water already did. "I've only done this once before."

A collection of emotions goes through me.

Of course he's been with other women—how could he not? He's older than me, more experienced, and one of the most beautiful specimens of *man* I've ever seen. I know I'm not the only woman who's wanted to feel him between her thighs.

Yet his words still make my chest pinch and my stomach squeeze. I don't much like the thought of him stretching someone else, preparing her to take his cock.

"So," I say softly, trying to pick my words with care instead of letting them spew out in a fiery volcano, like they usually do, "you've been with a human before?"

He nods once. "Yes. Though it was many years ago now."

I reach for the bar of soap still held in his hand and ease it into mine. Then, with a gentleness I didn't realize I possessed, I start working the soap into his chest, along his collarbones, and down his thick arms. "What happened?" I whisper, not looking up to meet his dark eyes.

Cairn doesn't reply for a long time. When I *do* finally glance up, he's not looking at me. He's staring at a point on the wall, forehead furrowed slightly, as though he's reliving old memories. His long curls hang loose, framing his face and strong jaw.

"You don't have to tell me," I say. "I'd understand if—"

"It's not that," he says softly. One of his hands finds my bare back, and he begins tracing his fingers along my skin slowly, as if he's lost in the past. "It's just that I've not thought about it for a long time. It's . . . odd, unearthing what I've left buried." Now his eyes meet mine. He shifts slightly in the tub, stretching his legs out longer. His head cants slightly to one side as he regards me. "I was engaged to be married."

Another bolt of surprise goes through me. It serves to remind me of the age difference between us. It's like he's lived this whole big life, and mine is only just getting started.

"But you didn't go through with it?" I take his hand in mine—it's so big in comparison—and work the soap into his forearm, then his wrist, where I can feel his heartbeat through the tender skin.

"I would have," he says. "But she decided not to. She called it off before we were wed."

I'm not sure I like that answer. The silly, jealous part of me wanted him to say that *he* decided not to marry her. Keeping my eyes down so he can't see the tangled emotions I'm working to unravel, I say, "Why?"

He sighs, long and low. Then, as if it's the most natural thing in the world, he says, "Her family wouldn't accept me because I'm a minotaur, so she broke it off with me."

Now my eyes flash to his, and my hand stills with the soap. "What?"

The emotion inside me turns quickly to anger, heat flooding my veins. I know—have always known—that there are people in the world who judge others on how they look or where they were born instead of judging them based on their character. But how *anyone* could toss Cairn aside like that . . .

My mind flashes with images: Cairn raking leaves, the small smile that curled across his lips when the red fox licked his chin, the gentleness with which he prunes plants and tucks them into the soil to keep them warm for the long winter ahead.

Around us, the water grows warmer as my fire magic simmers.

"What an asshole," I finally say, not pausing to consider how Cairn might respond.

But he surprises me when he lets out a hearty laugh. It makes the water slosh all around us, and for a moment, it's like I'm a boat in a tropical storm, getting tossed this way and that.

His arms come around me, and he eases me into his lap, my knees spread along either side of his hips. Close up, I can see little water droplets clinging to his beard and glimpse my funny warped reflection in the winking metal of his nose ring.

"Thank you for that," he says. His voice is buoyant, and his lips are pulled into a small smile. "I've wanted to hear someone say that for a long, long time."

Despite my anger and simmering jealously, I can't help but to smile. "Asshole, asshole, asshole," I repeat. My bare arms wrap around his neck, and I press my chest to his. "I'll say it as many times as you want."

Again, he traces my back with his fingertips, making

goose bumps rise along my skin. His eyes seem to search mine, though for what, I've no idea. Then his hand wraps around the back of my head, and he pulls me in, pressing his mouth to mine.

His lips are soft and warm, his beard ticklish against my skin. I hold tighter to him, hugging his neck like I'll never let go.

When he pulls away from our kiss, his mouth is quirked into a smile. Softly, he says, "I have a surprise for you."

CHAPTER 27
CAIRN

LYRA SITS IN THE MIDDLE OF MY BED, DRAPED in another one of my sweaters. She looks slightly comedic, like she's no more than a head poking out of what appears to be a big puddle of knit fabric. Her crimson gaze follows me as I go to my closet and pull out a small brown box with a red ribbon wrapped around it and knotted into a bow.

With the box in my hands, I suddenly feel a twinge of nervousness, perhaps even embarrassment.

Is this ridiculous? I'm not so sure she even likes gardening.

I'm doubting myself now, worrying that she'll open the little box and the excitement will vanish from her eyes, replaced with disappointment or even pity.

Well, she does still have another semester and a half worth of community service, I think, comforting myself with the logical approach to my gift. *So, they'll be helpful either way.*

"Cairn?" she says from behind me.

I glance over my shoulder. She's still sitting in the middle of my bed, legs crossed, damp hair woven into a chunky braid that hangs down her back.

Too late now.

I already told her I had a surprise for her, and her crimson gaze flicks to the package held in my hands, so there'll be no going back.

I turn away from the closet and cross the bedroom, then take a seat on the edge of the bed. The mattress dips beneath my weight. "It's not much," I say, still holding the little box. "When I saw them, I thought of you."

With some reluctance, I hold the box out to her.

She takes it with a level of carefulness that reminds me of when she was transplanting the sniffleblooms. I can see in her the ability to be calm, balanced, in control. She might not yet see it in herself, but I know it's there.

Lyra cradles the box in her lap. For a moment, she just stares down at it, and as my nervousness mounts, I wonder what she's thinking. I hope she's not expecting much . . . If she is, the gift will most certainly be a disappointment.

I twiddle my thumbs in my lap and hope she can't hear the rapid galloping of my heart.

Her fingers find the red ribbon, and they brush it softly. She pulls it loose in slow motion, letting the silky material fall into a spiral around the box. Then she lifts the lid and peers inside.

Oh, she's going to hate them. Such a bad choice. I should've just gotten her chocolate instead.

She blinks. She tips her head. She reaches into the box and withdraws the gloves, holding them up in the dim golden candlelight illuminating the bedroom.

"Gardening gloves?" she asks with a curious lilt to her voice.

Nodding, I clear my throat. "They're charmed with magic to be fireproof. So . . . no more catching the greenhouse on fire."

As soon as the words leave my mouth, I regret them. I intended for them to come out like a joke, but I'm not sure I nailed the delivery.

But Lyra's eyes glitter, and she looks back down at the gloves with a new sort of appreciation.

"They're fireproof?" she whispers.

I nod again.

She clasps them to her chest, and this time when her eyes meet mine, they're twinkling with moisture. "They're perfect, Cairn."

I blink in surprise. "Really? You . . . like them?"

After untangling herself from my bulky sweater, she crawls across the bed and wraps her arms around my neck. Her breath is featherlight against the shell of my ear as she whispers, "I *love* them. Thank you." Then she presses a kiss to my cheek.

My heart swells to the point I think it might squeeze out of my rib cage and drift into the autumn night.

Keeping one arm around my neck, she reaches out and snags up the red ribbon from where she dropped it onto the bed. "Can I keep this too?"

A laugh rumbles out of me. "I suppose."

Her lips pull into a smile, making her freckles crinkle. After wiggling into my lap, she turns so her back is facing me, then holds up the ribbon. "Will you tie it into my hair? Make a bow like you did around the box." She dangles the ribbon in the air, letting it hang from her fingers until I take it from her.

"I'm not very good," I mumble, already wondering how I'm going to get this thin ribbon around her braid with my big fingers.

"As long as you do it," she says lightly, "it'll be perfect."

Yup, there my heart goes again, feeling like it wants to explode.

As I start to wrap the red ribbon around the end of her braid, I wonder how I got here. How'd I go from being annoyed at the prospect of having to babysit a troublesome fire witch to having her in my lap, to knowing what her lips feel like against mine, to wanting to feel her pussy stretch around my cock?

I banish that last thought quickly; she must be sore from earlier this evening, and I already covered her in my cum, to the point where we both had to bathe. She needs to rest.

Narrowing my eyes in focus, I somehow am able to get my clumsy fingers to wrap the ribbon into a quaint bow at the end of her pretty red braid. I sit back to check my work, then mumble, "It's done."

Lyra pulls her braid around to check my work. Her fingers brush along the ribbon, and she turns her eyes up to meet mine. "Can I stay with you tonight?" she whispers.

The rain has slowed, but it still patters softly outside and against the thatched roof. The bedroom window is open just a crack, keeping us cool and carrying in the delicious scent of fall and woodsmoke from the Samhain bonfire.

I hadn't considered for even a moment sending her out into the rain, making her walk back to the castle in my over-size sweater. I'd have to be the biggest ass in Wysteria.

Lifting a hand, I trace my thumb along the ridge of her cheekbone, mapping out her freckles in my mind. "Of course," I whisper.

Her eyes glisten. And then she kisses me.

LYRA IS BEAUTIFUL WHEN SHE SLEEPS. HER MOUTH is open slightly, and she breathes deep and even. The furrow that often mars her brow is gone, leaving her forehead perfectly smooth.

She lies next to me, one hand draped across my bare chest, the other curled up under her chin. She looks so delicate in sleep, so soft. So gentle.

Yet I know she can be anything but.

We've been working together for half a semester, and already I've seen subtle changes in her—focus and concentration, the effort she puts forth to control her fire, the determination I so often see etched across her face.

Yet right now, all I see is peace.

Slowly, I use one finger to brush a soft, bouncy curl from her cheek. She shifts a bit in sleep, breathing changing, and for a moment, I fear I've woken her. But then she settles right back in, one hand still lying on my chest, right where my heart beats.

I know this is dangerous, that we—I—shouldn't be doing this. Lyra is already skating on thin ice with Headmistress Moonhart, and if anyone so much as suspects something untoward is going on between us, it could result in her losing her place here. As for me, I could easily lose my job, my home, all the quiet peace I've built here on the outskirts of the academy.

But . . . would that be so bad? a small voice asks me.

My gaze lifts from Lyra and lands on the doorway leading into the sitting room, where the letter Milo sent me is held inside the drawer in a side table.

After bumping into him in Wysteria the other day, I put quill to parchment and filled out the application he'd sent over. And though I still don't have high hopes of hearing back from the Columbine Conservatory, the thought that I might be able to do something more, learn something more, has my chest squeezing in nervous anticipation.

If I were to get the job, it would mean leaving here. Leaving *her*.

My eyes flick down to her, curled beside me, breathing softly, skin like cream in the silver moonlight cutting through a gap in my curtains.

If I left here, what would that mean for us?

Oh, there's an us *now?*

The thought startles me. Up until tonight, I'd still been resisting, telling myself I couldn't let this spark between us burn out of my control. But now it has. And in my heart, I want to kindle it, to throw logs onto the fire, to pray before it and dance around it and watch as the flames lick the sky.

In my head . . . I know this is dangerous. For both of us.

But I don't know what to do, don't know how to pull away now, how to stop this thing that's already taking on a life of its own.

Lyra shifts again, and this time, her crimson eyes blink open slowly. She looks up at me, sleepy and bleary, and yawns.

"Cairn?" she whispers.

"Hmm?" I brush my fingers across her cheek, then down the column of her throat.

"Is everything okay?" She blinks again. "Can't sleep?"

"Everything's fine," I whisper. "Go back to sleep."

"And you'll be here when I wake up?"

My heart twists into shapes it hasn't for many, many years. "Of course I will."

Lyra gives me a sleepy smile, then scoots closer, curling her small body around mine.

And though I close my eyes and try to find sleep, it evades me for a long while. Mostly, what I find is worry.

CHAPTER 28
LYRA

AIRN WAKES ME EARLY THE NEXT MORN-
ing, pressing kisses to my forehead and along
the curve of my ear. I'm so warm curled up beside him, cuddled under his blankets while the
cool autumn air gives my nose a slight chill. I
don't want to move. I want to lie here beside him forever.

"Time to get up," he says softly, his breath brushing the
sensitive skin along my neck.

"Why?" I grumble, refusing to open my eyes. If I keep
them closed, maybe he'll lie back down and let me fall
asleep again.

"You have to get back to the castle before everyone wakes
up," he says.

And that makes all my cozy, sleepy fantasies come crashing back down.

That's right. Last night was the Samhain festival. I'm
in Cairn's hut. And I'll need to get back to my dorm room
without anyone realizing I spent the night here.

And the girls ... Ugh. They're going to know something's up now. Hopefully they're not worried about me; I didn't tell them I might not come back to the dorm. But I didn't even know myself.

That's bound to be a fun conversation.

"Come on," Cairn says, and he shifts beside me, making the mattress dip. His lips brush my forehead again, soft and warm. "I'll make you a latte."

That gets me to open my eyes. I blink up at him, and he's stunning. His bare chest is lined with firm muscle, and his beard is full and wild. It's still too early for the sun to gleam through the window, so Cairn is mostly cast in shadow, his horns curling over his head.

"What kind of latte?" I grumble, trying not to let on that that's *exactly* what I need to entice me to get out of this perfect bed.

His lips pull up on one side. "Vanilla and cinnamon."

I squeeze my eyes closed and groan. Then I push myself up and let out a big yawn while stretching my arms over my head.

"Okay," I say sleepily. "I'm up. Where's my latte?"

I SIT ON THE COUCH IN THE DARKNESS OF THE early morning, watching the red-orange flames dance in the hearth as I wait for Cairn to make that latte he promised me. He's in the kitchen, hooves clicking across the worn hardwood floor. As he works and I watch the fire, the scent of vanilla and cinnamon starts to drift through the cozy little hut, making my mouth water.

"Here you go." He walks into the sitting room a short while later, and I look up from where I was staring, mesmerized, into the flames. Reaching down, he offers me a teacup with what look like moonflowers painted on the side.

I arch a brow and ask, "Did you make this?"

Cairn sinks into the armchair across from the couch and nods. "I'm no artist, clearly."

I let out a tired laugh. "I think it's lovely."

Then I look into my latte. And freeze.

"Um . . . Cairn?"

He sips his latte and looks into the fire. "Hmm?"

"There's . . ." I look into my cup again, then back at him. "Something yellow floating in my cup."

He laughs, and the sound is warm and rumbly. "I make coffee with dandelion root. The petals are good for you." His brown-eyed gaze slides to mine. "Don't tell me you're afraid."

A pulse of heat goes through me. "Of course I'm not afraid. It's just a flower." I look into the cup again, where the pretty yellow petals float atop the creamy frothiness dotted with cinnamon.

Okay, maybe just a little bit afraid.

Cairn stares at me and takes a very deliberate sip of his latte. Then one of his brows lifts in the corner. "Well?"

I swallow down my nervousness, lift the cup to my lips, and take a little sip.

The flavor is slightly earthy—probably from the dandelion root—but the vanilla and cinnamon soften the bitterness.

And the flower petals aren't so bad after all.

"What's the verdict?" Cairn asks. He tips his head at me, his horns and nose ring catching the firelight.

I don't even have to lie. "It's delicious."

His smile is small and perhaps even a little bit proud.

We go back to sipping our lattes in the quiet, watching the flames as they dance in the hearth.

And as we sit there together, a weird feeling starts to pull at my chest. It's a feeling of warmth, safety . . . *belonging*. It's a feeling I think I've always subconsciously searched for—the knowing that someone wants me, that they'll not abandon me.

Not like she did.

My gaze slides slowly to Cairn. He's leaning back in his armchair, staring into the fire, sipping his latte like he's got all the time in the world. Being here with him, in this little hut with the thatched roof, makes me want to never leave.

But as the sun starts to rise over the horizon, its golden fingers reaching for the windows, I know it's time to go, even if it's the last thing I want to do.

I finish my latte—it tasted better with every sip, and I'm already wanting another one by the time I rinse the hand-painted cup in the basin in the kitchen—then look down at myself and realize I'm still just wearing one of Cairn's oversize sweaters, with no pants under it. And it's not like I can wear my Samhain dress back to the castle; that would draw way more attention than a bulky sweater and some bed head.

"Um," I say as I step back into the sitting room. Cairn looks over at me from his armchair. "What should I wear?"

He tips his head and regards me with a thoughtful expression. After reaching up to scratch his beard, he offers me a little smile. "I think I might have an idea."

AND THAT'S HOW I END UP TRUDGING BACK TO THE castle in Cairn's sweater, a pair of baggy trousers that are actually *shorts* on him, and my black boots from the festival last night. Cairn let me borrow a knapsack, and my dress and new fireproof gloves are tucked inside. I know I must look a mess—his clothing drowns me, and I have to keep pulling the trousers up, because despite the twine Cairn tied through the belt loops, the trousers just want to slide down—but at least I'm not in a skimpy black dress, which would just *scream* that I never made it back to my room last night. And knowing my luck, I'd probably run into the headmistress on the way to my room.

I make it into the castle, and the hallways are quiet and still. The scent of breakfast from the dining hall twirls through the air, and my stomach growls. But I have to get back to the room first. I won't be able to eat until I see Juniper and the girls and explain where I was last night.

On my way up the twirling stairs of the north tower, I pass a few students who seem to be heading out to exercise in the crisp air. They give me curious looks but don't stop to talk.

Then I reach room NT33, and there's a dragon standing right outside.

Raelan narrows his dark eyes when he sees me and immediately shifts his broad frame to face me, arms crossed over his chest. His piercing gaze quickly assesses the baggy clothing I'm wearing.

"Lyra Wilder," he says, voice stern. "Where the hell were you last night?"

Raelan likes to act like he's not just Alina's bodyguard, but mine and Poppy's and Maeve's as well. It's equal parts annoying and endearing.

"Sheesh, *Dad*. Didn't realize I had a curfew."

Raelan purses his lips. "You know how worried they all were?"

A pang of guilt goes through me. I was afraid of that—but it certainly wasn't on my mind last night while Cairn had me spread on his kitchen table . . .

Before I can respond, the door flies open, startling me. Alina stands there, blue hair hanging around her light brown cheeks, eyes blazing like crystallized fire.

"How did you—" I start to ask.

Oh, the mate bond.

She must've realized I was here based on something she felt through her connection with Raelan. That still freaks me out.

"*You*," Alina says, pointing at me. "Get in here." That same angry finger points at one of the couches. "And explain yourself." Her cold blue eyes narrow. "And what you're wearing."

Well, I guess I knew this was coming. I *did* kind of hope they'd all still be asleep and I could slip in and pretend I'd been here all along, that I came back last night after staying out late at the bonfire. But that's obviously not happening.

With a last glance at Raelan—though he's obviously not coming to my rescue—I step into the room.

Juniper is perched on the back of the couch, and when she sees me, she squeaks and immediately climbs down and scurries across the floor. I stoop to pick her up and hold her to my cheek.

"Where were you?" she asks, putting her paws on my face and nuzzling her nose and whiskers against me.

And she's echoed by Maeve and Poppy, who wear varying expressions of anger and relief.

I drop the soft knapsack Cairn lent me onto the floor by the door, then pull off my boots and pad barefoot into the sitting room, feeling all their eyes on me. Hell, even Isis and Yuki seem to be glaring. But Isis always kind of looks like that—snake eyes and all.

"You don't want to eat breakfast first?" I ask. They're all a little less grumpy once they've got food in their stomachs.

"Lyra," Alina says slowly, voice simmering as she follows me into the sitting room. "Sit. *Now.*"

I sit.

Maeve and Poppy sit down on the other couch, but Alina remains standing over me. She crosses her arms over her chest.

"Where were you? Why didn't you come back? We were worried sick about you."

"Yeah, Raelan said . . ."

Alina just narrows her eyes, waiting for my explanation. The room is so quiet as they stare at me, all I can hear is the crackling of the flames in the hearth and the soft *tick, tick* of the clock on the wall.

"Okay," I say, then let out a big sigh. I move Juniper into my lap, where she cuddles up against the palm of my hand, her fur warm and soft against my skin. "I was with Cairn last night."

Alina blinks. Poppy's cheeks go pink. Maeve just tips her head back and lets out a sudden startling laugh.

Juniper nibbles my finger and mumbles, "I should've known."

"Cairn?" Alina echoes. "The *groundskeeper*?"

I avert my eyes and nod.

"Are those his clothes?" She points at me, though the finger is slightly less angry now.

I nod again.

There's another moment of tense silence. Alina continues to stare down at me.

Then, with a big whooshing sigh, she collapses onto the couch next to me, looking both tired and relieved. "You," she says at long last, putting her fingertips to her temple like I'm causing her a headache, "have a *lot* of explaining to do."

"Can I at least do it after breakfast?" My stomach grumbles as if to prove my point.

But Alina shakes her head. "Nope. Now."

"Okay, wait." Maeve sits forward on the couch and levels her storm-purple eyes on me. "He did *what*?"

I just finished telling them about last night, including my stretching session with Cairn. Now Maeve is acting like it's the most interesting thing in the world, while Alina just shakes her head some more and Poppy looks like she's not sure whether to be horrified or not.

"He stretched me," I say again. "You know . . ." I mime the movements he did with his thumbs, and Maeve laughs again while Poppy covers her eyes and Alina puts a palm to her forehead in obvious exasperation. "He said we have to before he'll fuck me."

"Lyra Wilder," Alina cuts in, "you *cannot* fuck the groundskeeper."

My gaze flashes to her. An ember flickers to life in my belly. "Why not?"

"You know why not. It's forbidden for students and faculty to have romantic relationships. If you get caught, you could get *expelled*."

"And he would probably be fired," Poppy adds.

"And the whole purpose of your community service with him is to *not* get kicked out, remember?"

I clench my teeth and glance away from Alina, choosing to stare into the fire instead. "Of course I remember."

"Then why are you taking this chance? It's dangerous for *both* of you."

My fingers stroke Juniper's soft fur aimlessly. "I know."

I'm not sure what to say. Alina's not wrong, but I can't bring myself to accept what she's saying either. The thought of not touching Cairn again, not kissing him and being held by him and waking up beside him, makes my stomach feel queasy.

"Do you really like him?" Poppy asks. She's mostly been quiet—she tends to get shy when we talk men and sex—but right now she's looking right at me, holding my gaze despite her cheeks still blushing pink.

I bite my lip. Glance into the fire. Bite my lip again.

"Oh my goddess," Maeve says. She leans into the cushions and tosses her arm over the back of the couch. "You do. You've fallen for the minotaur."

Without saying a word, I nod.

Because I have. At first, I thought he would just be some grumpy asshole I had to put up with every Saturday. I just wanted to get through my community service and be done with it. But slowly, I started seeing him, *really* seeing him, and he started seeing me. And now I can't go back, even if I know I should.

"I know it's risky," I say, letting my eyes flick to Alina. Some of the anger has gone from her gaze, but her lips are still pursed into a stern pout of disapproval. "But I don't want to stop. And I don't think he does either." My shoulders rise and fall on a sigh. "I really like him. More than anyone else I've been with. And he sees me." I bite my lip again, rolling my thoughts around before putting them into words. "This might be weird, but it feels *real*. He feels real."

All three girls regard me in the quiet. I wait for Alina to reprimand me some more. But instead, she lets out a long sigh.

"Shit," she mumbles. "Leave it to you to fall for a faculty member. I expected this from Maeve, not you."

This gets me to laugh. "Yeah, I know."

Maeve just arches a brow and smirks at us.

Suddenly, Alina leans forward and snakes her arms around my neck, pulling me into such a sudden hug that Juniper tumbles out of my lap and onto the soft couch with a squeak. Alina squeezes me tight and mumbles, "I'm sorry I was so mad. I was just so worried about you. You can't do that to us again."

"I know. I'm sorry." I put my arms around her waist and return the hug. "I won't. I promise."

With a sigh, Alina removes her arms from my neck and reaches down to give Juniper an apologetic scratch behind the ear. "Sorry, Juniper."

Juniper squeaks to me, and my lips pull up on one side. "She says you owe her a cinnamon bun."

Alina smiles for the first time since I walked through the door. "That's fair. I'll get you one at breakfast."

"Speaking of breakfast"—Maeve pushes to her feet and stretches her arms overhead—"can we go? I'm starving."

"I suppose Lyra has been thoroughly reprimanded," Alina says, lips pulling into a sideways smile. But then it slips a bit, and her eyes look troubled again. "But remember what we said. You have to be careful." She puts a hand on my knee. Her skin is a bit cold from her frost magic as she gives my knee a squeeze. "If you get caught, who knows what'll happen . . ."

"I'll be careful," I promise her.

But despite my promise, a little seed of worry and doubt has planted itself in my gut, and I'm concerned it's there to stay.

CHAPTER 29
CAIRN

FTER LYRA LEAVES, MY HUT FEELS . . . empty. This space, which always feels so warm and welcoming, seems too quiet without her here, too peaceful—if there is such a thing. It's unsettling enough to get me up and heading out to my garden in an effort to distract myself from thoughts of her.

The rain last night left everything soaked, and water droplets cling to the crunchy blades of grass and the plants that remain in my garden, not yet having been harvested. I'll need to pull the cart up to the castle today so the kitchens can deal with all the mugs and mead kegs, but it's still too early for that.

I grab a wicker basket from atop the bistro table and breathe in the rain-scented air. It calms my heart, if only a small amount, and helps put me at ease as I kneel beside a raised bed full of carrots and plush-leafed spinach. These plants like a bit of cold, so they'll last well into the late days of fall.

I pluck spinach leaves and pull bright orange carrots from the dark earth, and I try to think about anything except Lyra Wilder.

Unsurprisingly, it doesn't work.

No matter how hard I try to focus on the task at hand, her crimson eyes keep flashing in my mind, and her moans from when I had my fingers inside her echo in my ears.

Witchcraft, I think with a huff.

I've never had a smidgen of interest in *any* student. And up until I met Lyra, I never thought I would. I'm a man who follows rules, who likes to color inside the lines and not make any waves. I keep my head down, keep to myself, and live a safe, quiet life.

But she's changed all that.

I signed a contract when I accepted the job here, and part of that contract included a clause explicitly stating I'm not to have a relationship of any kind with any student— and now here I am, trying and failing to forget how amazing Lyra's hands felt around my cock, how she stroked me until I couldn't hold myself back. Then we bathed together, and I told her about my failed engagement, and she slept beside me, leaving behind the sweet scent of soap and *her*.

I let out an audible groan.

What have I done?

I've fucked up, that's what. I allowed her to wrap me around her little finger, and though she might not know it yet, I'm pretty sure I'd follow her to the ends of the earth if she asked me to.

Finishing up with the carrots and spinach, I move to the bed of red beets and pull a few of those as well, gently brushing the dirt from the dark purple-red roots. I can chop these up later and roast them, then add them to a bed of spinach leaves and diced carrot.

Does Lyra like beets? I wonder.

Then I remind myself that I shouldn't care what Lyra likes—she should be Miss Wilder to me, not the fire witch I want to toss into my sheets and ravage until we're both too exhausted to move.

I am absolutely hopeless.

"Good morning."

I nearly jump out of my hide.

Whipping my head around, I find Lysandra Moonhart standing there, her pale eyes sweeping over my garden as the morning sun makes her silver-blue hair twinkle.

"Headmistress," I say, trying not to let on how badly she startled me. She's the last person I need around when I'm thinking of all the inappropriate things I want to do with my student helper. I stand from beside my bed of beets and roll out my shoulders. "You're here early."

Her smile is quick and easy. "I hope I'm not intruding. Knowing you, I figured you'd already be up and working on something." She flicks her gaze across the garden, then toward my hut.

Am I imagining the curious look in her eyes, or is she looking for something—or *someone*—specific?

Does she know?

"Would you like to come in?" I offer, gesturing toward the hut like I have nothing to hide. "I'll make some tea."

She nods once. "That would be lovely."

We head inside, and immediately, I start scanning the space, looking for any hint of Lyra. The air still smells of her, just slightly, but Lysandra is a witch, not a minotaur, so I hope she can't smell it.

I clop into the kitchen and set the basket full of fresh produce on the table, double-checking that I didn't miss any stains when wiping the table down this morning. Thankfully, I don't find any damning evidence.

"Lavender?" I call out to Lysandra, who's already making herself comfortable in the sitting room. Every time she visits, that's her tea of choice.

"Please. Thank you, Cairn."

Why is she here? I wonder as I pull the jar of lavender tea off the high shelf. *Is this about Lyra?* I reach for my teacup, the one I used this morning to drink dandelion lattes with Lyra, and realize with a bolt of fear that Lyra's clean cup is sitting there right beside mine. If Lysandra *is* looking for some sort of evidence that the fire witch has been here, that little detail may have intensified her suspicions.

Covertly, I put the cup Lyra used back on the shelf—for some reason, I feel like it's hers now, like no one else should be given the permission to use it—and grab another one for the headmistress to use.

When I finally make it into the sitting room, teacups in hand, I'm wound tight with anticipation. Lyra was sitting on the couch just an hour or two ago, sipping a latte and looking sleepy and beautiful in my oversize sweater. Now Lysandra is in that exact spot. What if she looks down and spots a curly strand of red hair? What would I say? I could tell her Lyra just came in for a cup of tea, or that she hurt herself and needed a bandage. That one's true—she did sit right there on the couch while I bandaged her wrist after she slipped and fell.

I sink into the armchair across from the couch and level Lysandra with what I hope is a calm, curious look. Obviously, she's here for a reason. We've always been friendly, and she's one of the only faculty members I regularly interact with, but it's in no way normal for her to come out to my hut so early in the morning like this. There's something on her mind.

"I heard whispers through the pumpkin vines," she says at last.

Whispers? Something about Lyra? About Samhain last night? My stomach turns. I knew it was foolish to allow her to help me with the booth, in clear sight of everyone still milling around the bonfire. And to allow her to come back to my hut was beyond foolish.

It was that dress. It bewitched me.

I need to stay focused. I can't let myself accidentally reveal anything to the headmistress.

"Pumpkins tell lies," I finally say, and this gets Lysandra to crack a smile.

"Sometimes they do. But I think these ones were telling the truth." She takes a sip of her tea and hums in approval.

"The truth about what?" I flex my fingers around my cup of tea and try to take easy, even breaths. No need to get worked up. I still don't know if she has any idea about Lyra.

Lysandra looks up at me. Her frosty eyes are cold and clear. "They said you're considering a . . . change in career paths."

The rapid pounding of my heart skips a few paces.

Career paths?

Oh. *Oh.*

This isn't about Lyra at all. It's about the Columbine Conservatory.

The sigh I let out is long and deep. "I apologize for not telling you about the position. I was convinced to put in an application"—Milo's smiling face pops into my mind—"but I don't have high hopes they'll take any sort of interest in me."

"Well, I think you're quite wrong." Lysandra tips her head. "Because the conservatory has already reached out to me. You put me down as a reference?"

I almost cringe. I'd forgotten about that. "I should have asked first. I—"

Wait. Did she say . . . ?

"They reached out? About my application?"

Lysandra's lips pull into a small smile. "They did."

"And . . . And what did you tell them?"

She laughs now, almost spilling her tea in the process. "Well, wouldn't you like to know." One of her silvery-blue brows arches playfully. Then her expression sobers somewhat. "So it's true, then. You're considering leaving us?"

I hadn't expected to have this conversation so soon, if at all. Truthfully, I didn't even think my application would get far enough to warrant anyone bothering to reach out to Lysandra regarding a professional reference.

"I . . ."

She's staring at me, gaze focused and unyielding. Somehow, it makes me feel like I'm a student sitting in her office after having misbehaved in charms class. I take another deep breath.

"I don't know. I didn't think they'd be interested."

"They are interested, I can assure you of that. And if they do offer you the job, will you be leaving?"

My throat squeezes closed. Words don't want to form into coherent thoughts, let alone sentences.

Why is that such a difficult question to answer?

Maybe it's because I still haven't answered it for myself. I keep taking this a day at a time, trying not to get my hopes up. I know what it feels like to have all your plans come crashing down around you, and since last that happened to me, I've tried hard not to let it happen again. As long as I don't hope or wish too hard for anything, it can't be stolen away from me.

"I don't know," I say at long last.

Lysandra narrows her eyes a bit, though not unkindly, then takes a sip of her tea. She stares into the lavender brew for a moment before saying, "Whatever you decide, I came here to tell you that I support you, Cairn. I love having you here, but Coven Crest isn't all that's out there for you. So, if you do decide to take the job, I want you to know that there will be no hard feelings here. Only well wishes and good tidings."

Her words make me blink. Then blink again. My throat squeezes a little tighter.

"You're not upset?" I ask, voice husky with emotion.

Lysandra laughs then. "Of course not. I'm certainly in no rush for you to leave—goddesses know hiring is terribly tedious—but if you do decide to take the job, I'll be nothing but happy for you." Her eyes flash mischievously. "And hopefully you'll be able to get me into the conservatory with a friends-and-family discount, hmm? I do love walking through their gardens." She laughs again, the sound friendly and floaty.

And despite the tension still squeezing my chest and throat, I somehow manage a chuckle as well. "I'd do my best, Headmistress."

Lysandra sips at her tea and smooths her skirt over her knees. Her gaze goes to the fire still crackling in the hearth. "How are things going with Miss Wilder?"

My stomach almost turns itself inside out. I remind myself to breathe. She doesn't know what's been going on between me and Lyra. She's just checking in, touching base. Nothing to be worried about.

I sip my tea, using it as a means of hesitation as I try to calm the galloping of my heart. Then I clear my throat. "It's going ... well."

Lysandra flicks a gaze at me. "You sound surprised."

My shoulders lift in a shrug. "I suppose I am."

That's true on multiple fronts. Nothing about Lyra Wilder has turned out the way I expected it to.

"She helped me transport sniffleblooms the other day," I say, trying to focus on truths without drifting into dangerous territory. My brain provides an image of Lyra working at the garden bench, a furrow between her fiery brows, lips pulled into a focused pout.

The image almost makes me smile—until I quickly wipe it away.

"Oh no." Lysandra sits up straighter. "How'd that go?"

Unbidden, another laugh slips out of me. "Great. I thought she'd sneeze all the way back to the castle, but she didn't. Not one sniffle."

"Wow." Lysandra raises her eyebrows in an impressed look. "I'd never have guessed. And she's not burned anything down? Set anything aflame?"

I shake my head. "No. She's . . . Well, she's been a help." I tighten my fingers around my cup and take another sip. "She's working hard."

The headmistress hums thoughtfully. "I'm happy to hear that. You were my last hope, you know." Her eyes soften when I look over at her. "I really didn't know what to do with her—I wasn't certain this would even help. So . . . thank you, Cairn. I appreciate you doing this."

I'm not sure what to say, so I just nod and respond with a grunt.

"All right, I suppose I should get out of your hair now." Lysandra finishes up her tea and stands from the couch. "Let me know when the conservatory reaches out."

I push out of the armchair and look down at her. "You mean *if* they reach out?"

Lysandra's smile is small and knowing. "No. I mean *when*." She puts her empty teacup into my free hand, pats me on the arm, and moves to my door. "And I'll meet with Miss Wilder soon. If you're leaving, I may need to set up her community service with another faculty member." She waves a hand, her rings sparkling in the thin morning light, and then she's gone, opening the door and drifting off into the autumn air.

I stand there in my hut, frozen in place.

Set her up with another faculty member? That'd mean we'd have no reason to see each other—at least, no reason that the academy would find appropriate. Then anytime she came to my hut, there'd be the potential of her—*us*—getting caught.

My jaw tightens.

After all these years, how is it that one fire witch has made it feel like my whole life is getting uprooted? And why is it that I can't bring myself to make it stop?

With another grunt, I clomp into the kitchen to rinse out the teacups, and I wonder what the hell I'm going to do about Lyra Wilder.

CHAPTER 30
LYRA

I USED TO DREAD MY SATURDAYS WITH CAIRN. Now I spend the whole week being excited for them, looking forward to the early-morning walk down to his hut, hoping I might have the chance to steal a touch or a kiss when we're alone.

Today's no different. We spend the morning raking more leaves and mulching more garden beds. I never noticed how much landscaping there is around the academy until Cairn started assigning me wheelbarrows of mulch and telling me where to put it. Now I realize just how extensive the work is that Cairn has done around here. Plants and flowers are tucked into almost every nook and cranny around the castle, and he cares for them all. These days, whenever I see ivy crawling up the stone or broad-petaled flowers reaching for the sun, I think of him.

Well, honestly, I think of him most of the time. Especially since Samhain.

My pussy isn't sore from being stretched anymore; it took a couple days for the slight ache to fade, and now I'm hungry for it again. Even now, as I watch Cairn rake leaves, his tunic stretched tight across his broad chest, his horns curling over his head in the thin gray light, I think about how his fingers and thumbs felt inside me, how heavy his cock was in my hands.

He looks over at me, his dark eyes meeting mine with a jolt, and a little tingle of anticipation dances through my low belly.

"What is it?" he asks, voice deep and rumbly.

I give him a small smile. "Just admiring you."

Despite the beautiful brown tint of his cheeks, I can still see his skin flush red. He flicks his thin tail and glances around—I already know no one's out here in the cold—then meets my eyes again. "You're supposed to be raking," he grumbles, but I can hear a hint of bashfulness in his tone.

I heft my rake and quickly attack a few colorful leaves, stepping closer to Cairn with every scratch of the metal tines along the moist ground. By the time I get the leaves added to his pile, I'm only an arm's length from him—close enough I can smell woodsmoke clinging to his clothes and hair. He must've been sitting beside the fire this morning, perhaps with another steaming dandelion latte.

I wish I could've been with him.

As I look up into his dark eyes, a bit of sadness settles over me. Alina's voice echoes in my mind: *You have to be careful. If you get caught, who knows what'll happen . . .*

I don't want to get expelled, and I really don't want Cairn to lose his job. But I want him so badly. And the simmering look in his eyes tells me he feels the same way.

How do we make this work? I've got two and a half more years at the academy. Will we have to sneak around for that long, hiding our nights together and being nervous someone could find us out? That might be fun for a little while, but in the long term . . . Would it even be sustainable?

I bite my lip. Cairn's gaze follows the movement, and his nostrils flutter as he lets out a deep sigh.

"Do you have anything to eat?" I ask. I'm not actually hungry—well, not for food, anyway—but if by some chance someone is listening in, it'll sound innocent enough. "I'm not sure I can rake another leaf without having some brunch first."

Cairn glances around again, acting more cautious than usual. I wonder what has him so on edge. He doesn't find anyone watching; I've already looked. Then he nods. "Let's get this pile picked up, then we'll take a break to eat."

One more leaf pile, I tell myself. *Then I can get him alone.*

WELL, AS IT TURNS OUT, CAIRN MADE US CLEAN up *three* more leaf piles, and now I actually am hungry. My stomach grumbles pathetically as we walk back to his hut. The air has grown colder, and thick dark clouds have moved in, ushered along by a bone-chilling wind. There's a scent of moisture to the air, and if Maeve were here, she'd probably tell me a storm's about to hit. But that's just fine with me. I wouldn't mind an excuse to get trapped in Cairn's hut for a while.

Please, weather gods, send a deluge to strand me here forever!

Cairn wipes his hooves on the doormat, then opens the door for me and steps to the side, gesturing for me to go first. I do the same, wiping the mud and leaf matter off my boots, then slip into his hut.

The air is warm and smells of fresh-baked bread. Immediately, I yank off my boots, then pad across the wooden floors in my thick socks in search of the fluffy goodness Cairn must've baked this morning.

I find it sitting on a bread stand in the center of the kitchen table—the table where Cairn spread my thighs and made me cum so hard my legs shook. The reminder makes my cheeks tingle with heat.

"Take a seat," Cairn says as he appears in the kitchen beside me. His arm brushes mine lightly as he moves past me. "You like cinnamon toast?"

I scoff. "Of course I like cinnamon toast. Who doesn't?"

Cairn tosses a glance back at me. "People who are allergic to cinnamon."

I roll my eyes and plop myself down into a chair at the table. "You're no fun."

His lips pull up on one side as he fetches a couple small plates, a shaker of cinnamon, and a little jar of sugar. He returns to the table and cuts us two slices of bread, then smears them with butter and sprinkles cinnamon and sugar over the top. My mouth waters. My stomach grumbles again.

"You really are hungry," Cairn says as he puts one of the plates in front of me. "Did you eat breakfast?"

I shake my head and take a big bite of the still-warm bread. It's fluffy and almost melts in my mouth, and the cinnamon sugar makes me sigh in happiness. Around the bite, I say, "No."

Cairn takes a seat across from me. His dark eyes narrow slightly. "Why not? I've told you to eat breakfast before you come."

I shrug. After swallowing down my bread, I give him a small smile and say, "I was too excited to see you."

There his cheeks go again, turning a little bit red. Is this a new thing, or was I just not paying enough attention before to see the way the color dances so beautifully across his skin? I decide I like it. A lot. It makes me want to say more things that'll make him blush.

"So . . ." I take another bite of bread and tip my head at him. He looks at me like he's worried about what I'm going to say next. That's probably fair. "Have you missed me?"

His laughter is sudden and wonderful. He leans back in his chair, making it creak a bit beneath his weight, and then reaches up to scratch his beard. "It's not been so long since we last saw each other."

I give him a little smirk. "Is that a yes? You can admit it."

One of his brows pulls up in the corner. I hold his gaze as I finish up my slice of cinnamon-sugar bread, not letting him off the hook so easily. When I don't break our stare, he shakes his head and lets out another deep sigh.

"Yes," he says at long last. The word is quiet, like it's supposed to be a secret. "I missed you."

My heart squeezes so hard I think it might pop. I lick the sugar from my fingers, then push up from my chair and twirl toward Cairn before plopping myself into his lap and wrapping my hands around his strong neck. He sits back suddenly, blinking in surprise.

"I knew it," I say. My fingers play with the soft brown curls along his nape. Then my gaze lifts to his horns curling over his head. They're ridged slightly, and their tips are tapered and sharp. I start to reach for one, then pause and say, "Can I . . . ?"

He gives a small nod.

Slowly, I continue to reach out. When my fingers meet Cairn's horn, he softens a bit, some of the tension going out of his body. I touch the base of the horn first, where it meets his head and is covered by his thick dark hair. It's warm, perhaps from the blood flowing beneath. Then my fingers dance up the curling length. The horn is smooth between the ridges, and it's cooler the farther from the base I go. It narrows into a sharp point, and I brush my thumb across it, feeling the slight bite against my skin.

"They're amazing," I whisper, admiring how even the gray autumn light slipping through the kitchen window makes them gleam.

Cairn huffs out a little breath. "You think so?"

"Mm-hmm." I let my fingers glide back down the curling horn, and Cairn shivers. I glance down at him. "Can you feel that?"

He nods. "The closer to the base, the more I can feel it." *Hmm.*

I glide my fingers around the base of his horn, noting how his eyelids flutter closed for a moment. "And does it feel . . . good?"

Since I sat down on him, Cairn has kept his hands off me, one curled into a fist on the table and the other alongside his thigh. But now he reaches for me, his warm fingers finding the dip of my waist. He tips his head a bit so he can meet my eyes. "Everything you do feels good."

Now he's the one making my cheeks warm.

I shift atop him, letting my legs fall along either side of his hips. He tenses up again, and beneath me, his length twitches.

Sliding my hands down his warm, firm chest, I whisper, "Can we do it again?"

I know full well he's aware of what I'm asking, but he plays innocent. "Do what again?"

In reply, I take his hand and guide it from my waist up my chest, settling it over my breast. "Stretch me."

His cock twitches again, his nostrils flaring and his tail flicking my calf. The pad of his thumb brushes my nipple through my sweater, and he squeezes it softly.

Then he abruptly clears his throat and drops his hand, making me pout.

"No. We've got more mulching to do. And raking. Mulching and raking."

Mother Nature must have a soft spot for me, because no sooner have the words left his lips than thunder rolls, long and deep, the rumble rattling the windowpanes. Cairn's eyes meet mine, and then he takes me by the waist, lifts me as if I weigh no more than a loaf of bread, and sets me on my feet. He pushes up, and his hooves clop along the wooden floor as he strides to the kitchen window and looks out.

Even from where I'm standing, I see the flash of lightning illuminate his face.

And then the rain starts to fall. It's a light patter at first, a gentle dance across the thatched roof. But it doesn't take long for the storm to arrive in full. It's a loud thrum across the roof, and the view outside Cairn's kitchen window is already becoming obscured by rain and fog by the time he pulls away from it and shoots a look at me.

"Are you sure you're not a storm witch?"

"I'm sure." I give him an innocent smile. "But one of my roommates is."

He leans back against his kitchen counter and crosses his arms. "Did you plan this?"

"Of course not."

That's not a bad idea though . . .

He snorts. Maybe he doesn't believe me.

Socks whispering across the floor, I ease toward him. He looks at me warily as I stand before him, so small compared to his height and width.

"So . . . I guess the mulching and raking will have to wait."

He arches one brow.

"And I'd hate to get soaking wet walking back to the castle in this storm. Plus, I could get hit by lightning. And you said yourself you missed me, so I know you don't want me to get fried out there. Guess I'll just have to stay, wait it out. The headmistress would understand."

"Please," Cairn grumbles, shaking his head, "let's not speak of Lysandra."

"Okay, no more talk of Moonhart. How about," I say as I take one of his hands and start to tug on him, trying to guide him toward the sitting room, "we talk about what you're going to do to me, hmm?"

His eyes narrow further, and though he resists me for a moment, he does eventually push away from the counter and start slowly following me toward the sitting room.

The fire has burned low, and I hurry to toss another log on and shoot a few fresh flames dancing across the wood with my fire magic.

Then, before Cairn can give me another excuse for why we can't do this, I hurriedly rush from window to window, pulling the curtains closed. When I'm done, the sitting room is dim, lit by the firelight as the rain pours and thunder rumbles above us.

"Lyra," he says softly.

I know he's about to tell me we can't, that we have to stop.

Before he can, I reach for the waistband of my trousers—the ones I wear to work with Cairn, with the stained knees and muddy cuffs—and loosen the cord, then push the fabric down around my ankles.

Cairn watches without speaking as I step free of them and kick them aside with my foot.

Next, I take hold of the bottom of my sweater, and with one motion, I pull it off over my head. That, too, falls into a heap on the floor.

Now I'm just wearing my warm socks and cotton undergarments, the fabric so thin I know Cairn can clearly see the peaks of my nipples even from across the room.

Still, he says nothing. But there's a straining against his trousers that he's making no effort to hide.

Each step slow, I move across the sitting room toward him. He stares down at me, the firelight reflecting in his glassy dark eyes.

"I know you want this," I say as my palm finds his hardening length and I start to stroke him through the fabric. His breath hitches. "And it's okay. We're not doing anything wrong." I run my thumb along his tip; it's already warm through his trousers. His eyes squeeze closed. "Don't let them ruin this."

Cairn pushes his hips forward, grinding himself against my palm. His eyes flash open. And then he's guiding me backward across the sitting room, lifting me by my hips and holding me to his chest as I wrap my legs around his waist. The way he holds me, I feel like I'm weightless, held aloft by the ocean waves.

His dark gaze meets mine. And before I can catch my breath, he kisses me. His lips taste of cinnamon and sugar, and he smells like earth from working outside this morning. The heat from his kiss travels through my veins, setting every inch of my body alight.

With what feels like very little effort, Cairn sinks slowly to the rug in front of the fire. He lays me down, my back cradled by the softness of the rug, all without breaking our kiss. And when he does finally pull away, allowing me a moment to breathe, it's only to pull his tunic off over his head and horns. His brown skin gleams in the golden light of the fire, contrasting against mine as he reaches for my lightweight cotton panties.

They come off with a whisper, and then I'm lying bare before him. His gaze is hungry as it settles between my legs.

For a moment, I worry he'll resist again, that I'll have to beg and plead until he finally gives in. But blissfully, I'm wrong.

Cairn presses a thumb against my clit, which is already pulsing with warmth, then slips one finger inside me. It's thick, but there's little resistance—I'm already wet and waiting.

I close my eyes as he pushes his finger deeper, thumb rubbing circles against my swollen clit.

"Are you sore?" he asks. "From last time?"

I don't bother to open my eyes, just give my head a slow shake side to side. "No. Not anymore."

"But you were?"

"Mm-hmm."

He makes a rumbly sound from deep in his chest. Concern? Approval? Maybe both. I don't know. I'm too focused on the feel of his finger inside me.

Cairn shifts forward, one hand still working me while his other presses into the rug beside my head. Now I open my eyes, if only to look up into his.

Eyes dark, he stares back at me. And when he adds a second finger, pushing it into me alongside the first, he doesn't break our stare.

I flinch, just a little, and he goes slower, giving my body time to adjust to him.

"How long," I whisper, voice hitching as he resumes the slow finger thrusts, "will it take until I'm ready?"

His lips pull up slightly. "You asked me that last time."

I give him a pout. "And you still don't have an answer for me."

Inside me, Cairn scissors his fingers, stretching me until I gasp. "Only you can answer that."

Then I want to do it now, I think, though by the way I'm already gripping his fingers, I know we can't.

With determination, I say, "Add another."

One of his brows arches. "We've only just started."

"Just do it. I'm ready."

He regards me for a long moment. Then, finally, he does as I say.

CHAPTER 31

CAIRN

S HE'S SO DEMANDING FOR SUCH A SMALL witch. But I'm more than happy to do as she says.

I pull my fingers out of her—they glisten in the light of the fire—then add a third and start to ease them inside her. There's more resistance this time, her pussy squeezing tight. Lyra's crimson eyes close, and a small wrinkle of pain forms in her brow.

"Is that too much?" I ask.

She shakes her head, but the furrow remains. "No. Don't stop." She lifts one leg and uses her foot to stroke my cock through my trousers, making me moan. "If I'm going to take *this*, I have to make it through a little pain."

I don't want to cause her pain, yet the idea of pushing inside her, sheathing my cock in her tight, wet pussy, makes me harden and throb. Lyra must like the idea too, because her pussy gets a bit wetter, and it yields just a fraction to the pressure I'm putting on it. Instead of trying to force my fingers inside, I lavish more attention on her swollen clit, rubbing it with my thumb, teasing it until she's panting and trying to push her hips up against me. I rub a little more.

And then my three fingers slip all the way inside her.

She gasps. It's a tight fit, but they fit nonetheless.

"Fuck," she groans as I start to move them, pumping in and out slowly. Her cheeks are flushed red, her eyes pinched closed.

I admire her freckles, her pale skin, the curve of her lips and column of her throat. She's exquisite, and I almost laugh when I think of our first day together, the anger that danced in her eyes and pulled those perfect lips into a firm pout.

So feisty, my little fire witch.

My witch? I blink at the thought.

Is that what she is? Is that what I want her to be? *Mine?*

My head may not want to accept the implication, but my heart and body do so willingly, and I find my fingers working her a bit faster.

"More," she whispers.

I don't think she can take more. Her pussy is already so tight around my fingers.

"I don't think—"

"More, Cairn. I have to be ready for you." A little shimmer of red and orange dances across her skin—her fire magic?—but she doesn't seem to notice; her eyes don't even open.

I still resist. This is already enough. I don't want to hurt her.

"We should go slow," I say, "so we don't—"

Now her eyes open, and they're alight with flames. Lyra pushes up onto her elbows, knees and legs still spread before me. She reaches down between us, where my fingers are still knuckle-deep inside her, and she uncurls my pinky. It's my smallest finger—it won't add much by way of girth—but when she lines it up with her pussy and makes me push it inside, another furrow forms in her brow, and she flinches at the stretch.

I should stop.

"*Don't* stop," she says.

My eyes narrow. "Can you read minds too?"

"No." She settles herself back onto the rug, breathing hard. "I just know you."

Those words make my chest warm in a way I didn't expect. It's been years since I was intimate with anyone, and longer still since I felt seen, *known.* But this witch can pull words right out of my mouth, can anticipate what I will say or do before I can do it.

She knows me. She wants *to know me.*

That realization alone almost makes me cum, even without her so much as touching me.

But it scares me too. Because what if she changes her mind? What if—

Lyra's pussy tightens around my fingers, squeezing me as her low back arches off the soft rug. Her moans stop, her breath hitching. Beneath my thumb, her clit is swollen and hot.

Then she cums, hard. Her pussy spasms and clenches, her clit throbs, and I can't resist the urge to capture her mouth with mine. As our lips move together, she reaches up to wrap her arms around my neck, her fingers playing through my hair as mine still work inside her.

She presses her tongue into my mouth, making me moan. *Goddess, this witch . . .*

When her breathing slows and her pussy softens, I ease my fingers out of her, not missing the way she winces as they slide free.

Breaking our kiss, I look down between her legs, where my fingers are slick with her wetness and my cock is bulging against the front of my trousers.

"Are you okay?" I ask her.

"Mm." She tickles the nape of my neck with her fingers, then traces the edge of my collarbone. "Better than okay."

"I didn't hurt you?"

The look she gives me is more smirk than smile. "Are you always such a worrywart?"

I sit back from her and hold her shimmering crimson gaze. "When it comes to you? Yes."

The smirk falls away. She regards me with something deeper in her eyes, and for a moment, I fear she might cry.

Maybe I really did hurt her.

Then she surprises me yet again as she turns herself over on the rug and pushes up onto all fours. Her beautiful round ass is right there in front of me, slick wetness tracking down the insides of her thighs.

"What are you doing?" I ask.

"Take your pants off," she demands.

I shake my head, the shadows cast by my horns moving across her. "No. You're not ready. I'll just—"

"Cairn Axton, by the goddess, just do what I say. It'll be all right. I'm not asking you to fuck me."

I narrow my eyes. "Then what are you—"

But her sharp gaze cuts my words short.

I push up onto my knees and yank my trousers down. An audible groan slips out of me when my cock leaps free, the tip already glistening with moisture.

Lyra looks back at me, and her tongue darts out to wet her lips. "I want to feel you here," she says, then makes my heart beat double time when she reaches up between her legs to touch herself. "Come on. I'll show you."

I'm still not quite sure what she wants, but I ease up behind her anyway, taking her hips in my hands and pushing my cock between her legs. My tip drags through her slick folds, and she uses her fingers to guide my cock into the tight space between her thighs, but not inside her.

Oh.

Now I understand.

She wants me to fuck her folds and thighs, not her pussy.

That I can do.

I tighten my fingers around her hips and thrust against her. Her pussy lips drag at my cock, still slick, and I can feel her swollen clit each time the head of my shaft pushes against it.

Her ass is soft, and I grab a handful of it, making her gasp. Between my legs, my balls swing, heavy and tight with pressure. It's not going to take much for me to paint her in cum. I need to distract myself, to make this last longer than thirty blissful seconds.

The fire flickers beside us, hot and comforting. It tosses light across Lyra's pale skin, turns her a shade of shimmering gold.

Fuck, she's beautiful.

Her curls are messy and tangled, and when she glances back at me through them, I get a little jolt up my spine. She's beautiful *and* wild, like a fairy creature in a hidden wood, dancing through the trees right outside your line of vision. Yet somehow, she's here with me, letting me touch her, taste her. Letting me *know* her in a way I've known so few.

She narrows her eyes a bit, challenging me. I renew my hold on her hips and buck against her, thrusting hard and fast, using the slickness between her legs to get myself there. My balls swing and slap her, making her moan, and she drips more wetness onto me. The sensation and the sound make me tip my head back and let out a low, sustained groan.

Then I dig my fingers into her hips, pull my cock from between her legs, and bellow as ropes of cum explode from me, painting her sweat-slick back with each pulse of my shaft and balls. I've been thinking about her so much lately, have been on edge and hungry since our last time together, and now I dump everything I have across her pale, trembling body, until she's a canvas of my cum.

I realize, perhaps too late, what a mess I've made of her. But as she tosses her hair and looks back at me, lips pulled into a catlike smile, I get the feeling she doesn't mind at all. In fact, I think she's pleased. And now she has an excuse to get me into a hot bath with her again.

Not that I'm complaining. And the rain's still falling, droning against the thatched roof, so we should still have time before anyone even considers where we are or what we're doing.

I grab my tunic off the floor and use it to wipe Lyra clean—or as clean as I can get her with such a small amount of fabric. When I'm done, she pushes onto her knees and turns to face me, her arms coming up to loop around my neck, a softness to her body now as she droops against me. I expect her to kiss me, but instead, she nuzzles her face into the side of my neck, right up under my chin.

Against my chest, I can feel her heart beating. My arms wrap around her, pulling her snug against my body, and I hold her like that until my heartbeat starts to meld with hers, until I can no longer determine where mine starts and her ends.

And deep in my chest, under my ribs, there's a dull ache. And I know what this ache means.

It means I'm hers now, means my string is wrapped around her firelit finger. And it means everything is going to get a lot harder from here forward. Because for me, there's no going back. My peaceful life here is no longer.

Now it's all Lyra.

CHAPTER 32
LYRA

I'M DEFINITELY SORE NOW, TO THE POINT WHERE after taking another bath with Cairn, I have to settle myself onto the couch delicately, wincing a bit in the process.

Four fingers—that's all it took to make me ache like this. Yet I still can't deny I want to feel more, want to feel all of him. I realize, though, that I'm not yet ready, and I'm grateful to Cairn for taking his time with me, for making sure when he *does* finally fuck me, it'll be good for both of us.

He's still in the bedroom, getting dressed, so I'm alone for a moment, and I take this chance to look around his sitting room, noticing and appreciating all his little knickknacks. I've been in here multiple times, but usually not alone, and whenever Cairn is around, my gaze is always on him, drawn to him whether I mean for it to be or not.

On the mantel above the fire are little wooden statuettes, a few hunks of crystal quartz, an amethyst the size of my fist, and bundles of herbs I don't know the names of. The walls hold more herbs, these tied upside down, their flowers and blooms still vibrant with color. I recognize the lavender and white sage, but again, many of the others are unfamiliar to me.

I should've paid more attention in Botany 101 . . .

My gaze traces across Cairn's armchair, and a little smile pulls on my mouth when I remember him sitting there with a steaming dandelion latte—which sounds *so* good right now. Maybe I'll ask him to make me one, and I can enjoy it before the rain stops and we have to head back outside and act like we didn't do what we just did.

Cheeks tingling at the memory, I glance down at the side table standing next to the couch. And lying atop it is an envelope and a letter. My eyes track quickly across the words scrawled onto the paper. I don't mean to pry—that's not my intention—but with each word I read, my chest squeezes a little tighter.

The Columbine Conservatory? Isn't that on the other side of Wysteria?

I recall visiting it once, with all its beautiful plants and abundant orchards. But that was a long time ago. And it's also many miles from here.

Is he . . . leaving?

The possible implication hits me hard.

All at once, I'm struggling to breathe. My chest feels like it's being twisted and wrung like a wet rag, and I reach up to grip my sweater with trembling fingers.

Breathe, Lyra, I tell myself. *Focus on something. What can you see?*

225

I tear my eyes away from the letter and stare at the bundle of lavender on the wall.

What can you hear?

The rain patters on the thatched roof, the fire crackles gently, and in the back bedroom, the floor creaks beneath Cairn's weight as he moves about.

What can you smell?

Smoke. Earth. Rain. That comforting mix of smells that's distinctly *him*.

Slowly, the tightness in my chest starts to abate, the racing of my heart slowing to a painful thrum.

This isn't like that, I remind myself. *Not like when she left.*

Ever since my mother abandoned me and Papa, I've had these moments. They don't happen often, and when they do, I can usually calm myself quickly. When I was young, they used to terrify me—and Papa. But together, we learned how to handle them, how to ease me back from the panic that sometimes grips my chest and makes my vision go shadowy at the edges.

Hooves clop down the hall, and when I look up, Cairn is standing there in the wide, tall doorway, wearing a fresh tunic and trousers, smiling down at me.

I try to smile back. I don't think it works.

Immediately, Cairn's face falls, his forehead furrowing in concern. "What's the matter?"

I don't mean to glance at the letter on the side table, but my eyes do it anyway, betraying me. And I hear the small surprised breath Cairn takes.

So, he didn't mean for me to find out.

Why does that make it so much worse?

"I...I..."

What am I even trying to say? I'm not sure, but whatever it is, the words get stuck on my tongue.

With a heavy sigh, Cairn sinks onto the couch beside me, making the cushions dip and tipping my body toward him. He tries to ease an arm around me, but I pull away. I don't want to be held by him right now. I want him to tell me the truth.

"The conservatory," I whisper. "Are you going?"

There's a flash of pain in his eyes when I scoot away from him, but he masks it quickly. "I don't know," he says, gaze moving from me to the letter on the side table. "I applied on a whim, but I haven't heard back." His broad shoulders rise and fall with a shrug. "Didn't want to mention anything or get my hopes up. It's nothing official."

I think he's trying to make me feel better, trying to make it sound like it's not a big deal, nothing to worry about.

But it *is*. Because it means he might leave. Means I might be here, at the academy, for another two and a half years without him.

Why does that make me feel like crying?

I clench my teeth and curl my fingers into tight fists beneath the sleeves of my sweater.

And why didn't he tell me before? Why didn't he tell me he applied?

He says it's because he didn't want to get his hopes up, but inside me, a voice whispers, *He doesn't think you matter enough to know.*

Trying to disguise the discomfort between my legs, I push to my feet, then glance back down at him. "We should get back to work."

His eyes meet mine. They look confused. But again, he wipes the emotion away before I can dig too deep into it.

"It's still raining."

I shrug. "Never bothered you before."

He blinks, mouth opening but no words coming out.

Then I pull on my boots, yank my hair back into a messy bun, and open the door.

Because I'd rather be outside working in the rain than sitting in here, being reminded of the things that I know will soon be snatched from me.

Like I expected, even this wasn't meant to last. And even Cairn is going to leave.

CHAPTER 33
CAIRN

I THOUGHT NOT TELLING LYRA ABOUT THE CON-servatory was a good thing, a smart thing. They proba-bly won't want to hire me anyway, so why say anything at all?

But clearly, I made a grave error. Because Lyra is dif-ferent now, like she's become a stranger.

As the days and weeks pass, she stops showing up early, and she's not visited me during the week again. While she's here, she's on edge. I can feel her chaotic energy simmering in the air around us while we work. And just last week, she accidentally set fire to a bed of purple irises. If she'd been wearing the gloves I gifted her, it wouldn't have been a prob-lem. But she refuses.

I was so shocked, so startled to see the flames dancing across the precious blooms, that I hesitated to act. The flames chewed through everything before I could think to stop them. And even now, when I pass the bed, with its dead plants and ashy soil, I can't help but to feel that this is all my fault. I did something wrong, and Lyra is letting me know—whether she means to or not.

I've been gearing up to talk to her, to try to clear the air between us. But I've not yet been able to bring myself to try to bridge the gap.

It snowed last night—the first snow of the season—and this morning we're both wearing thick cloaks to ward off the chill while wielding shovels and trying to clear all the walkways so the afternoon sun can help melt the snow and ice away.

But whenever I draw near to Lyra, she moves away from me. And she does it so smoothly that if I weren't paying attention, I'd probably not notice a thing.

She's avoiding me. Even her gaze refuses to meet mine.

My heart squeezes so hard that it makes me clench my teeth.

I have to talk to her. I can't let this frigid distance between us grow into something that can't ever be mended. I'd never forgive myself.

I've just finished shoveling one of the paths that winds through the garden, and Lyra is finishing up with a path that leads to the big greenhouses. When I'm done, I pause to watch her.

She shovels with a furrow in her brow, her lips pulled into a firm frown. Against the stark white of the snow clinging to the ground and the structures around us, her red hair is a beacon, so bright and beautiful that it makes me ache to reach out and touch it, to tangle my fingers in it like I did that afternoon on the rug before the fire.

She's not touched me since that day. And if I thought I was hungry for touch before I met Lyra, now I'm starving.

With a grunt, she hefts a shovelful of snow off the path, then pauses and straightens up, stretching out her back. Her eyes find me, and I'm not ashamed that she caught me staring.

The frown she wears turns into a barely restrained scowl. "What?" she snaps.

It's just one word, but it's full of simmering venom.

"Let's take a break," I say, trying not to let on how painful each of her sharp glares is. "I'll make us something warm to drink."

Something flickers through her eyes. If I'm not mistaken, it looks like sadness. Then she slams the windows in her gaze closed, tearing her eyes from mine before I can see too much.

"No thanks. I've got plans this afternoon. Let's just hurry up and finish."

I've never been struck by an arrow before, but each of her words lands like one, piercing me deep.

I really fucked up. Dammit, Cairn.

Without looking around to ensure no one is watching us, I take a wide step toward her and say, "Lyra, look at me."

She doesn't. But I know she's listening, because the furrow in her brow deepens.

"Lyra. Please?"

The word comes out laced with pain, and she must hear it, because she finally relents, turning her face so I can meet her eyes. But she doesn't say a thing, just stares at me, the distance between us feeling like it's stretching into a yawning chasm.

"What's wrong?" I ask.

And I know I've fucked up again when anger flickers in her crimson eyes.

Before she can say anything, I hold up a hand. "I'm sorry. I know what's wrong. You're angry with me about the letter. But—"

"You don't have to apologize." She takes a long breath, then lets it out in a whoosh, steam billowing around her lips. "It's not like we're friends or something. And you'll be leaving soon, so I'll be out of your hair in no time."

More arrows land true. I'm surprised I'm still standing.

"Lyra, that's not—"

"Are we done here?" She casts her gaze around at all the freshly shoveled walkways. As the morning sun climbs higher in the sky, the paths are already starting to melt. "Like I said, I've got plans, so if we're finished up, I'd like to go."

I want to tell her that no, she can't go. She has to stay here and talk to me, has to understand why I didn't tell her.

But the look she gives me is so sharp that I know I'd just cut myself on her, would just be setting myself up to bleed.

So instead, I bite back my pain and give her one firm nod. "Yeah. We're done."

Her eyes flash.

That was a bad choice of words—and not at all what I meant.

"Fine." She takes a few steps down the path toward me, thrusts the shovel into my hand, and turns on her heel. As she whirls to walk away, her smell washes over me, and it reminds me of the morning I woke up beside her, the way the morning light touched her freckled face, the scent that clung to my pillow even days after she'd gone.

But then she's walking away, boots clipping out an angry rhythm on the stone walkway.

And before I can fix this, can figure out what words will mend the pain I've caused her, she pulls open the door to the academy and vanishes into its darkness, leaving me standing by myself in the snow.

Alone. Like I've been for so many years. Except now, it doesn't feel safe or comfortable.

It feels lonely. And it feels cold.

A STONE HAS SAT HEAVILY IN MY STOMACH ALL DAY, ever since this morning. No matter how busy I keep myself—setting up cold frames in my small back garden, reshoveling paths that don't need to be shoveled, baking a fresh loaf of bread—I can't seem to get Lyra's angry eyes out of my mind.

I'm standing in my sitting room, staring out the window at the moonflowers clinging to the shadows along the edge of the forest line, when there's a sharp rap against my door.

Immediately, my heart soars, hoping foolishly that it might be Lyra.

But my head knows better. And when I open the door thirty seconds later, it's not a freckled redhead who's standing there. It's the mail carrier.

"Letter for you, Mr. Axton," he says. He pulls a crisp parchment from his shoulder bag and offers it to me.

Without taking it, I know where it's from. The envelope looks familiar now. The mail carrier narrows his eyes in confusion, holding the letter out a bit farther. "Sir?"

I grumble something incoherent and take the letter from his outstretched hand. "Thank you."

He tips his soft cap to me, then goes on his way. Slowly, I close the door behind him, then stare down at the envelope in my hand.

It's from the Columbine Conservatory.

And I'm not sure what I hope for it to say.

Do I want them to offer me the job? If they do, what will I decide? Will I stay here, hoping I can cling to the peace I've carved out for myself? Or is peace even possible now that my eyes always look for Lyra, now that every flash of red in my periphery has my heart squeezing and yearning?

Or will I leave?

I clench my teeth, muscles along my jaw feathering. Either way, regardless of what the letter says, I have to open it and find out.

But first, tea.

I pour myself a cup, trying not to pay attention to the ache in my heart when my gaze lands on the hand-painted cup that Lyra drank from when she was here. I push away the image of her sipping the frothy dandelion latte, then smiling when she realized it didn't actually taste like dirt, as I'm sure she feared.

Shaking my head, I take my tea to the kitchen table, but even then, all I see is Lyra lying back on it, knees spread for me. I promptly snatch the letter off the table and go sit in my armchair instead.

Already, Lyra is everywhere. How is it that she permeated my life so quickly? Like a rapidly spreading plant, she twined her vines and petals all around me, and I feel trapped now—trapped in thoughts of her, in my desire for her.

Maybe I should leave either way . . . Maybe it'd be better for both of us that way.

I sit in my armchair and put my tea on the table beside me. Then I hold the letter in both hands and stare down at it like I might be able to ascertain what it says without having to open it.

The parchment is thick, and whatever is inside feels dense.

If it's a rejection letter, why waste so much paper on me?

I call to mind what Lysandra said when she came to visit me: *They are interested, I can assure you of that.* The conservatory reached out to her, was curious enough about me to actually contact her as my reference.

Maybe Milo had something to do with this. He was so excited when we sat down for a drink at Boar and Badger, going on and on about how great it would be to work together again, this time in a professional capacity. And I can't deny that I did get a spark of excitement at the prospect.

I love my life here, love my job and my garden and my thatched hut. But there are times when I feel underappreciated. The students don't often stop and wonder who shovels the walks every morning so they don't have to trudge through snow, don't think about who tends the grounds and cares for the plants that make the campus so beautiful. But at the conservatory, that might be different. People visit the conservatory to appreciate the beauty and abundance, and given what Milo said to me, the community gardens would be a place where I could teach others what I know, where I could focus on growing foods that will feed people's bellies and souls.

Even now, thinking about it makes me warm with excitement.

But Lyra's face is right there as well. And she warms me in a different way. She makes me excited to wake in the mornings, wondering if I'll see her. She makes me hungry in a way that only she can sate.

Will I be able to leave her?

I reach for my cup of tea and take a sip. It's already lukewarm, which means I've been sitting here staring at the letter for quite some time. Now the only thing left to do is actually open it.

With fingers on the verge of trembling, I rip through the flap of the envelope, not bothering to reach for my letter opener, like I usually would. Before I can stop myself, I pull the letter free, unfold it, and allow my eyes to track across the page.

They . . . They want to hire me.

Me. A minotaur groundskeeper with so very little to offer. Yet they're offering me the job.

I read further, and my stomach pinches.

They want me to start this spring, right after the holiday break, which means I'd only have a very limited time left here.

Limited time left with Lyra.

If she even wants to be around me anymore.

I let out a heavy sigh and drop my head back against the headrest of my armchair, then stare up at the ceiling.

And I ask myself, *What the hell am I going to do?*

CHAPTER 34
LYRA

EVERYTHING FEELS ... WRONG. AFTER MIDTERMS and Samhain, I had so much hope, so much excitement. But somehow, it's all blown away like leaves on an autumn wind. I keep thinking about that letter sitting on Cairn's side table, wondering what's going to happen, wrestling with the emotions writhing inside me.

I know I'm being selfish and hotheaded. I care about Cairn—of course I want him to have a job he enjoys, do something that gives him purpose.

But I'm also sad and jealous and left feeling like I don't mean to him what he means to me. If he really cared, wouldn't he have told me? Wouldn't he have wanted to talk to me about it? Maybe he was afraid of this very thing happening: me getting upset, making a fuss, tearing the fragile thing we have—had?—into little pieces.

Why am I doing this? Why am I acting this way?

I felt like I'd made so much progress with controlling my magic and my emotions. But all it took was this one thing to derail me. Now my fire's acting up again, and so close to final exams . . . This could be it for me. If I mess up again, I might be packing my bags and not coming back.

Where I'm sitting in the deep window in my secret alcove, I pull my knees tight against my chest and wrap my arms around them. Juniper sits beside me, looking out the window at the snow-frosted trees in the Mistwood. Her little ears perk up, and she turns to look at the stairwell.

"Someone's coming," she says.

Great. Just what I need: another student seeing the volatile Lyra Wilder pouting around, probably thinking about what she's going to burn down next.

"Lyra?" comes a familiar voice.

I sit up a little bit. A moment later, a blue head appears as Alina climbs the stairs. I tense up, waiting to see Raelan walking right behind her, but he's not there.

Alina comes to stand next to me where I'm sitting in the window. She props one hand on her hip and arches a frosty brow. "I thought I'd find you here. Hi, Juniper."

Juniper squeaks out a small greeting.

"Where's Raelan?" I ask.

"He and Yuki are out playing in the snow." Her lips pull up a bit on one side. "I figured you'd be more willing to talk if Raelan wasn't here, so I sent him away for a bit."

A short laugh slips out of me. "I'm surprised he allowed that."

Her expression softens. "Raelan knows you're upset. He cares about you too." Alina settles herself into the window near my feet, leaning back and turning her gaze to the frosted woods outside. "So, are you ready to talk about it?"

I cross my arms. "There's nothing to talk about."

Alina flicks her gaze at me. "Why do you do that?"

"Do what?"

"Act like I don't know you, like you can hide your feelings from me. You can't, you know. You wear everything on your sleeve, even if you pretend like you don't. And I know you're sad and mad about something. Please tell me what it is." She reaches out and puts a hand on my knee. Her sky-blue eyes hold my gaze, imploring, begging.

"You could just order me to tell you, *Princess*," I grumble.

Alina smiles. "I could. But you still wouldn't listen to me."

My shoulders rise and fall with a sigh. "That's true."

"She's worried about you," Juniper says from beside me. She crawls up into my lap, then up to perch on my knee so she can look me right in the eye. "Alina's your friend. It's okay to let her in."

Now both Alina and Juniper are staring at me. Looks like there'll be no worming my way out of this one.

"Fine," I grumble, then let out a whooshing sigh. Juniper squeaks approvingly and jumps off my knee to go look out the window again. I focus on Alina. "I found out Cairn applied for a job at the conservatory."

Alina tips her head. "You mean the Columbine Conservatory? In Wysteria?"

I nod.

"It's beautiful there. My father and I used to go every year when I was young." She smiles like she's reliving a fond memory. Then she asks, "But what's wrong with that?"

"If he gets the job, he'll leave." As emotions rise in my chest, I clutch the sleeves of my sweater in my fists. "And I'm not good with people leaving..."

Understanding glistens in Alina's eyes. Without warning, she leans forward and wraps me in a hug. I go stiff at first—I've never been one for physical affection—but she just keeps holding on, and slowly, my body relaxes.

"Him leaving the academy to get a job doesn't mean he's leaving *you*," she says, her breath rustling my hair. "It just means he's trying to do something good for himself. And maybe even for you too."

"How is that good for me?" I ask, resting my head against hers, softening to her arms around me.

Alina squeezes me again, then sits back slowly so she can look into my eyes. "Because maybe then you can actually be together. You know that so long as he's here, you can't be seen publicly together—at least, not romantically." Alina finds one of my hands and takes it in hers, unwrapping my tight fist so she can hold my fingers. "That's not a real relationship, having to hide how you feel about each other. But if he's no longer working here . . ." She gives my fingers a gentle squeeze. "Then maybe you can create something real. Something that'll last."

Something that'll last.

I think, in some ways, I've been looking for that since my mother left. She taught me that even the things that are supposed to be there forever can walk out the door at any moment, can choose to leave you behind in search of something bigger and better—or just different.

And this job at the conservatory, it feels bigger and better. Of course Cairn would want something like that. But will he still want me? That I'm not so sure about.

"I don't really want to talk about it," I say, pulling my hand from Alina's and turning to look out at the snow clinging to the tops of the pine trees.

Alina goes quiet for a while. Maybe she's mad at me. I've never been good at friendships. I've never been good at any sort of relationship, except with Papa and Juniper.

But then she just says, "Raelan and I are going to spend part of the holiday at that little cottage—you know, the one I told you about?"

"The one you found together after that mess with Tristan?"

In my periphery, she wrinkles her nose, maybe remembering that evening and the events that followed. "He'll be getting out of prison soon," she says. "Warren, I mean."

Warren, right. I forget sometimes that Tristan wasn't even his real name. The Veiled Hand like to be secretive that way.

"I think they should just leave him there," I grumble. "Let him turn to dust."

She shakes her head at me and lets out a sigh. "He was helpful. He led Grandfather to the *real* culprit behind all that. So now the person responsible can face justice." Her fingers curl into fists in her lap, and her eyes narrow as she stares out the window at the snow-tipped trees. "If something had happened to Raelan," she whispers, "I don't know what I'd have done."

I don't think any of us like reliving that night, but Alina likes it least of all.

"You okay?" I say after an extended silence.

She shakes her head a bit and blinks the faraway look from her eyes. "Yeah, I'm fine. What was I saying before?"

"You're going to the cottage."

"Oh, right." She smiles while tucking a strand of blue hair behind her ear. "You're welcome to join us. You can come stay if you'd like. The forest is so peaceful, especially in the snow."

My shoulders rise and fall with a shrug. "I don't know."

What I really want is to see my dad, to wake up in my bed and to smell the terrible coffee he brews before going out to work in his woodshop. I want to be somewhere that doesn't feel like it could change at any moment. Somewhere that I feel I can depend on.

The air around me grows colder, and when I look over at Alina, her lips are pulled down. I think I hurt her feelings without meaning to.

"It's not that I don't want to visit," I explain. "I really just want to see Papa. It feels like it's been forever since I was home."

The chill in the air from Alina's frost magic disperses. She nods. "I understand." She squeezes my knee, then stands up. "Just know that you're always welcome. And I'm sure Raelan would love to give you a bucket and watch you mop the floors."

This makes me smile, and it feels good. "That dragon can scrub his own floors, thank you very much. If I visit, it'll be to do absolutely nothing."

"Sounds like a good way to spend the holiday." Alina gives me a real smile, then lifts a hand. "All right, I'll go. But don't be late for dinner. They're serving apple pie for dessert tonight. Yuki already tried to sneak in and steal some."

My stomach grumbles at the thought.

"I won't. I'll be back soon."

Alina descends the stairs, and once she's gone, I resume staring out the window. The snow is starting up again, falling from the gray sky in a slow, silent dance.

"Come on," Juniper says from beside me. She tugs the sleeve of my sweater with her tiny paws. "Let's go get some apple pie. That always makes you feel better."

I glance down at her, and she's staring up at me, whiskers twitching.

I don't think pie is going to fix this. I think Cairn is the only one who can make me feel better.

But I don't tell Juniper that. Instead, I scoop her up and kiss the top of her warm brown head, feeling comforted by her familiar smell. "All right, let's go. It feels like a dessert-before-dinner night anyway."

Juniper climbs onto my shoulder and tucks herself under my hair. "Exactly what I was thinking."

I push up from the window seat, but my eyes are drawn once more to the snow flurrying outside the window.

Everything Alina said about me and Cairn is true. So, then, why didn't it make me feel better? And why does the thought of Cairn leaving still make me feel hollow inside?

As I start down the stairs, I'm left wondering if I'm meant to be alone. If the people I love are destined by fate to leave me.

CHAPTER 35
LYRA

NOTHER FEW INCHES OF SNOW FELL last night. Autumn has been fighting a losing battle since Samhain, but as I look out the window in my mathematics classroom, watching fat snowflakes drift from the gray sky to blanket the frozen ground, I know that winter has officially claimed victory, and it's here to stay.

While Professor Burke drones on and on about trigonometric functions and tables—I will literally *never* need this in the entirety of my life—I start to think about Cairn.

We've barely spoken since I found that letter, and I know it's all my fault. He's tried to mend things, has tried to reach out across the flames I've surrounded myself with, but I haven't let him succeed. I've been too consumed with my own anger and hurt and feelings of betrayal.

Last night, I dreamed of watching the moonflowers in Cairn's garden bloom, but when I turned my head to smile at him, he wasn't there, and the hand that I thought had been holding his was empty and cold.

Despite the fire burning in the hearth in the corner of the classroom, I shiver. I don't usually feel cold—my fire magic keeps me warm—but I've been chilled for days.

I'm still staring out the frosted window, wondering if I may see a glimpse of Cairn through the ice, when all the students around me burst into motion, closing their heavy math books, slinging their bookbags onto their shoulders, and chatting about *anything* but trigonometry as they flee from their desks.

I'm one of the last students to leave the room, still in a bit of a daze. My feet feel slow and heavy, weighed down right along with my heart.

"You smell that?" Juniper asks from my pocket. We're not supposed to bring our spirit companions to class, so she keeps herself mostly concealed in the inside pocket of my robe, with just her nose poking out.

I sniff the air, and my stomach grumbles. "Potato soup," I say wistfully.

"And fresh bread," Juniper adds.

Mathematics was my last class today, so I'm going to hurry back to the dorm, then meet up with the girls so we can go stuff our faces together in the dining hall.

The other students have already abandoned this hallway, leaving it empty and quiet. I'm just about to go around a corner when I hear voices up ahead.

"The Wilder girl's been awfully cozy with the minotaur lately, from what I hear. Someone saw them going back to his place on Samhain."

My pace slows, boots falling silent on the stone floor.

The voice is female, but it's not young enough to be a student—a professor, then.

She continues, "What exactly is she doing for community service?"

There's a chuckle from whoever the professor is talking to, and then an older male voice says, "If he's caught, he's toast. They'll cut him loose before word even has a chance to get out. You know Moonhart hates scandals."

"You'd think he'd be more careful," the woman says, her voice getting quieter, like they're walking the other way from me down the hall. The last thing I hear her say is, "Just a matter of time."

In my robe pocket, Juniper goes very still. My fingers curl into fists, and I have to actively fight down the heat and fear rising inside me.

They know.

Someone saw us on Samhain. I was certain it wouldn't be a problem—I was helping him with the booth, and then the storm hit. Of course we had to go somewhere to wait it out. And I'd assumed—stupidly—that everyone was too drunk on honeyed mead to pay any attention to what Cairn and I were doing.

But like so many times before, I was wrong.

My stomach drops. Suddenly, potato soup doesn't sound very appetizing. Nothing sounds very appetizing.

This could ruin him, I think. *I could ruin him.*

That's not what I want—it's never been what I want. Even though I'm angry with him, with myself, with the mother who abandoned me, I don't want him to suffer because of me, don't want him to be cast out, labeled as something he's not. I'm not sure I'd be able to forgive myself if that happened to him.

"Are you okay?" Juniper asks softly, pulling me back to the present, where I'm still standing frozen in a narrow hallway in the mathematics corridor, my bag weighing heavily on my shoulder.

"I . . . I . . ." My hands itch with heat. Fire wants to spew from my fingertips, but I hold it in. "I don't know what to do. If they've found out . . ." I bite my lip. "Have I ruined everything?"

"Of course not." There's a bit of movement, a tugging on my robe, and then Juniper climbs up to perch herself on my shoulder, hidden beneath my curls. Her fur is soft against my skin. "Nothing's ruined. But he needs to know." She puts her paw on my neck; she's warm from being tucked inside my pocket. "You'll figure it out together."

I give a small nod of my head. "Okay. Yeah." I take a deep breath, trying to steady myself. "But I have to tell him soon. Tonight. I can't wait until Saturday."

Part of me is relieved at having an excuse to go see him, a reason to set my hurt aside for long enough to look into his eyes, to hear his voice, to breathe in his woodsmoke scent. But the other part of me wonders if it even matters anymore, if there's anything to warn him about.

Because I might have already burned down everything that once blossomed between us. And it might be too late to heal the damage I've caused.

B E CAREFUL," POPPY TELLS ME AS I PULL ON MY thick winter cloak. "If there're already whispers going around, you can't afford to be spotted."

"By *anyone*," Maeve adds. She's draped on the couch, watching me from over the cushions. Poppy is sipping tea while Alina paces in front of the fire in the hearth.

Suddenly, Alina stops. "I have an idea."

I arch a brow at her while reaching for one of my boots. "What's that?"

She whirls to face me. "Take Raelan with you."

I narrow my eyes. "Why?"

Alina tips her head at me. "Because he's a shifter. He's got impeccable hearing, and he'll be able to get you to Cairn's place without anyone seeing you."

"Can he bring her back?" Poppy asks. "Don't forget, you still have to get back *in* without being spotted." She taps her fingernails against her teacup. "Goddess, I don't know about this, Lyra. What if you're seen?"

Pulling my boot on with a huff, I reach for my other one. They've all got a point. And it might be annoying having to sneak around with Raelan, but if it means protecting Cairn from more faculty gossip, then I've got to at least try.

"All right." I yank my other boot on, then pull up my hood. "Get your dragon," I tell Alina. "It's time to go."

AND THAT'S HOW I FIND MYSELF SHUFFLING QUIETLY through the empty halls of the academy, Raelan one stride ahead of me. Despite his size, he's able to move silently, and he's already saved me *twice* from being spotted by a professor walking through the halls.

I admit to myself, begrudgingly, that this was a great idea on Alina's part, and Raelan is actually *really* helpful.

We're coming up at a hallway junction, and Raelan pauses, holding an arm out to stop me. He's carrying a bundle of fabric in his other arm, though I'm not sure what it is. He tips his head, listening, then ushers me back into the shadows between a broad-leafed potted plant and a tapestry depicting the academy's moon-phases crest. His body puts off heat as he stands near me, and I wonder if it's the dragon inside him, keeping him warm. My fire magic is not so different, though lately, it's been erratic again, not listening to me and behaving badly, like a child who's had too much candy and refuses to be put to bed.

In the hallway, I finally hear boots on stone; Raelan's hearing really *is* amazing. I wonder how far away they were when he first picked up on the sound of their footsteps.

Whoever it is, they don't bother to pause or investigate our hallway; they just walk right by, humming a little as they go.

Once they're gone, I let out a breath. "Okay, dragon, let's get on with it. I don't have all night."

When Raelan glances down at me, there's a bit of gold glowing in his eyes.

His dragon again?

"You're welcome to go on without me," he says, sweeping his arm out in a mocking gesture.

I roll my eyes and cross my arms beneath my heavy cloak. "No. You're actually kind of helpful."

"Kind of?" Raelan asks as he resumes our brisk walk through the castle. He doesn't even stop to look either way down the halls before we cross through them, I assume because his hearing—and maybe his smell?—is so strong that he already knows no one is there.

Candles burn in sconces along the walls, making our shadows dance as we make our way slowly toward the castle's garden exit. Before leaving the north tower, we decided that going through the main entrance into Coven Crest would be too risky; so, instead, we're opting for the doors that lead into the garden.

When we get there, the hall is quiet, and Raelan has to slowly unlock the heavy door before pushing it open. Immediately, a burst of cold air sweeps in, making my cloak flutter around my calves. We step out into the night, our boots crackling the crust of frozen snow.

The moon is mostly obscured by clouds, which makes it easier to move across the garden undetected. Raelan still has us move cautiously around the outskirts of the courtyard, then under the barbican, which has another locked gate he has to open from the inside. Once I'm finally on the outside of the castle walls, I breathe a sigh of relief.

I'm so close now.

Raelan knows which direction to go to Cairn's hut, and I glance up at him and arch a brow as we walk. "You know where he lives?" I ask.

A small sideways smile pulls on Raelan's mouth. "I was here last year. Ended up . . . borrowing some clothes." He holds up the bundle of fabric, as if that explains everything.

I narrow my eyes. "What?"

But Raelan doesn't answer, just presses ahead through the snowy field.

When we arrive at Cairn's hut, the windows are glowing softly, candlelight illuminating the curtains drawn over the glass. I step up to the door, then hesitate, glancing at Raelan.

"Do you . . . ?" I point toward the closed door.

He shakes his head. "No. I'll wait out here. But will you give these to him?" He hands me the bundle of fabric, then slips his hands into his pockets and leans against the side of the thatched hut. "The cold doesn't bother me much. And I'll keep an eye out, just in case."

I stare at him for a moment. He stares back.

"What?" he asks, voice edged in suspicion.

I let out a breath, and the cloud of steam floats between us. "Thank you," I finally bring myself to say. "For . . . helping me."

Raelan's shoulders soften a bit, and he gives me a small smile, then tips his head toward the hut. "Go on, then."

I grip the fabric Raelan handed me, squeezing my fingers around the soft bundle. Then I turn to Cairn's door and knock firmly—before I can lose my nerve.

On the other side, I hear hooves clop across the floor, slow and heavy. I take a breath.

The door opens, bathing me in firelight, and my minotaur looks down at me.

CHAPTER 36
CAIRN

LYRA WILDER STANDS ON MY DOORSTEP, CHEEKS flushed, crimson eyes shining in the light cast by my fire and candles. And off to the right, I find an unfamiliar man leaning against my hut, shimmering flecks of gold in his eyes. When I scent the cold air, I detect an odd smell coming from him. Not fully a human, then.

"That's Raelan," Lyra says. "He helped me get here without being spotted."

This draws my gaze back to her. She's bundled in a sweater and boots, the hood of her winter cloak pulled up over her red hair.

"Why are you—"

"Can we talk inside?" she asks, her breath steaming out around her lips.

I glance at Raelan again. He gives me a subtle nod, then turns away, as if to give us privacy. Does he . . . *know* about us?

What's going on?

Moving back, I pull the door open wider, then try to control the rapid beating of my heart as Lyra steps inside. Raelan doesn't move. Guess he's staying out there.

I close the door. When I turn, Lyra is still standing in the entryway, looking like a stranger, like someone who hasn't been here multiple times, like someone who hasn't shared my bed and laughed with me in the bath.

It hurts more than it probably has a right to.

"These are yours." She holds up a bundle of fabric.

I eye it. "My what?"

"Clothes, I think." She bends to set them on a narrow bench in the entryway. "Raelan said he . . . borrowed them? I don't know. He asked me to return them."

My clothes. The ones that were stolen from the clothesline last year.

What an odd witch this Lyra Wilder is. And it seems she keeps odd company as well.

Not sure what that says about me.

Now she's just standing there, staring at me. It makes my skin tingle with heat.

"Do you . . . want something to drink?" I ask.

She gives me a small smile and a quick nod of the head.

I move into the kitchen, and she follows, albeit hesitantly. She takes a seat at the table while I pour us each a cup of tea—I use the hand-painted moonflower cup for Lyra, the one that hasn't been used since last her lips touched it.

When she sits there, does she think about the way we touched each other that night, the pleasure we experienced at each other's hands? Because that's what I think of. It's the only thing I see. And it's made eating meals at my kitchen table almost impossible.

The calming scent of lavender twirls around me as I turn and set two teacups onto the table.

"Thanks," Lyra says softly, not meeting my eyes.

This is so unlike her. I'll admit I've not known her long—only a few months—but I've never known her to be shy or timid. She's quite the opposite.

Sinking into the chair across from her, I sigh and decide to get on with it. "Why are you here? What's going on?"

Lyra stares down into her cup of tea, the steam dancing around her freckled cheeks. "I overheard a couple professors talking in the hallway today," she says. "And they . . ." Finally, her striking crimson eyes meet mine. "They were talking about us."

Something tight snakes around my stomach and squeezes. "What did they say?"

"That I've been cozy with you, and someone saw me come back with you on Samhain. And then one said . . ." She hesitates, glancing away again.

"Said what? Just tell me."

A furrow forms in her brow. "He said Moonhart hates scandals and that you'll be toast if you're caught."

My stomach squeezes tighter.

Of course, I should have expected this. Especially after Samhain, after we interacted so freely in public. This shouldn't be a surprise.

"Do they know for sure?" I ask, curling my fingers into fists upon my thighs.

Lyra tips her head, looking unsure. "It sounds like they suspect, but I don't think they know for sure. But that's why Raelan helped me sneak out tonight—it would be bad for anyone to see me here like this."

I turn her words over in my head for a moment, trying to push through the stuffy cotton that my warring emotions of fear and desire are causing to cloud my thoughts. "Why was it so important for you to tell me?" Turning my eyes toward her, I make myself stare at her, even though looking at her hurts. "Why not wait until Saturday, when it was safe?"

Lyra's jaw feathers. I'm not quite sure what goes through her head, but she sits up a bit straighter. "Because I know this is my fault. And I wanted to tell you. To warn you. If anything happened to you because of me . . ." The furrow deepens. "You deserved to know."

You deserved to know.

Without meaning to, I look into the sitting room, where my job offer from the Columbine Conservatory is lying on the table beside my armchair.

She deserves to know, a voice whispers in my ear. *I have to tell her, regardless of what I decide.*

I push to my hooves. Lyra's gaze follows me as I walk into the sitting room to retrieve the letter. Then I set it on the table in front of her.

She doesn't read it. Instead, she just stares at it, at the inked script on the front of the page. Then her eyes move slowly to me.

"What's this?"

I have to tell her.

"It's from the conservatory. They've offered me the job." I hesitate, then add, "And they want me to start in the spring."

A flurry of emotions flashes through her eyes, then settles on something that looks like a mix of sadness and pain. "So . . . you're leaving? Just like that?"

I hate the way her voice trembles, just a little bit. *Tell her the truth*, I say to myself.

"I haven't decided yet."

She looks down at the letter again, then slides it away from her across the table. There's a tense moment of silence. Then she says, "Well, you should. Take the job."

My eyes narrow. "You mean that?"

She shrugs, feigning nonchalance, but she can't hide her truth from me—not like she used to be able to. I see the tension in the skin around her mouth, the way her fingers are curled into tight fists.

"Whatever this was"—she gestures between us roughly—"we knew it had to end eventually. It was just temporary."

I blink. My mouth opens, but the look in her eyes steals the words from my tongue.

She looks like she's breaking, and I don't know what to do, don't know how to fix this.

"Lyra, I never—"

She pushes to her feet and flashes me a fake smile. "This is probably a good thing for both of us. It'll be better this way." She moves toward the door, her sweet scent trailing behind her. As she reaches for the door handle, she says, "I'm going to talk to Moonhart, ask her to discontinue my community service so I can focus on finals. I'm sure you'll be busy preparing to leave." Her gaze quickly flicks around my little hut, then back to me. "And a clean break would be best. So . . . goodbye, Cairn."

The door opens, letting in a swirl of icy air that tosses Lyra's curls around her shoulders. Then, just like that, she's gone. The gentle click of the door closing echoes in my ears.

Should I do something? Should I chase after her? Is it foolish to want to try to make this work when so many things are trying to keep us apart?

I stand there, frozen in indecision, until I know Lyra is long gone. And then I look at her cup of lavender tea, sitting untouched on the table, and I feel lonelier and colder than I have in a very long time.

CHAPTER 37
LYRA

Sitting in Headmistress Moonhart's office, I focus on keeping my face as friendly as possible, trying not to let on how my emotions are whirling like a tornado inside me.

"You're asking me to discontinue your community service?" One of her icy brows arches in the corner. "You know that wasn't the agreement, Miss Wilder. You're to complete one year of community service and prove to me that you can control yourself and your magic."

"I understand," I say, keeping my tone low. "And I've been working hard, and I think it's helping. But with finals coming up, I could really use the extra time to study, and you know, so many study groups are on Saturdays." I give her a small smile. "And I'm not asking to cancel the community service—I understand why it was assigned to me. I'm just asking if we can pause until finals are over, then I can start up again next semester."

If I'm even still a student here . . .

I'm not sure if the headmistress knows that Cairn is thinking about leaving. If she does, she doesn't make any indication of it to me.

But this is what I need. He's leaving, and I need to separate myself from him. I can't keep working alongside him every week, watching the gentleness with which he tends to the plants, wishing I could tuck myself into his arms and never have to leave.

It was temporary, I tell myself. *Just like everything else in my life.*

Headmistress Moonhart steeples her fingers and regards me through thoughtful narrowed eyes. I try not to let her see what I'm hiding, try not to let her hear the words I'm not saying.

"Please, Headmistress. I'm not going to mess up again. I just want to work hard, pass my finals, and start fresh next semester." I dare a glance into her icy eyes. "I won't let you down."

Her gaze softens. "You're not letting me down, Miss Wilder. This has never been about letting me down." She sighs softly. "This is about trying to help you, trying to set you on the right path. It's never been about punishing you."

I give her a tight nod and stare down at my hands in my lap. Silence stretches between us, making the ticking of the clock on the mantel that much louder.

Finally, after what feels like a lifetime, she pushes to her feet, drawing my gaze up. "Very well. I'll allow you a hiatus from your community service. Focus on your classwork, study hard, and control that fire. I want to see you back here next semester."

This time, the smile I give her is genuine, even if it's hiding my pain. "Thank you, Headmistress. I will."

AFTER THAT, MY DAYS START TO BLEND TOGETHER. I used to look forward to my weekends, to my uninterrupted time with Cairn. Now every day is the same. Wake up early, trudge through my classes, study on the weekends, fall into bed, repeat. The days are gray, the snow a constant reminder of the impending end of this semester. And maybe the end of my time at the academy.

It's a Saturday—our last weekend before finals week—and I find myself sitting near the window in our dorm room, staring out the frosty glass as snow falls lazily from the cloud-covered sky. And even though I shouldn't be, I'm thinking about Cairn.

Typically, I'd be with him right now. But those days are done. Still, I can't help but wonder what he's doing. With the snow falling like this, he's probably out shoveling, trying to keep the paths clear around the campus. I remember the last time we shoveled together, the cold shoulder I gave him when he tried to reach out to me.

My own voice echoes in my mind: *It's not like we're friends or something.*

My brow furrows, eyes narrowing as I stare into the winter sky.

It was a cruel, hurtful thing to say. I saw the look in Cairn's eyes when the subtle verbal attack found its mark. Part of me wants to feel guilty for it, but the other part feels it was the right thing to do—for both of us. He's leaving,

I'm here for another couple years (hopefully), and whatever we were, whatever we had, wouldn't have lasted anyway. The longer it went on, the more painful it would have become.

It's better this way.

"Lyra!"

A burst of snowy air wraps around me. The ice fractals twinkle before my eyes, and I blink, sitting back from the window and jerking my gaze to my roommates, who're all perched in the sitting room, schoolbooks open before them.

"Hello? Are you listening?" Alina asks.

"Uh, yeah." I blink and wave her frost magic away, making it disperse into the warm air. "Sorry. Just a bit . . . distracted today."

We've been studying since returning to our dorm after breakfast. Yuki and Juniper are asleep on the rug in front of the fire, snoring pleasantly; Isis is curled around Maeve's neck; and my mind is anywhere but on semiotics.

Alina takes a deep breath, then sighs, her shoulders rising and falling with the movement. "I think we could all use a break," she says.

"What kind of break?" Poppy asks without looking up from her textbook—looks like something about divination, one of Poppy's strong suits.

Alina, Maeve, and I exchange looks, and a smile starts to curl across my lips.

At the same time, the three of us say, "Runeball!"

THIS HAS BECOME SOMEWHAT OF A TRADITION FOR us. When classwork becomes too overwhelming or we've been cooped up in the castle for too long, we like to come out here onto the runeball field and fool around, tossing the arcane sphere to one another, running and laughing and letting out all the stress that so easily builds up in this academy.

And this time, Poppy joins us.

"Poppy!" I call. "This one's yours!"

My hands tingle with warmth, and I send a burst of flame from my fingertips. The energetic blast lights the arcane sphere on fire and shoots it into the air, flying in Poppy's direction.

"You've got it!" Alina calls.

"Run for it!" Maeve adds.

But the ground is slick, and I watch as if in slow motion as Poppy's boots slip out from under her and she goes plunging right into the snow with a *thump*.

"Poppy!" the three of us all call at once, our cloaks snapping around our ankles as we run for her.

But someone else makes it there first, stopping us in our tracks.

"You okay?" the orc asks, kneeling next to where Poppy is now sitting in the wet slush, righting her glasses and wiping snow from the frames.

She tips her head in his direction, and if not for her cheeks already being pink from the cold, I'm pretty sure they'd be flushing like crazy right now.

"F-fine," she squeaks up at him.

The student holds out his hand, and Poppy hesitantly takes it, allowing him to pull her to her feet.

"Thanks," she whispers, then hurriedly pulls her hand away and starts trying to wipe the slushy snow from her cloak, looking anywhere but at him.

I share a conspiratorial glance with Alina.

Hmm.

"Aric," Maeve says, striding forward.

The orc looks up, and his smile makes his protruding tusks that much more prevalent. "Hey, sis. What're you girls up to?"

"Blowing off steam." She bends over to pick up the arcane sphere from where it fell into the snow. Tossing it in her hands, she tips her head at him. "You wanna play?"

"Ha!" Aric crosses his huge arms across his chest. "I'm not sure you could keep up."

Even from over here, I can see the challenge flicker in Maeve's stormy eyes.

We've been to all the runeball games over the past two years, and I know what a proficient player Aric is. But that doesn't stop Maeve.

"You think it's always like this with them?" Alina whispers to me.

I nod. "Yup."

"We can take you on," Maeve says. Then she props one hand on her hip and looks back at us. "Right?"

"I-I think I'm gonna sit this one out," Poppy says. She's still wet and starting to shiver.

Immediately, I walk over to her, then hold out my hands, using a bit of fire magic to radiate warmth. It makes Poppy smile.

"Thanks, Ly."

"Alina? Lyra?" Maeve presses. "Come on. Let's show him how it's done."

I'm always up for a little friendly competition—plus, it'll help me stop looking around, wondering if I might catch a glimpse of Cairn somewhere near the runeball field. I thought I saw him on our walk down here, but it just turned out to be Professor Stone bundled up in way too many cloaks, the shadow of him in my periphery playing tricks on my mind.

"I'm in," I say. I narrow my eyes at Maeve's stepbrother. "Get ready to hurt, orc."

"*Ly,*" Alina says, shooting me a sharp look.

But Aric doesn't seem to mind. He lets out a big laugh. "Great. This should be fun."

CHAPTER 38
LYRA

A S IT TURNS OUT, *I'M* THE ONE WHO hurts from the epic runeball game against Aric. Poppy returned to the dorm to warm up and dry off, but Maeve, Alina, and I stayed to wage battle against the orc. And we lost spectacularly.

Even now, bouncing along in Alina's carriage days later, my muscles are still sore.

"We made it through," Maeve says as she slumps against the plush cushions. There are dark circles under her eyes from staying up too late this week studying. We pulled a couple all-nighters in prep for our finals, and I think we're all feeling it.

Except for Poppy.

She didn't need to pull any all-nighters—in fact, I'm pretty sure she didn't even have to study and just wanted to sit with us during our companionable suffering. Even now, she looks rosy cheeked and well rested, sitting tall beside me, looking out the window as the Mistwood rolls by.

"So, what's the deal with your community service?" Maeve asks. "Are you starting again next semester?"

Next semester.

Our finals haven't been marked yet, but somehow, I get the feeling I passed. I should be more excited and relieved, but all I feel is . . . numb.

Isn't this what I've been working so hard for? To control my magic, to cling to my place as a student at Coven Crest? So, why do I feel so disheartened?

Cairn's face hovers in my mind. Finals helped to distract me from my thoughts of him, but now that they're over and we're returning to Wysteria for our holiday break, I worry that he's going to be constantly on my mind.

"I think so," I say. "That's what Moonhart said, at least."

But will Cairn be gone by then?

I recall what he said last time I spoke to him, about the conservatory wanting him to start this coming spring. Does that mean he'll be gone by the time I return to campus?

The realization sweeps over me like someone just dumped a frigid bucket of water onto my head.

Alina reaches over to touch my knee. "You okay? Your cheeks just went white."

I pull my knee away from her, leaving her hand hanging there in the space between us. "Fine. Just exhausted." I look down at Juniper, who's perched in my lap, grooming herself. "I'm just ready to go home."

In my periphery, my roommates exchange looks, but they say nothing.

And I keep quiet the rest of the ride back to Wysteria.

HOME. I'M FINALLY HERE.

Alina's carriage dropped Poppy off at the café first—I was tempted to run inside and buy something sweet to eat—then me. Now, I wave as the carriage starts away, with Alina, Maeve, Iris, and Yuki looking out the frosty window at me. When they're gone, leaving nothing but tracks in the snow, I turn and start up the cobblestone walkway to the house, the one I grew up in and know like the back of my hand.

After stepping inside, I push the door closed behind me, set my bag down on the floor in the hallway, and take a deep breath. The air smells of woodsmoke, strong coffee, and cedar from Papa's workshop.

Even Juniper seems comforted by the smell, given the way she crawls onto my shoulder and sniffs at the air. "Think he has any of those glazed donuts?" she asks.

Papa has a soft spot for donuts, and he usually keeps them around to have with his morning coffee.

"I hope so."

After wiping my boots on the mat by the door, I walk into the kitchen. Papa isn't there, but the donuts sure are.

"Yes!" Juniper says.

A smile pulls on my lips as I snag a donut for myself and rip a big chunk off for her. The vanilla glaze makes my fingers sticky. Then I move through our tiny cramped house, glance into Papa's bedroom—it's empty—and continue into the narrow yard in the back, where his

269

workshop is. The snow underfoot has been packed down by Papa's boots, so I know he's been coming and going from his shop, as usual.

I pull the roller door open, and Papa looks up from what he's working on—intricately carved corbels, by the look of it. As soon as he sets eyes on me, his mouth pulls into a grin, and he crosses the workshop in just a few wide steps.

"Ly!" His arms come around me, though he's careful not to squish Juniper in the process.

I hug him back, breathing in the smell of sawdust and coffee that clings to him everywhere he goes. "Hi, Papa."

"Oh, I'm so glad you're home." When he pulls back from me, there's moisture in his eyes, and I laugh a little as he reaches up to wipe the tears away.

"You miss me that much?" I ask. "We've gotta get you a girlfriend, Papa."

He pinches his lips and ruffles my hair, probably getting wood shavings in my curls. "What? You mean to say you didn't miss me?"

The humorous smile falls slowly from my lips. Now I'm the one whose eyes are going glassy.

"Of course not," I say with a barely concealed sniffle. Then a couple tears fall onto my cheeks, and next thing I know, I'm wrapping my arms around his middle and pressing my head to his warm chest.

His laughter rumbles in my ear. "Come on. Let's have a bite to eat, and you can get me caught up on everything you've been up to. And you too, Juniper. Did you find those donuts I left out?"

Juniper crawls from my shoulder onto Papa's shoulder, where she can often be found when we're at home. She snuggles her face against his cheek, and he laughs.

"Yup, I can smell the sugar on you already," he says.

Papa slings his arm around me, grabs his mug of strong coffee off his workbench, and takes me back to the house, where he proceeds to pour me a cup of tea and serve me another glazed donut.

And despite how messy everything is in my heart right now, it comforts me. Being here, being with Papa, feels safe and familiar.

But I still can't get Cairn's face from my mind, no matter how hard I try.

CHAPTER 39
CAIRN

THE STUDENTS HAVE ALL LEFT THE CAMPUS, and it's quiet around here now—no laughter or conversation, no boots crunching over the leaves or snow. Just me and Coven Crest and the bite of cold in the air.

Despite the academy being closed for the semester, there's still plenty for me to do. This is the time of year when I work *inside* the academy—oiling squeaky door hinges, tending to the indoor plants, washing the windows so they shine despite the gray outside.

I keep myself busy, working hard, but no matter how much I sweat or how many tasks I check off my to-do list, Lyra's face is never far from my mind. When I shovel snow, I see her. When I pour tea, I see her. And when I sit in my armchair and stare into the fire at night, I can almost swear I *feel* her—the warmth of her skin, the softness of her mouth. The pillow she once slept on no longer smells of her, and I'm not sure whether to be relieved or not.

Today was a cold day—colder than most. The Mistwood is frosted over, ice clinging to the pines, and now that night has fallen, I move around my hut, pulling the drapes closed to trap the warmth from the fire inside. But as I grab hold of the drapes in the sitting room, something outside the window catches my eye.

The moonflowers are blooming, glowing silver against the cloak of darkness that is a winter night. And something about the ethereal light beckons to me.

I close the drapes, then grab my cloak from a peg by the door and fasten it about my neck before heading out into the cold.

As I step into the snow and close the door behind me, the quiet of the night settles like leaves falling to the earth. The air is crisp and sharp, with the unmistakable freshness only winter can bring. It chills my nose and lungs as I breathe in deep, and steam puffs around my face as I let it out with a sigh.

Hooves crunching across the snow, I make my way toward the blooming moonflowers. As I draw near, I appreciate their light and the way it glows and reflects off the snow around their bases, turning everything a shimmering shade of silver and blue.

I kneel before them, and immediately, another memory returns to me.

Lyra sitting with me on a blanket, watching the moonflowers bloom and glow. The wonder in her eyes as she first watched them unfurl. Then her weight in my lap, her fingers dragging through my beard, the heat of her body and the press of her lips against mine.

Still kneeling, I bury my head in my hands and let out a growl.

What is wrong with me? Why did I allow this to happen?

I knew this could only end badly, knew it would just be messy and painful and wrong. But I let it go on anyway, let myself believe that maybe, somehow, it would work. After all these years, these feelings are unearthing my memories of my ex—the looks on her parents' faces when she introduced me to them, the horror when they realized their daughter wished to marry a beast, a monster.

They didn't know me. Didn't want to know me.

But Lyra knows me. And yet it still didn't work out. It's like love isn't meant to be—at least, not for me.

When will I accept that?

As I kneel there in the snow, a cold wind twines through the trees, rustling the moonflowers and sending one blossom drifting down to settle upon the snow. My eyes follow its movement. It glows for a short while, clinging to life, but like all things, it eventually succumbs, its glow fading until it falls dark.

I reach for it, scoop the delicate flower with its creamy-white petals into my palm. And as I cup it there, I realize something.

Nothing lasts forever, no matter how badly I might wish for it to.

And it might be time for me to stop gripping and just . . . let go.

My gaze lifts to my hut. The windows glow with very subtle firelight, the drapes drawn and still. Smoke puffs from the chimney in a steady stream, drifting up into the night sky until it slowly disperses and vanishes from view.

I love it here. I've settled into this place, my roots growing deep into the earth. I've never wanted to be anywhere else. But now I have a chance, an opportunity at something different.

Will I let my fear hold me back?

Another cold wind dances around me. It snags the moonflower from my palm and sends it spiraling through the air. I track its movements with my eyes until the wind steals it from view, carrying it somewhere I can't follow.

With a deep sigh, I brace my hands on my thighs and push to my hooves. My cloak shifts and settles about my fetlocks, buried deep in the snow.

I tip my head back and regard the sky, with its thick cloud cover and fleeting glimpses of stars.

And I know what I have to do. I just hope it's the right decision for both of us.

CHAPTER 40
LYRA

I'VE GOT A POT OF LEFTOVER VEGETABLE SOUP heating up in the kitchen, and Juniper is taking a nap on the couch while I sweep the scuffed hardwood floor. Papa is already coming in and out from his workshop, dropping wood shavings everywhere he goes.

Honestly, I think, *how does he survive around here without me?*

The thought causes a ball of guilt and anger to form in my gut.

Was it selfish to want to attend Coven Crest? Papa raised me on his own after Mama left us. He worked hard every day to give me the best life he could. But as soon as I was old enough to leave, that's exactly what I did.

Just like her.

I left him here, with his burnt coffee and his floors dusted with cedar shavings. I left him in the quiet of this place, my room empty, my bed never slept in.

Am I like her? I wonder again.

Her blood—her fire magic—burns through my veins, yet I can scarcely even recall her face. In my memories, she's little more than a red-haired phantom, a specter moving at the edges of my awareness, the deafening click of a door closing, never to be opened again.

When I was younger, I asked Papa about her. He told me what he could despite the pain I could see in his eyes when he spoke of her, the woman who once loved him and then left him.

And for some reason, recalling this makes me think of Cairn. Will that be all I am to him? A fire witch who touched him, who wanted him, and then who left him?

No, I tell myself, sweeping with a bit more fervor, sending puffs of dust and wood shavings swirling through the afternoon light. *He's leaving me, not the other way around.*

The Columbine Conservatory is on the other side of Wysteria—close enough to travel to but too far to visit regularly. Cairn working there would mean I'd only get to see him every so often, wouldn't get to sneak down to his hut anymore or curl up with him in front of the fire after a difficult day in class.

Am I being selfish about this too?

My eyes narrow, and I sweep just a bit harder. The dust stands no chance against me and my broom.

I leave Papa, then I leave Cairn, and all the while, I'm upset that she left me.

I almost want to laugh. Then I do laugh. But it quickly turns to tears. They track down my cheeks and collect along my chin before dripping off, pattering onto my sweater as I continue to sweep.

I'm not like her! I want to scream.

"Lyra?" Juniper says in a sleepy voice as she wakes from her nap. "What's that smell?"

But I don't listen. I just keep sweeping. And I barely even realize when smoke starts to twine up from the thick bristles of the broom.

Then the entire head of the broom bursts into bright red-orange flames, startling me enough that I drop it and jump back. The fire licks across the old, worn wood of the broom, devouring it before I can even think to try to use the water magic I've been learning to douse the flames.

Juniper's squeaking like crazy. But I'm still frozen, staring at the flames as they crackle, when the back door opens and Papa calls, "Ly?"

The smoke must alert him, because he comes sprinting into the room behind me, his boots thumping loudly on the wood floor. Then he's grabbing an old knit blanket off the back of his armchair. He throws it atop the flaming broom and starts hurriedly stomping the flames out, turning them to smoke and ash. Now I'll need to clean that up too.

And when he's done, I'm still standing there, tears tracking from my eyes.

"Lyra?" he says, breathing hard, chest rising and falling rapidly. He's got wood dust in his beard. "What happened?"

What happened?

I look down at my hands. They're warm, still tingling with magic.

"I . . ." I sniffle, and my eyes mist over with more tears. "I set it on fire. But I didn't mean to. I'm sorry. I'm so sorry."

Papa steps forward, and as his arms come around me, I start crying with more fervor. Then words start pouring out of me, unbidden.

"Why'd she leave us?" I ask between sobs. "Why'd she leave *me*?"

His arms tighten around me, the way they have since I was young.

"She wanted something different, Ly," he says. One of his hands starts stroking my curls, the other still holding me close. He smells like coffee and cedar, like home. "And we can spend the rest of our lives feeling abandoned by her. Or"—he pulls back and puts his hands on my shoulders, looking into my teary eyes—"we can accept that she left, and we can move forward. I know it's painful. Goddess, do I know." A look of hurt flashes through his brown eyes, and his fingers tighten slightly. "But what's done is done. She might not be here, but *we* are." He uses one thumb to wipe the tears from my cheek. "I'm so sorry she hurt you like this. But it wasn't personal. She didn't leave because of *you*. She left because of *her*."

"Have you," I say between sniffles, "forgiven her?"

Papa's eyes narrow as he stares at me. The smell of smoke still hangs in the air around us. Then his lips pull up slightly in one corner. "I think I have. But you haven't, have you?"

I tighten my fingers into fists and give my head a small shake. "No . . . I'm still mad at her."

"And you have every right to be." He cups my face with his hand, and I lean my cheek into his palm. "But you don't have to be. Anger is exhausting. It weighs you down, becomes a bag that's heavier to carry with each passing day.

And though what she did will never be gone from your memory, you can choose to put that bag down, Ly. Choose to leave it where it lies. Your anger, while valid, doesn't change anything. I learned long ago that finding my joy was much more important than holding on to my hurt."

Papa's voice is soothing, his hand on my cheek a comfort I didn't realize I needed. And his words help to slow my tears.

Reaching up, I use my sweater sleeve to wipe the moisture from my eyes and cheeks. "When did you become so insightful?" I ask, a hint of humor to my voice.

He gives me a smile. "Well, I've had a lot of time to think without you here."

At that moment, another whiff of smoke tickles my nose. Papa gets a confused look on his face and glances down at the blanket on the floor, but the broom hasn't burst back into flames again.

"What's that—" he starts to say.

"The soup!" Juniper calls.

"The soup!" I echo.

I scurry into the kitchen, where the pot is boiling over, sending bubbly broth cascading down into the flames. This time, I'm able to call on the water magic I've been practicing in my elemental class, and the flames are doused in seconds, hissing as they die.

Papa's boots thump softly behind me, and I turn to find him leaning in the doorway, arms crossed. With a look of exasperated humor, he shakes his head and says, "I've got a better idea. Grab your boots. We're going out to eat."

CHAPTER 41

CAIRN

INALLY, IT'S A SUNNY DAY. THE SUNLIGHT makes the snowy courtyard shimmer like fairy dust as I walk the cobbled path—which I shoveled yesterday—up to the castle. The snow blanketing the campus is pristine, with only a few animal tracks dotting the fluffy layer of white. Everything is quiet save for the occasional plop of snow falling from the pine boughs and the click of my hooves on the sun-warmed cobbles.

When I enter the castle, the scent of sage and old books washes over me. I tap the snow from my hooves, then cross the marble-floored entryway, heading toward Lysandra's office.

Some professors return from the holidays early, and some opt to stay at the castle year-round, but I've yet to see anyone since the students left. Anyone who is still around is keeping to themselves. This leaves me free to walk the hallways alone, with only my thoughts to keep me company.

This is the right thing, I tell myself, my fingers tightening at my sides. *It's time to move on. To move forward.*

When I arrive at the headmistress's office, the door is closed, as I expected it would be. Reaching into the inside pocket of my cloak, I remove the letter I wrote last night. This isn't the most professional way of handing in my resignation, but it'll have to do. The conservatory wants me to start right after Yule, so I'll need to pack up my little hut and be on my way before the spring semester begins.

Stooping, I slide the letter under the door, and as soon as it's out of my fingers, I know the decision is final.

After all these years, I'm leaving Coven Crest Academy.

With a drawn-out sigh, I straighten up. My gaze remains on the closed door for a moment, and then I turn to walk away.

And almost bowl right into the headmistress.

"Gods above!" I snap, my heart nearly leaping from my chest at her sudden and silent appearance.

She, as usual, is unflustered, her hair coiled neatly atop her head and her dangly blue earrings barely swaying despite me having almost run her over. She didn't even jerk back.

Witches . . .

"Cairn," she says. "It's unexpected to see you here. Though always welcome. Please, join me for something warm to drink."

Shit. Now I'm going to have to explain the letter, to have to look into her eyes and tell her that despite everything she's done for me, all the opportunities she's given me, I'm going to be leaving.

It's not what I want to do, but I know it's the right thing to do.

So I give her a nod. "Sure. I'd love to."

I step aside, my hooves clacking on the stone floor. Lysandra procures a key from deep inside her robe, then opens the door. The windows in her office allow the daylight to illuminate the space, and the letter I slid beneath the door is like a beacon, sitting there on the floor with the wax seal glowing in the light.

"What do we have here?" Lysandra uses a brush of wind magic to send the letter twirling up into the air and right into her outstretched hand. She quickly scans the front of the envelope, then regards me over her shoulder. "Seems we have much to talk about."

Again, I nod.

We both shed our cloaks, hanging them on pegs by the door. Lysandra strokes Barron's feathers as she passes him where he's resting on his perch near the fire, and he closes his bright yellow eyes and lets out what sounds like a rumbling purr.

"So, what kind of conversation is this?" Lysandra asks as she places a kettle over the flames flickering in the hearth. When she turns to face me, she's smiling. "Meaning, should we be drinking tea or mulled wine?"

I can't help but to give her a smile in return. After all these years, Lysandra still impresses me with her ability to read people—to read me.

"Wine," I say.

Her blue eyes sparkle. "I was hoping you'd say that."

A SHORT TIME LATER, LYSANDRA SERVES ME A MUG of mulled wine—it smells of honey and clove and cinnamon, and the brandy makes my nose tingle when I take a deep breath.

Definitely the better choice for this conversation.

Lysandra sinks into the armchair across from mine. We're near the fire, close enough that it can warm us despite the chill in the castle. She takes a sip of her drink, then sighs and sinks into the cushion's embrace.

"Okay, I'm ready." She levels her icy eyes on me. "What's the letter say?"

I take a deep breath, then bolster my courage with the wine. It's strong—pleasantly so.

"It's . . . It's my letter of resignation."

"Hmm." Lysandra takes another sip of her drink. "You've accepted the job, then?" The smile she gives me is soft and knowing, and it puts me immediately at ease.

"I have. And this . . . comes as no surprise to you?"

She lets out a breathy laugh. "Yes and no. I was hoping you'd take the job, but I wasn't convinced you would." Her silver-blue hair twinkles in the daylight streaming through the windows behind her desk. "What led you to this decision?"

My lips open, trying to reply, but I freeze up.

What led me to this decision? What changed everything, shook me so deep into my roots that I decided I was ready to pull loose from the earth and try something new?

There's only one answer I can give with any semblance of truth to my words. And if what Lyra said is true, and professors have already been whispering about us, then I expect Lysandra already knows all about it. I was a fool to think I could hide anything from her. After all, she's the headmistress for a reason.

"Lyra Wilder," I say, then quickly wash her name down with a swig of hot wine, as if I can burn the sweetness of those words from my tongue.

It only partially works.

Lysandra casts her gaze into the fire. "She came to me," she says. "Before finals, she asked to take a hiatus from community service. I knew something was wrong."

"Did she . . . say something?" I ask, realizing only after I've said it how suspicious it makes me sound.

"No. But she didn't need to. I know you've grown close." She swishes her wine and takes a sip. "Barron's been keeping an eye on her for me."

On his perch, Barron lets out another deep rumble. I think he's falling asleep. Guess this conversation isn't nearly so interesting as flying around spying on everyone. Meddlesome owl.

Again, I open my mouth to say something, but I'm not sure how to speak without digging myself ever deeper into this hole. So I just sip from my mug and turn my gaze to the fire.

But even there, I find Lyra. My mind plays tricks on me, making me think I see her in the dancing flames, and I have to blink the vision away lest I get lost in it.

"Does she know you're leaving?" Lysandra asks at long last, after an extended silence falls between us, disrupted only by the crackle of flames and Barron's rhythmic snoring.

"She . . . does."

"And she didn't take it well?"

I flick a gaze at Lysandra and shake my head. "She's upset with me . . . for deciding to leave."

"Of course she is. She's young, Cairn. And like many young people, she can't yet see the forest for the trees."

I slowly arch a brow at her. "The forest being?"

She finishes her wine, then turns fully to face me, leveling me with such a strong stare that I wonder if she just pinned me to the cushion with magic.

"The forest being your relationship. She's so focused on the here and now that she can't see that this is actually a good thing—for both of you. Should you have chosen to stay here, the relationship would've had to end. You know me well enough to know I couldn't have allowed such a thing to continue."

That's all it takes to make me feel properly scolded. My cheeks warm, and I give her a small nod.

"But now that you're leaving, well . . ." Her shoulders rise and fall with a shrug beneath her blue winter dress. "There's nothing to be done. As soon as you leave this campus, you're free of the rules that bind you." She sits forward a bit. "Free to be together."

I slowly arch a brow at her. "You sound oddly supportive of this, Headmistress."

Her laughter is light, softened by the wine. "I know you, Cairn. And Lyra might disagree, but I know her too. And you're good for each other, regardless of the differences between you. You needed her to dig you up, to transplant you into a new plot. And she needed you to help her learn stability. From you, she can continue learning how to put down roots, to ground herself and her magic. You're exactly the fit for each other that I hoped for."

Now my eyes narrow. "Did you . . . plan it like this all along?" I ask.

"Of course not." Lysandra goes to sip from her mug, but there's no wine left, and a pout tugs on her lips. "Let's just consider it a happy surprise."

I shake my head, my horns casting shadows onto the rug beneath my hooves. "I've never known you to be surprised by anything, Lysandra. And somehow, I doubt you're starting now."

She just gives me another one of those knowing smiles, then holds up her mug. "How about another?"

A laugh rumbles out of me, and I sigh. "Another one sounds great."

CHAPTER 42
LYRA

SIDE BY SIDE, PAPA AND I WALK THE COBBLED streets of Wysteria, just like we've done since I was a little girl. But today, instead of going to one of the cafés we usually frequent, I grab him by the crook of his elbow and guide him toward my new favorite café: the Wandering Cup.

"What's this place?" Papa asks as I pull open the door and usher him inside to the chiming of the little bells.

Immediately, I'm overwhelmed with the smells of coffee and cocoa and baked goods. My mouth waters.

"The mom of one of my roommates owns the place. Just wait and see. Layla makes the best strawberry shortcake I've *ever* had." Then I turn and call out, "Poppy? Layla? You here?"

Their cat—I'm not sure Poppy has ever told me his name—sits in the front window, next to the plants reaching for the winter sunlight. He flicks his ears at us and blinks slowly.

There's a rustling in the kitchen in the back, and then Poppy's familiar face appears in the doorway.

"Lyra!" Her eyes crinkle as she smiles, and she uses a knuckle to push her glasses farther up the bridge of her nose. "Hi! What are you doing here?"

"Came to get something to eat. And I figured I'd bring my old man along."

"Hey," Papa says, reaching up to rustle my hair. "Watch who you're calling old."

Poppy comes out from behind the counter and offers Papa her hand. "It's nice to meet you, Mr. Wilder. My mom's here too. She'll be out in just a second. She was almost done frosting a carrot cake."

"Perfect." Papa shakes Poppy's hand, then looks at me with a warm smile. "I'll order for us both if you two wanna chat, catch up."

I'm about to ask why we'd need to catch up—we've not been on holiday *that* long—when I remember the fire I set to the broom, the tears I shed before we left the house. It'd be nice to talk to Poppy about it, especially because she knows what's really going on, unlike Papa.

I'm definitely not ready to tell him about Cairn—if there's anything to tell at all.

"Yeah, okay. Strawberry shortcake for me."

"Got it." Papa nods in Poppy's direction. "Go on. See you in a bit."

I shrug, then turn to Poppy. One of her lavender brows has a little arch in it, but she doesn't ask. Instead, she says, "Come on, my room's up here."

We walk through the kitchen—I catch a fleeting glimpse

of Layla and raise my hand to wave—then climb a narrow set of stairs to the Waverlys' apartment above the café. I've never been up here before, but Poppy's mentioned it, so I knew she and Layla lived here.

The space is quaint and cozy, and the air is pleasantly warm from the fire flickering in the hearth. All around me, the cheery yellow walls hold a multitude of painted images, bundles of herbs, and other knickknacks—little shelves with figurines, stones, and sticks of incense. Everywhere I look, there's something new to see and be curious about.

"Through here," Poppy says. She kicks off her shoes near the door, so I do the same, and then I follow her to a small room overlooking the cobbled street at the front of the shop. People walk down the road or ride in carriages, bundled up to fend off the cold. And all across the city, smoke plumes puff from chimneys, all the fires fighting to keep the homes and shops warm against winter's chill.

"So," Poppy says, sitting down on the end of her perfectly made bed, "what's going on?"

With a sigh, I turn and sink into Poppy's big bay window. It's full of plush pillows and thick knit blankets, and a narrow end table stands nearby, weighed down with more books than I'd probably read in a year—though I'm sure Poppy will read them all during the holiday, plus some.

I wiggle my toes under one of the blankets and lean back against the wall. "I set a fire again. At home."

Poppy doesn't say anything at first. Her pale purple brows pull low over her eyes, and she stares at me like I'm spent tea leaves in the bottom of her cup in tasseography class. I've never been particularly good at divination—or any of my classes, for that matter—but Poppy excels at it, probably because she's a dream witch, with lots of practice interpreting things that at first glance don't seem so clear.

"What happened? Were you upset about something?"

"Yeah, about a million somethings," I grumble, then nibble on my bottom lip and look out the window again. Down on the cobbles, a mother pushes a stroller, with another young child toddling along at her side.

Did Mama ever go places with me? Did she ever want to?

With a sigh, I say, "I was thinking about me, and my mother, and Cairn . . ." Saying the words out loud makes my stomach pinch at the reminder of all the pain. "It just set me off, I guess. Papa had to put out the fire. Then I burned the soup. So here we are." I toss her a glance and a big smile, but I don't think she's buying it. Now that we've been roommates for a year and a half, it's become exceedingly more difficult to hide my real feelings from the girls. Most of the time, they see right through me. Then I add, "It feels like I'm moving backward, like I'm sliding down a slope, and I'm going to be right back where I started this year. One more fire at the academy, and I'm done. And now, with Cairn leaving, I . . ." These are words I've not said aloud to anyone, words I've scarcely allowed myself to even think. "I'm afraid I'm just going to get worse. He grounded me, helped me. But without him, I feel weak. Dangerous . . ." I fiddle with the soft tassels on one of the knit blankets in the window seat. "I don't want to hurt anyone."

Poppy tips her head at me, short lavender hair framing her light brown cheeks. "I don't think that's the case at all."

I arch a brow at her. "No?"

She shakes her head. "No. You've made so much progress, Lyra. And Cairn might've helped, but *you* did that work. And . . ." Her smile is small and soft. "And you're allowed to miss him. It doesn't mean you're weak."

Miss him . . .

Of course I miss him. But I'm also afraid to miss him, afraid of the pain of caring for him and wanting him when he's so far away. It would be safer to cut things off, to set fire to the feelings I have for him and let them burn to ash that blows away in the winter wind.

"I don't know," I say, wiggling my toes farther under the warm blankets. I've still been struggling to stay warm, like my fire magic is feeling just as gloomy and blue about Cairn as I am.

"Do you want to be with him?" Poppy's voice is gentle, coaxing.

"I . . ." I furrow my brow, bite my lip, try to come up with an answer that won't feel like a lie but won't make me face the truth either. But with Poppy staring at me like that, her eyes focused and intent like she's staring right into my soul, I suddenly feel like there's no point in lying—to her or to myself. It's too exhausting. "I do. And I don't want to lose what I found in the gardens. Not just him, but the new me." Tears start to well up in my eyes for the second time today. "I was doing so well, Pops. And now . . . I'm afraid."

Poppy stands from the bed and comes to sit beside me in the bay window. "You're not going to lose anything. But you might have to fight for it." Her eyes are twinkling when I meet her gaze. "I've never been in love"—her cheeks flush pink—"but from what I can tell, it doesn't always come easy. I mean, look at everything Raelan and Alina went through last year. You've got to work for it. And I think this connection you have with Cairn is worth fighting for, Ly. Do you?"

My mind flashes through my memories of Cairn: images, conversations, the kisses we've shared. And a warmth starts to blossom in my chest as I realize that the reason I learned to control my magic around him is because he always made me feel safe, grounded. When he looked at me, spoke to me, laughed with me, it felt real, and it felt like we had something that would last. But now that I'm afraid of him leaving, my magic is acting up again, becoming as erratic as the emotions swirling in my chest.

"What if it doesn't work out?" I whisper to Poppy.

She smiles at me and puts a warm hand on my knee. "You'll never know if you don't try." Her smile grows. "And I've never known you to give up on anything you put your mind to, Lyra Wilder."

Now I'm starting to smile too, and the tears welling along my low lashes slowly start to dissipate.

I don't want to be reckless, but I also don't want to isolate myself because I'm afraid of those I love leaving me. Mama left Papa behind, but he's not closed himself off, hasn't become bitter and resentful. He still laughs and smiles and finds joy in every day. That's what I want too—to finally take off this burden of weight I've been carrying around with me ever since my mother walked out that door.

I don't want her to drag me down any longer.

And what I *do* want is Cairn.

If he'll still have me.

Leaning forward, I wrap my arms around Poppy and give her a firm squeeze. She smells like honey and cinnamon, probably from whatever she's been baking today.

"Thanks, Pops," I whisper. "I think I know what I need to do."

CHAPTER 43
CAIRN

TODAY IS THE WINTER SOLSTICE, THE SHORT-est day of the year. The campus is quiet, a soft snow is falling, and my fire has been burning nonstop to keep the cold at bay.

Since my conversation with Lysandra, I feel more sure than ever in my decision to take the job at the Columbine Conservatory and leave Coven Crest behind. The only thorn still pricking at my heart is the one with red hair and sharp crimson eyes.

Lyra Wilder.

No matter how I try, I can't seem to get her off my mind. Even now, as I'm going through the belongings in my hut, trying to determine what to take with me into my new life, I find my thoughts drifting to her.

Even though this will be good for both of us, I can't shake the feeling that there is so much left unsaid. She didn't give me the opportunity to explain, and now she's gone, and I'll not be here when she returns.

Will she think of me? I wonder as I take hold of the end of the blankets on my bed. *Will she miss me like I miss her?* I give the blankets a hard flap, intending to set them straight so I can make the bed, and the movement sends something flying into the air before it twirls to the ground without so much as a whisper.

My brow furrows. I step around the bed, looking for what just fell, and my gaze homes in on a silky red ribbon.

It's the ribbon that was wrapped around the gift box I gave Lyra, the one she asked me to tie around the end of her braid that night she stayed with me. It must've fallen out of her hair, and I'm only just now finding it.

Hooves thumping on the wood floor, I round the bed, then stoop to pick it up. It's soft against my fingers and brings back memories of that night—memories I've been trying very hard to push down, to repress so they can't rise up to bite me.

But now it all rushes in, along with the truth of my feelings.

I want Lyra. I want her so bad it makes my bones ache. And I'm going to miss her terribly when I leave.

I'm still holding the ribbon, tracing my fingers along its softness, when a knock sounds on my front door.

Immediately, I lift my head.

Who could that be?

I know Lysandra left a few days ago, returning to Wysteria to be with her family for the solstice, and none of the other professors who're staying here over the holiday ever come to visit me. As far as I'm aware, there's no one else still on campus.

Enclosing the ribbon in my fist, I turn from beside the bed and walk into the living area. Outside the windows, snow softly falls, and I don't hear anything except for the crackling of flames in the hearth and the gentle tick of the clock.

My hand wraps around the door handle, and I pull it open.

A shock of red greets me.

Red hair, red eyes, cheeks flushed with pinkish red.

It's . . . *her.*

My heart squeezes.

What is she doing here?

My gaze flicks up, over her shoulder. There are tracks through the snow, and in the distance, I see a wagon trundling back down the road toward the Mistwood. But I see no one else.

Just Lyra Wilder. Standing on my doorstep. Looking up at me with snowflakes caught in her eyelashes.

"Hi," she says, breath steaming out around her mouth.

I swallow hard. "Hi."

Lyra shuffles her boots a bit in the snow that's already accumulated on my doorstep, and I realize I've not yet invited her in out of the cold. I was so shocked to see her standing there, I froze up. Quickly, I step back, holding the door open.

"Would you like to . . . come in?"

Her smile is quick and beautiful. It cuts right into me. "Please."

She taps off her boots, then steps into my hut. As I close the door behind her, I'm overwhelmed with the fresh smell of snow and pine, which must cling to her from her trip through the Mistwood.

Lyra removes her cloak and hat—releasing her wild red curls—and her rat, Juniper, pops her head out of Lyra's pocket. Next, she pulls off her boots, then sets them beside the door. When she's done, she turns her gaze up to meet mine.

And I have no idea what to say, except for, "Uh . . . what are you doing here?"

Her smile falters a bit. "I have a lot to say to you. Do you mind if we sit down? Maybe have something warm to drink?" She rubs her hands together, bringing a small flame to life in her palms, using it to warm herself.

I watch the flame dance, casting subtle light across her freckled face. And when she smothers it between her palms, it sends up a tiny twirling puff of smoke.

"Of course." I gesture for her to step into the kitchen. "Any requests?"

"Dandelion latte!" she says as soon as the words leave my mouth.

A smile tugs on my lips, a chuckle slipping out of me. "Okay. I can do that."

I'm still holding the ribbon in my fist, and I drop it into the pocket of my knit sweater after Lyra turns her back to me to walk into the kitchen.

Lyra takes a seat in a chair, and Juniper hops out of her pocket to scurry around on the table, sniffing for crumbs. But she won't find any—one of the ways I've been trying to distract myself from thoughts of Lyra is by cleaning everything I can get my hands on. The kitchen table is so spotless that the wood gleams a little in the gray light coming through the kitchen window.

Lyra pulls her legs up, tucking her knees into her chest and resting her chin atop them. As I get started on the lattes, gathering up the spices I'll need, I can feel her gaze on my back. We're both quiet as I brew the dandelion-root coffee, and still we say nothing as I sprinkle cinnamon into each cup and drizzle a little bit of honey on top. I take my time, finding myself hesitant about sitting down and having to look her in the eye.

Why is she here? What does she need to say so badly that she ventured all the way to Coven Crest from Wysteria? And in the snow no less.

Finally, there's nothing else I can do to the cups except turn and put them on the table. So, I take a steadying breath, then do just that.

"Careful," I say to Lyra as I set the cup—*her* cup, the hand-painted one I've not touched since the last time she drank from it—in front of her. "It's hot."

One of her brows pulls up, and I recognize the humor in her eyes. But instead of joking with me, she just says, "Thanks." She wraps her hands around the cup and takes a sniff of it while I sit down. She lets out a long sigh. "I've been craving one of these since—"

Her words cut off.

Since the morning after we spent our first night together. I've been craving something since then too, but not a latte.

"Hopefully it won't disappoint," I say softly.

299

She tips her head at me. "I think that's impossible."

The look she gives me makes me wonder if we're still talking about the lattes.

Juniper squeaks something to Lyra, who then flicks a look at me and says, "Do you have any snacks?" At that exact moment, her stomach grumbles, making her cheeks flush red again. "It was a long wagon ride."

Grateful for another excuse to not have to sit at the table looking awkward and nervous, I busy myself with cutting a few slices of the bread I baked yesterday and dicing up what's left of my hunk of artisan nut cheese. I plate everything on a big platter, then return to the table and set it down.

And Lyra's already done with her latte—apart from the little bit of foam around the rim of the cup.

I blink at her. "Did you . . . drink that whole thing?"

She gives me a big smile. "Told you I've been craving one."

With a chuckle and a shake of my head, I sit down and gesture to the bread and cheese. "It's all yours."

Lyra and Juniper immediately dive in, and I take a moment to sip my latte while observing her, still wondering what she wants to say to me.

And what I'm going to say in return.

"What is this?" Lyra asks, her mouth partially full with a bite of cheese.

"Nut cheese. Got it at a little shop in Wysteria. Maybe I could show you—"

Lyra's eyes widen a bit, and I cut off the sentence before the rest of it can spill from my mouth.

Lyra made it very clear that she's done with me, with us, with whatever *this* was. And I've spent these last weeks trying to drill that into my head, though I obviously haven't done a very good job of it.

I clear my throat. "I could . . . tell you the name of the shop, if you want to go."

The look in her eyes dims a bit, like a candle slowly losing its flame. She brushes a few bread crumbs from her lips—though Juniper is still nibbling around—then sits back in her chair and gives me a look that say it's time to talk.

"What did you want to say to me?" I ask. Around my cup, my fingers tighten, and in my chest, my heart beats a little faster.

Don't do it, I say to the little flicker of hope tickling the inside of my rib cage. *Go away.*

"I—" Lyra bites her lip. Then she takes a deep breath and tries again. "I'm sorry, Cairn."

The little flicker of hope burns brighter at the sound of my name on her lips. Still, I say nothing, try not to betray anything I'm feeling.

"When I saw that letter, it felt like . . ." She holds up a hand, like she's searching for the right words, trying to pull them out of the fire-warmed air. Then she sighs and lowers her hand to the tabletop, fingers curling into a fist. She averts her eyes. "It felt like I was losing you. And that's why I started pushing you away, saying the things I said . . ."

I still feel the bite of her words, can still recall to memory the look in her gaze that day we shoveled snow together, when she told me we weren't even friends.

"And that wasn't fair to you. I should've told you how I *actually* feel."

Her eyes are still averted, her gaze focused on the platter of snacks, where Juniper is sitting up on her hind legs, a little chunk of bread held between her front paws.

Lyra lapses into a long silence—long enough that I realize I should probably say something. But my tongue feels like it's been tied in knots. What if I say the wrong thing? What if I inadvertently hurt her again and she leaves before I have the chance to make things right?

Just try. I can at least do that.

I take a deep breath, then force it out in a huff. "I've not been fair to you either, Lyra. I should have told you about the job, but . . ." I reach around to scratch the back of my neck. My muscles are tense, coiled and bunched up. "But I really didn't think I would get the job. And when they did offer it to me, I told you as soon as I could."

"I appreciate that," Lyra says, voice soft. "And I'm happy for you." This time when she meets my eyes, there's a sad smile lingering behind them. "I really am. I think this job will be amazing. You're going to love it."

She's saying one thing, but I still hear the hurt in her voice, still see the sadness in her eyes.

Finally, I'm able to push my fear away for long enough to reach across the table—being careful not to jostle the platter and Juniper—and take Lyra's small hand in mine. Her skin is warm to the touch, though not as warm as I remember it being the last time I touched her.

"I'm not taking the job to get away from you, Lyra. I . . . I don't *want* to be away from you. I should've said that first thing, when you saw that letter. But I was scared." I huff and shake my head, horns casting shadows over the table from the window at my back. "I'm not good at . . . at *needing* people. I've been alone for a long time, and it's made me scared to try anything new. But then you came along, with your fire and your snappy attitude"—that makes Lyra crack a smile— "and something changed for me. And it terrified me. Hell, it still does."

Slowly, Lyra squeezes my fingers with hers. "It terrifies me too." Her shoulders soften a bit, drooping down. "After my mom left, I stopped trusting people. And that's probably not an excuse, I know. But it changed things for me, made me hesitant to connect with people when I knew they could leave me. And when I heard about the job, I just felt like it was happening all over again, like you were going to walk away and never look back. So I tried to pull away from you. Tried to act like it didn't matter." Tears start to well up along her lower lashes. "But it *does* matter," she whispers. "*You* matter."

"Lyra, I—"

"Wait!" She holds up a hand to stop me, then uses it to scrub the tears from her eyes. "I'm not done." She sniffles, then finally meets my gaze. Her red eyes are made more vibrant by the glassiness from her tears, and they burn right through me. "The way I acted was wrong. I should've just told you that I didn't want you to leave. It's still selfish, but at least it would've been the truth. The truth is that . . . that I'll miss you, Cairn. And I don't want to lose you."

More tears slip from her eyes, and I abandon the warmth of my latte cup to reach out and wipe them from her flushed cheeks. Then I cup her face in my hand and say, "I'm going to miss you too. And I don't want to lose you either. But the conservatory isn't so far. And you know we couldn't keep this up here. Moonhart already knows about us, and—"

Lyra jerks up. "What? Moonhart knows? Why didn't she say anything?"

I shrug. "Probably because I'm taking the job. I won't be an employee here anymore, so . . ."

A long silence settles between us. Juniper stops eating, and her eyes dart between me and Lyra like she's watching an intense runeball match.

"So, you're leaving," Lyra says slowly, like she's choosing each word carefully, "but you still want to . . . ?"

With another deep sigh, I push up from my chair, then reach down and guide Lyra out of hers. She's so small beside me that she has to tip her head way back as I reach down to cup her cheeks in both my hands. "I still want to be with you. Hell, I want to *actually* be with you, without having to sneak around and be worried that someone might see. I want to take you to that cheese shop I mentioned, and spend holidays with you, and not have to hide how I feel. I don't know what this is, but I do know that I don't want to give up on it. I want to keep trying." I stroke her freckled cheeks with the wide pads of my thumbs, my brown hands a stark contrast against her pale face. "Do you?"

Lyra stares up at me. Her crimson eyes reflect the winter sunlight coming through the window, and this close up, I can see the bands of yellow and gold encircling her irises. Her lips part. I hold my breath. And for a moment, she says nothing. Her gaze holds mine, and I swear I can almost see something softening in her eyes.

Like she's finally letting down her walls for me.

And I'll be damned if I don't do the same.

Finally, her lips move, but instead of forming words, they press together, and then she's pushing up onto her toes.

And she kisses me.

It feels so, so good. She's like the first cool sip of water after a long, arduous journey, the feel of collapsing into a deep mattress after a full day of back-breaking work beneath the summer sun. I can't get enough.

I slide my fingers from her cheeks to the back of her head, tangling my fingers in her hair as I taste her lips with my tongue. She tastes of cinnamon and vanilla, both spicy and sweet.

It's oddly fitting for Lyra Wilder.

Our kisses are coming faster now, breaths gasped each time we break for air. She grasps the hem of my sweater in her fists and starts tugging on me, guiding me backward, out of the kitchen and into the hall that leads to my bedroom. It's not smooth, but we laugh each time we stumble, and I steady her with my hands around her waist.

We make it into my bedroom, where I didn't quite finish making the bed—but I suppose it doesn't matter now.

Lyra pushes me down onto the end of the bed—or gives me the hardest shove she can muster, and I play along—then closes the door behind her. She leans back against it, breathing hard, hair mussed from where my fingers were grasping it. She bites her lip.

"Cairn," she says softly. "I . . . I'm ready."

My brain is muddled from the fire in her kisses, and I can hardly focus on the words that come out of her mouth. "For what?" I finally bring myself to ask.

Still biting her lip, she pushes off the door and walks slowly toward me. She comes to stand between my legs where I'm still seated on the bed, her arms wrapping around my neck. Pressing her forehead to mine, she whispers, "To feel you." Slowly, she trails one hand down my chest, her fingertips finding my cock where it's already straining against my thick winter trousers. "To feel *all* of you."

Oh.

Oh.

I lean back, leveling her with a hard stare. "I don't know. I don't want to—"

"To hurt me." She tips her head to one side. "I know." With the hand still draped around my neck, she starts to play with the hair at my nape, drawing a rumbling sigh from me. "But we've got to at least try. And if it's too much, I'll tell you."

Now I narrow my eyes at her. "Promise?"

Lyra laughs, and it's more beautiful and more soothing than any piece of music I've yet heard. "I *promise*. So . . ." She gives me another little shove, guiding me back so I have to recline on my elbows on the bed. "Are *you* ready?"

Now it's my turn to laugh. And I tell her the truth. "I'm not sure I'll ever be ready for you, Lyra Wilder."

Her eyes shimmer with mischief. "Good answer."

Then she tugs the cord of my trousers free, grabs hold of my waistband, and guides the fabric down, giggling as I have to lift my hips to help her. As soon as the fabric releases me, my cock springs up, the tip already glistening.

And I barely have time to draw breath before Lyra crawls onto the mattress between my thighs, grabs hold of my shaft with one hand, and draws her tongue down its hard length, holding my gaze all the while.

This fire witch will be the end of me.

But I'll go happily into that unknown dark—as long as hers is the last face I see.

CHAPTER 44
LYRA

I HOLD CAIRN'S DARK GAZE AS I DRAG MY TONGUE along the underside of his shaft, my other hand stroking him slowly—or stroking as much as I can, given he's easily as long as my forearm and certainly just as wide.

The thought of taking him is just as scary as it is exciting, and I don't want to spend one more night wondering, waiting, *wishing*. Tonight, I'll get him inside me if it's the last thing I do.

Rising up, I lick around his tip, then suck what I can of his head into my mouth—as I expected the first time I saw him naked before me, I can't widen my jaw enough to get him fully inside. I suppose stroking and licking will have to do.

With each tug of my palm along his length and each swipe of my tongue over his engorged tip, Cairn lets out a shuddering breath. He's still propped on his elbows, but his eyes are closed now, and he has his face tipped to the ceiling, horns sprawling out beautifully on either side of his head.

And seeing him like this, I get an idea.

Sitting up on my knees, I scoot back, then stand so I can pull off the thick winter tights I'm wearing under my chunky knit sweater dress. Once they're on the floor, I grab my panties—cute little red ones I wore in hopes that *this* might happen—and pull them down slowly, enjoying how Cairn's gaze follows the movement now that he's opened his eyes again.

"Lie back," I say as I rejoin him on the bed, crawling up the length of his body, legs now bare beneath my dress.

Though he arches a brow, he says nothing, simply maneuvering himself back a bit so he's fully on the bed, me straddling his chest.

I remember the last time I touched his horns, the way his eyes fluttered closed as I let my fingers graze along the base, where his dark curls give way to the glistening onyx spirals.

Gently, I climb higher, and Cairn must finally realize what I'm going to do, because his gaze darts down, and he wets his lips in preparation.

Easing my knees along either side of his head, I grip him by the horns, hear him take a shuddering breath, and then lower my pussy onto his face.

His tongue is hot and wet and—

"Fuck," I groan out almost immediately, gripping his horns as his hands come up to wrap around my thighs.

Tightening his hold on me, he pulls my weight down, crushing me against his lips. As he drags his tongue over my clit, making me start to shake, I start gliding my hands along his horns, lingering as I get closer to their base. And with each thrust of my pussy against his mouth, we *both* moan.

Cairn sucks my clit into his hot mouth, making me gasp. Then his tongue finds my slit, and he pushes inside me.

And even his *tongue* is huge. Every part of this man feels like it was built to pleasure a woman.

How lucky am I to be the one in his bed?

Using his horns for stability, I rise onto my knees, then sink back down, forcing his tongue deeper inside me. At the same time, his fingers tighten on my thighs. They press into my flesh, and though I'm sure I'll have purple-and-blue bruises tomorrow, I like the ache of pain and feel myself get wetter each time I slam down onto his face.

My low belly is tensing, an orgasm building.

Not yet.

I want to ride this wave as long as I can before it crashes onto shore, leaving me spent and gasping.

So this time when I rise up off of Cairn's face, I look down at him between my knees and say, "I want you to fuck me now."

And he completely surprises me when he doesn't argue, instead just giving me a nod. "Flip over. Lie down."

I release his horns and carefully ease around them, collapsing onto the soft blankets and pillows. The curtains are still open, letting the thin gray sunlight illuminate the room. As Cairn sits up and carefully removes his sweater, the movement sends a smattering of dust motes floating through the beams of light, like every brush of his hand might scatter the stars in the sky.

I can't believe I just thought that. A little smile pulls on my lips. *I've totally fallen for this guy.*

Now completely and beautifully naked, Cairn turns to regard me. The muscles in his chest and shoulders coil as he crawls across the bed and positions himself atop me. With one hand, he reaches down and takes hold of the hem of my sweater dress, and I wiggle out of it, helping him to pull it over my head. The heavy fabric falls onto the floor with a thump, and my nipples pucker under Cairn's intense gaze.

"We're still going to take this slow," he says, his voice more a rumble than it is words.

I nod. "Okay."

Cairn looks nervous—more nervous than I feel.

So, as he positions his gleaming red head at my slick entrance, my knees spread wide to accommodate his broad frame, I whisper, "I trust you."

He pauses for a moment, his eyes catching mine.

And then he starts to push.

CHAPTER 45
CAIRN

I KNEW SHE'D BE TIGHT, BUT I HAD NO IDEA SHE'D be *this* tight.

As I start to push against her, Lyra catches her breath, and a delicate furrow forms in her brow.

"Tell me if—" I start to say, but then Lyra reaches up and places her fingers over my lips, silencing me.

"I know," she whispers. Her crimson eyes glitter in the gray sunlight slipping through my bedroom window. "Just kiss me."

She reaches up to wrap her arms around my neck, then pulls me down on top of her—though I have to hold my weight up on my forearms so I don't crush her body beneath me. Her lips find mine, hungry and demanding. I tangle my fingers in the hair at the nape of her neck, then turn her head to one side so I can press kisses along her jaw and down her throat. I nibble her soft skin, then trace my tongue across it.

And around the head of my cock, she gets wetter, allowing me to slide inside her just a fraction. Her breath hitches again, but she doesn't tell me to stop. And I know it'll upset her if I keep asking every five seconds if she's okay, so instead, I keep kissing her, moving my mouth to her collarbone now and tracing my lips along it.

Lyra wraps her legs around my waist, locking her ankles together. I shift my hips and pull out of her, then push in again, and her pussy accepts me with more willingness this time.

I'm a whole *inch* inside her.

This is going to take a while. But I'm not in any rush. I want to do this slowly, want to be delicate with her.

Still putting pressure on her, I pull back a bit to look into her eyes.

"What is it?" she whispers.

I use one hand to brush a curl from her freckled cheek. "I just . . ." The words get caught in my throat. I want to say them, but my fear is fighting to keep the words inside lest the truth come back to hurt me.

But I don't want to keep being afraid. I want to be brave. And I want Lyra to know how much she means to me.

"I just . . . care about you." My brows pull together a bit. "A lot."

Lyra's mouth quirks into a side smile. Does she know what I'm actually trying to say?

Her fingers find my cheek, and her skin is hot as she cups my face in her palm. "I care about you too. A *lot* a lot."

I think she understands, if the glimmer in her eyes is any indication.

With a small chuckle, I turn my face to kiss her palm. At

the same time, I slide a bit deeper into her, and Lyra lets out a small hiss.

Before I can say anything, she whispers, "I'm okay. Keep going." And her ankles tighten around my back once more.

So I keep going. I kiss and lick and suck her neck, her pale small breasts, the perfect divot at the base of her throat. She closes her eyes, allowing me to lavish her, to taste her, to try to soothe the discomfort she must be feeling. And though the sun is already changing position outside my window, casting its sunbeams in a different angle through the glass, I still don't rush.

I'm not sure how much time it takes, but my entire head is inside her now, and I'm just deep enough to start slowly, gently thrusting in and out. At first, I feel her pussy tighten up even more around me, her body coiling with the pain of stretching to accommodate my girth. So I move slower. And after a short while, her muscles relax again, the crinkle in her brow softening, and I'm able to slide a bit deeper.

With each slow thrust, my balls sway, thumping against her ass cheeks with a steady rhythm. One agonizing centimeter at a time, I sink a bit farther inside her. She has to tell me to pause at one point, to allow her tight muscles to relax around me once more, then gives me the okay to keep going.

And when I can't go any deeper, when her pussy has taken as much of my cock as it can hold, I smile at her.

"You're full," I say.

She lets out a tiny breathy laugh, and her words come out in a whisper. "I can tell."

She's taken about half of my length, and she's stretched so tight around my cock that I could probably get off on the squeeze alone. But I don't allow myself to.

I focus on her, gliding slowly in and out, pausing when her brow crinkles in pain. And after some minutes, the wincing gives way to sighing, and her body softens beneath mine, her pussy relaxing enough to let me truly fuck her—albeit gently. This is our first time, after all.

I tangle my fingers in her hair again, and she gets wetter as I start to pump her with a steady rhythm. My balls hit her harder now, and if her panted breaths are any indication, she likes the feel and the sound of it just as much as I do.

She tugs my head down with a demanding hand, crushing my lips to hers like I'm the air she needs to breathe. And though it terrifies me, I can finally admit that she's the same to me. I need her in my life, need to follow this winding unknown path for as long as my hooves will carry me, even if I don't yet know what lies at the end.

For Lyra, I will be brave.

She moans against my mouth, her pussy sucking at my cock, trying to milk out the seed I've been saving up for her. But I grit my teeth and hold myself back.

I want to get her off first. Always.

So I shift my weight onto one elbow, and without breaking our kiss or ceasing my deliciously slow thrusting, I reach down between our sweat-slick bodies to find her swollen clit. When I touch it, she gasps, her body jerking beneath mine. Now she's the one to break the kiss, arching her back and tipping her head on the pillow, eyes closed and brows pulled together.

Her body radiates heat as I stroke and rub her, filling her with my cock all the while. She drops her legs from where they were wrapped around my back, letting her knees fall open, like she's experiencing such pleasure that she can't even hold her muscles firm anymore.

Good. This is the kind of pleasure I want to heap on her. I want her so lost in ecstasy that she can scarcely remember her own name.

Like the afternoon I pleasured her on the rug before the fire, a magical shimmer of red and orange dances across her skin, and I smile.

Her pussy flutters around me, squeezing so tight I almost lose hold of myself, needing to grit my teeth harder and count backward from ten to keep myself from dumping my load inside her. I move my fingers slower now, touching her clit with a featherlight touch, drawing her pleasure out one brush of my fingertips at a time.

Lyra catches her breath, her whole body going taut.

And I watch her face as she cums around me. Her body trembles as her walls pulsate around my cock, sucking on it. She gets so wet I can fuck her with ease now. And before her orgasm can reach its peak, I shift atop her again, using one arm to lift her hips off the bed, angling her so I can slide as deep as she'll take me.

Still, I watch her. With each thrust and each slap of my balls against her ass, I study her face, the way her lips are open with a moan, the thrumming of the veins along either side of her neck. Her fingers are tangled in my blankets now, messy red curls draped across my cotton pillowcase.

Then she opens her eyes.

And the moment she meets my gaze, I'm done for. I can't hold back any longer.

I pull my cock out of her, and with a bellow I try and fail to contain, I dump everything I have onto her beautiful naked body. My cum spews in ropes from my tip, painting her as she pants beneath me, eyes wide as I tug my shaft, draining every drop I've saved up for her over these many days we've been away from each other.

And when I'm done, she's covered in sweat and cum, and so are my blankets. Which means I'll have to do the laundry today. But first . . .

I lean over Lyra again, capturing her lips, kissing them softly, relishing the taste. Then I kiss her cheeks, her forehead, each eyelid. "You," I whisper as I nuzzle my face into the side of her neck, "are pure magic, Lyra Wilder."

She laughs, though the sound is tired, drained of energy. I can tell she's completely spent.

So I ease myself off of her and the bed, then scoop her into my arms, cradling her body against mine. She wraps one arm around my neck, her eyes flicking up to meet my gaze.

"Where are we going?" she whispers.

"I'm going to give you a bath," I say, already moving around the foot of the bed and crossing the room toward the washroom. "Then I'm going to feed you. And then we can do whatever you want."

Her eyes flash with a hint of mischief. "So . . . we can do *that* again?"

I rumble out a laugh. "Anything but that. You'll need time to heal."

She pouts but doesn't argue.

With that, I carry my little fire witch into the washroom, where I intend to wash and kiss and worship every inch of her skin.

And I know in my heart that I will do everything in my power not to ever let Lyra Wilder go again.

CHAPTER 46
LYRA

I STAY WITH CAIRN FOR THE REST OF THE YULETIDE holiday, helping him pack up everything he owns into wooden boxes and big, solid trunks—which I have no hope in the world of being able to move, heavy as they are. At night, he makes us meals that put even the castle chefs to shame: chunky potato soup with crunchy rustic bread, vegetable stew with carrots he sends me to the garden to fetch from his cold frames, fire-baked butternut squash, and, of course, my favorite: vanilla-dandelion lattes.

"I like him," Juniper says to me the evening before Cairn leaves for the Columbine Conservatory. He's sitting in his armchair, a book about fungi (yes, *fungi*) propped open in his lap. But he fell asleep half an hour ago and has been breathing deeply ever since, head tipped back, eyes softly closed, chest rising and falling rhythmically. I'm sitting cross-legged on a blanket in front of the fire, practicing my elemental magic—letting flames flicker across my palm, then calling on a fine mist to douse them before sending a warm breeze dancing through the small sitting room.

This coming semester, I want to do better. I want to show my professors how important my education is to me, and I want Headmistress Moonhart to see how hard I'm trying and how much I appreciate her giving me the chance to fix the mistakes I've made. I don't just want to pass my classes—I want to excel at them, like Poppy.

Well, I'll never be as studious and smart as her, but I can still do my best.

Juniper is lying on the blanket beside me, her belly round and full after our big meal of tomato soup and fluffy rolls. I pull my gaze away from Cairn and meet Juniper's steady gaze. "I do too . . ." I whisper, keeping my voice down so as not to wake him.

Honestly, I *more* than like him. Every time I look at him, a warm feeling radiates through my chest, and I've started to feel like no matter what happens, if I have Cairn by my side, nothing can be *that* bad. It gives me an odd sense of safety and calm, something I've never felt before, despite Papa and my roommates and all the people in my life who care about me.

The feelings I have toward Cairn are just . . . different. In a good way.

Juniper stretches, then climbs up onto my knee and sits back on her hind legs, twitching her whiskers. "It's going to be okay, you know."

My brow furrows a bit. "What is?"

Juniper tips her head toward Cairn. "Him leaving."

Her words make my stomach pinch. But I take a deep breath and let it out slowly, then offer Juniper a small smile. "I know. I'm still going to miss him though."

I've been dreading him leaving, trying to cherish every moment we have together. And these past few days, I've felt so at home.

Now he's going to leave, but I'm going to be strong, and I'm going to remind myself that him leaving is not the same as him *abandoning* me. He's not my mother. But he is helping me heal from the hurt she caused me—or is at least providing me a place where I can do that on my own.

"He's going to miss you too. But I'll always be here with you." Juniper nuzzles her head against my hand, and I uncurl my fingers to scratch her gently beneath the chin. She looks up at me and twitches her whiskers again. "Even if I can't make lattes."

Her words make me laugh, and Cairn stirs awake. He blinks his eyes sleepily, then reaches his arms up over his head and yawns.

"Oops," Juniper says. She hops off my lap, then finds a puddle in the blanket that she can burrow into.

While she does that, I push to my feet, which are clad in a heavy pair of winter socks, and pad across the room to Cairn. He smiles up at me as I take the book from his lap and set it on the side table. Then I sink onto his lap, his arms coming around my waist as I wiggle myself into the warmth and security of his firm chest.

"How long was I asleep?" he asks, voice husky from just waking up.

I shrug softly. "Less than an hour. Not long."

His fingers trace patterns on my thigh where it's draped over his legs, and I let my eyes close, listening to the beating of his heart.

"Sorry. I didn't mean to fall asleep on you."

"It's okay." I cuddle closer to him. "You've got a big day tomorrow. You need your sleep."

He tenses up a bit, his fingers ceasing their movements on my thigh. "Lyra," he says after a long moment, "are you really okay with this? With me leaving?"

I sit up slowly so I can look into this dark eyes, where the fire behind me is reflected. "I am. I'm more than okay with it." Reaching out, I trail my fingertips across his warm brown skin, trace the planes of his cheekbones and the cut of his jaw. "I'm excited for you. And besides"—a smile curls across my mouth—"I have every intention of coming to visit."

Now it's his turn to smile. "How about for Ostara?"

Ostara is roughly three months away, a celebration of the spring equinox. In a way, that feels like a lifetime, but I know I'll have my hands full with my studies, and Cairn will need time to settle into his new home and job without me underfoot, distracting him and trying to constantly pull him into bed with me.

After our first time together, I was sore for days, but I'm feeling better now, and as I trail my fingers down his neck and across his chest, low heat begins to build in my belly.

"Ostara sounds good," I whisper. Leaning forward, I brush my lips softly against his, and beneath me, I feel his cock stir. "I'll miss you, you know."

His voice is a deep rumble as he says, "What will you miss?"

A smile tugs on my lips. "Your lattes, definitely."

He gifts me with a laugh, and the sound is rich and sweet. "That's all, huh?"

"No." I reach down beneath our bodies to touch his hardening shaft through the fabric of his trousers. "I'll miss other parts of you as well."

One of his brows arches in the corner. "Well, we *do* have one more night together . . ." Then his gaze flickers with concern. "If you're feeling okay, I mean."

Nodding, I wrap my arms around his neck, then press kisses along the column of his throat, his beard tickling my skin. "I am."

I love how careful he is with me. He always puts my needs before his own, is never selfish or demanding or impatient with me. And that just makes me want to give him more, to give him everything I have.

"Take me to bed," I say, my breath causing goose bumps to rise along his neck.

I don't have to tell him twice.

With ease, he wraps one arm around my back and one beneath my knees, then stands from his armchair, holding me like I weigh nothing in his arms.

"If my witch commands," he says.

"I do!"

Chuckling again, he starts toward the bedroom, and I tell myself to enjoy every one of these last few moments I have with him, because when the sun rises tomorrow morning, he'll be gone.

CHAPTER 47
CAIRN

HAT'S THE LAST OF THEM," I SAY AFTER HEFT-ing a heavy trunk into the back of the wagon that's come to take me to Columbine Conservatory. They sent it for me, and it's nice—a big covered thing that'll keep all my belongings dry, with hardy wheels that aren't impeded by the fresh snow that fell overnight.

I turn, and Lyra is standing there, Juniper on her shoulder. Snow drifts down from the gray-blue sky, catching in her curls and crimson lashes.

My heart pangs for her, a mix of pain and longing and . . . maybe something more.

Her gaze flicks past me, to the wagon and the waiting driver, who's bundled up against the cold and smoking a sweet-scented pipe while patiently waiting for me.

"Well," she says, "I guess this is it."

"I guess so . . ."

The snow falls silently, turning the world quiet.

It's now or never, I suppose.

I reach into the inner pocket of my heavy cloak and pull out a letter. I wrote it last night, after Lyra fell asleep. Now, I hold it out to her with some hesitation.

"What's this?" She tips her head and takes it from me.

And now that it's in her possession instead of mine, there will be no taking back what I said in the letter, no undoing it. It's done.

"A letter," I say. "But . . . wait until I'm gone to read it." My face tingles with a bit of warmth, and I hope she can't see it against my brown cheeks. I flick my tail and shift my weight in the snow.

Lyra arches a brow at me, and her lips pull up on one side. "All right." She slides it into her own pocket, then meets my eyes again. And a breath later, she's closing the short distance between us and wrapping her arms around my waist, burying her face against my chest. Even Juniper looks up at me with what I want to think is a touch of sadness in her glassy eyes.

"Take care of yourself," she says. "And don't do anything I wouldn't do."

That makes me laugh, and I reach down to embrace her, careful not to squish Juniper where she's still perched on Lyra's shoulder. "That won't be a problem."

Lyra pulls back just far enough to look into my eyes.

Now that I'm no longer an employee here, it doesn't matter who sees me with Lyra. So, without caring about the driver behind us, I cup Lyra's freckled cheeks in my palms and bend to press a kiss to her lips. They're a bit cold from the snow, but they warm beneath my mouth, and I try to pour all my thoughts and feelings into this one kiss. And I think it works, because when I pull away, tears are gathering along Lyra's lower eyelids, shining like little crystals in the winter sunlight.

I use my thumbs to brush the moisture away. "I'll see you for Ostara," I say softly. Then my lips tug up. "Don't forget about me in the meantime."

She shakes her head and lets out a small laugh. "Impossible."

Our breath mingles in the cold air, steaming around our lips in the space between us.

Then I hear a soft sound, a pattering of paws across frozen snow.

Straightening, I turn to look toward the Mistwood.

And crossing the pristine white blanket of snow is the red fox I nursed back to health earlier this year. He's headed right toward me, loping along at a smooth stride, no sign of the injury that once plagued him.

I take one step toward him, my hooves sinking deep into the snow, and then kneel to his level.

The fox approaches me slowly, something held in his mouth.

"What do you have there?" I ask, holding out my hand.

He drops something into my palm, and when I hold it up, I see it's a chunk of crystal quartz. The facets reflect the light, sparkling brilliantly.

"This is a lovely gift," I say, focusing my attention on the fox again. "Thank you, my friend." I hold out my free hand, and the fox allows me to stroke his fur and scratch him behind one ear.

Then he pulls away, flicks his ears at me, and lopes right back into the trees, disappearing from view as quickly as he came.

"What did he give you?" Lyra asks.

I push to my hooves, then hold the quartz out for Lyra to see. Her brows shoot up, and her lips pull into a smile.

"It's beautiful. And you know, a crystal gifted is ten times more powerful than a crystal that's bought."

I arch my brow. "I've never heard that before."

Lyra shrugs, and Juniper digs her claws into Lyra's cloak a bit deeper to avoid being unseated. "I'm a witch. I know these things."

I laugh, breath steaming out around my mouth in big white-gray puffs. "I suppose I shouldn't question you, then."

She gives a quick shake of her head. "No, you shouldn't." Then the joy drifts from her eyes, and she says softly, "Will you write? Once you're settled?"

With a nod, I reach out and squeeze her mittened hand. "Of course I will. And will you write back?"

Her lips quirk, just slightly. "If I have time."

"Good. Keep yourself busy. And *don't* burn Professor Fleur's greenhouse down this semester, all right?"

Lyra groans. "Don't remind me. I've still got making up to do for that."

"Better late than never."

"Mm." Her eyes meet mine again, and I know this is it. We have to say goodbye.

Even if I really don't want to.

"Ostara," Lyra says.

"Ostara," I repeat.

And then I kiss her one more time, trying to chisel the taste of her mouth into my memory. Stepping up into the wagon is one of the hardest things I've ever done, and staying in the wagon while it starts to roll away, leaving Lyra standing there in the snow, makes me feel sick.

Ostara, I think. *I'll see you again soon, my little fire witch.*

CHAPTER 48
LYRA

I HOLD MY TEARS AT BAY UNTIL ALL THAT'S LEFT of the wagon is tracks through the snow. Now Cairn's hut is empty save for the heavy pieces of furniture he couldn't take with him, and when I step into the sitting room and see the empty walls and bookshelves, it makes me finally break down.

Juniper sits with me while I cry on the floor in front of the crackling fire, nuzzling her wet nose into my cheek and neck. She doesn't say anything, doesn't try to comfort me with false platitudes. There's nothing she can say now that would comfort me. At least, until she crawls into my lap and nibbles the pocket of my cloak.

"Ready to read his letter?"

The letter. I'd almost forgotten.

I wipe my eyes with my sleeve, then reach into the deep pocket and slowly withdraw the letter Cairn gave me. He wrote my name on the front, in penmanship that's neither tidy nor messy, but somewhere in the middle. I trace my fingertips across the ink, smiling as I imagine him sitting at the table in the kitchen, using his quill to shape the letters that make up my name.

After spending much too long staring at the envelope, I finally get up the nerve to open it. Carefully, I swipe my finger under the wax seal, making sure not to rip the envelope or the letter inside. Juniper scurries onto my knee impatiently, pressing up onto her back legs like she's trying to read it before I can even get it out of the envelope.

With trembling fingers, I remove the letter from the sleeve and unfold it. Cairn's handwriting stares back at me. My stomach clenches in anticipation. Then I start to read.

> Dearest Lyra,
>
> It's the night before I leave, and you're asleep in my bed right now, snoring so loudly I can hear you from where I'm sitting at the kitchen table.

My brows immediately tug together. "I don't snore," I grumble.

"Yes, you do. And what's it say?" Juniper asks, reaching her paws out for it.

But I hold it up out of her reach. "Hang on. I'm not done."

> Yes, you do snore. I'd know.
> But jokes aside . . . I'm going to miss you, Lyra. When the headmistress first came to me to ask if I'd agree to facilitating your community service, I wasn't happy about it. Well,

I was pissed, to be perfectly honest. I thought you were going to be a nuisance. And in some ways, you were. But in more ways, you were exactly what I needed. I just didn't know it at the time.

I put down roots at Coven Crest, and I'll admit that I've been afraid of moving again, of trying something new for fear it may not work out. And I'm afraid even now, as I sit here the night before I depart. I'm afraid I won't be a good fit, or that they'll determine they don't want me after all, or that I'll arrive and they'll realize they made a mistake and send me on my way.

But because of you, I'm going to push through the fear, and I'm going to try something new.

You made me want to uproot myself, made me want to grow leaves instead of burrowing deeper into the earth. And I'll be forever grateful to you for that. If you hadn't come storming into my life, with your fire and your temper and those beautiful freckles, I'm not sure I'd have even been brave enough to consider this position, let alone pack up my entire life and leave the place I call home.

To leave you, Lyra.

It hurts just inking it onto this page.

But I don't want to give up. I want to fight for this. For you. And perhaps I've got my horns in the clouds, but I think this could be a good thing for us, because we both know that had I stayed at Coven Crest, things would've gone wrong eventually. The headmistress already knew about us, and she wouldn't have allowed it. But this way, we're free to be together - really together - without sneaking around or hiding (as fun as that was). And I want to know you in all the ways there are to know someone. I want to know everything about you.

But I'm not in any rush. I'm grateful for every moment I get to spend with you.

Every. Single. One.

So, I guess there's just one last thing I want to say. I'm scared to say it, but I feel I have to get it off my chest, so here goes.

I'm falling in love with you, Lyra Wilder. You're wild and fiery and so beautiful it hurts - really, it does. Right in the middle of my ribs. And you might not feel the same way back, but I want you to know the truth. And that no matter the miles separating us, you are always, always on my mind. That's not going to change.

Below, you'll find a moonflower seed. It's from the plant at the edge of the woods, the one we watched bloom together that night beneath the stars. I hope you'll plant it, and when it blooms, perhaps you'll think of me, and I won't feel so far away.

I'll see you on Ostara, little flame.

Please try not to burn anything down in the meantime.

With love,
Cairn

By the time I reach the end of the letter, more tears are tracking down my cheeks. One plops onto the parchment, and I hurriedly hold the paper away so I won't ruin it.

I want to keep this letter forever. I want to encase it in shatterproof glass and hang it on my wall, or sleep with it beneath my pillow.

At the bottom of the letter, there's a little folded-up piece of paper tied with twine and affixed to the parchment so it won't fall off.

"Will you snip this for me?" I ask Juniper.

She uses her teeth to cut clean through the twine, and the little paper bundle comes free. I set the letter down for Juniper to read and carefully unfold the paper. Sure enough, one precious moonflower seed waits for me inside. It's about the size of my pinky nail, and I clutch it in my hand like it's the most valuable thing in the world.

"Lyra," Juniper whispers, looking up from the letter to meet my eyes. "Do you feel the same? About Cairn?"

My lips are starting to tremble, and I know if I speak, I'll just start blubbering again, washing Juniper away with my tears. So instead, I nod. I nod so hard I make myself dizzy.

I'm absolutely, without a shred of a doubt, falling in love with Cairn Axton.

And there's nothing anyone can do about it.

CHAPTER 49
LYRA

UR SPRING SEMESTER STARTS TOMOR-
row, and the campus is already thrumming
with activity. I have to dodge students and
spirit companions as I walk the candlelit corridors, and everywhere I go, I hear laughter
and excited voices.

There's something about a new semester that feels so
promising, like a fresh canvas just ready and waiting to be
painted.

But before I can paint mine, there's something I need to
do. It's something I've needed to do for far too long.

I make my way out the side entrance into the gardens.
The weather deities have blessed us with a beautiful January
day, though it's still so cold that I have to pull my thick cloak
tighter around my body to ward off the chill despite the heat
from my fire magic.

The grounds are crunchy with snow—I guess the headmistress hasn't found a replacement for Cairn just yet—as

I cross the garden and pass the raised beds still frozen and dormant. When I reach the big greenhouse, with light reflecting off the glass, I pause and take a steadying breath.

I have to do this. It's the right thing to do.

Inside my cloak pocket, Juniper says, "I'm proud of you."

I stroke a finger over her warm fur, then take a breath and say, "Well, better get it over with."

Yanking open the door, I'm immediately bathed in warm air. The greenhouse is pleasant—so pleasant that I even consider taking my cloak off. And stooped over a raised bed two rows over is Professor Fleur.

She's muttering something to herself as she presses seeds delicately into the soil, giving them an early start to the growing season. She twists her wrist, and a little sprinkle of water falls on each newly planted seed. Her eyes flick up to meet mine as I approach.

And a storm cloud rolls through her gaze.

Yeah, I expected that.

"Miss Wilder." Professor Fleur straightens up and closes her fingers around the tiny seeds like she's afraid I might set fire to them, then dance on their ashes while cackling maniacally. Her pale green hair is twisted into a chignon at the base of her neck, and her green eyes narrow suspiciously at me.

Okay, fair.

"What can I do for you?" she asks, voice about as frigid as the weather outside the greenhouse.

Last semester, Professor Fleur could hardly bring herself to speak to me after I burned down her precious midnight lotus flowers, and I likewise could hardly bring myself to speak to her, though for me it was a matter of shame, and for her it was barely contained rage.

Even now, she looks like she wants to prick me with thorns, which I'm sure she's more than capable of with her earth magic.

"Nothing," I say, closing my fingers into fists at my sides, trying to brace myself. "I just want—no, *need*—to apologize for last semester."

Professor Fleur's brows rise, and some of the anger flickers from her eyes. "What?"

"I should have said it months ago." I hold her gaze. "I'm sorry for ruining your flowers. I know how much they meant to you. It was an accident, but that doesn't excuse what I did, and it especially doesn't excuse me from giving you a proper apology. I'm so sorry, Professor. If there's anything I can do to make up for it, I absolutely will."

"No." She holds up her free hand, the one not clinging to the seeds. "That won't be necessary."

I think what she *means* to say is that she doesn't want me any closer to the greenhouses than is strictly necessary. And I'm not taking any classes with her this semester, so she'll finally be free of me.

"But," she continues, lowering her hand and letting out a slow breath, "I appreciate the apology. I know it was an accident, Miss Wilder, and I hear you've been working hard since then to better control your magic. How is it coming along?"

I allow a small smile to pull on my lips. "It's . . . still difficult sometimes. But I feel better. Stronger." I picture Cairn and his steady patience, imagine roots curling down from the bottoms of my feet and into the earth, helping me to ground myself and my emotions. "At the very least, I'm learning the skills I need to control my emotions. And I've not burned anything down in . . ." Tapping my chin, I tip my head dramatically to one side. "Three days?"

Professor Fleur's eyes widen, and I quickly let out a laugh. "Kidding. I promise."

This time, I get her to smile. A little bit. "Well, thank you for coming, Lyra. It means a lot to me." She shifts her weight, and her gaze flicks toward the raised bed.

I can tell she's anxious to get back to work.

"I'll get out of your hair," I say, taking a step back. "But really, if you ever need anything, you know where to find me."

"The headmistress's office?" Professor Fleur asks with an arched eyebrow.

I blink at her, then realize there's a smirk trying to tug one side of her mouth up.

"I didn't know you could joke like that, Professor," I say as I walk backward toward the door. "It suits you."

She rolls her eyes and gives me a real smile then. "Goodbye, Miss Wilder."

I step out of the greenhouse and into the cold. As the door closes behind me, Juniper wriggles up to the top of my pocket.

"That went well," she says.

"Yeah. Better than expected."

"Since you're having such good luck, maybe we should stop by the headmistress's office."

My gaze cuts down to her. "And why would we want to do that?"

"It'll show her your initiative. Better than hiding out and waiting for her to call on you."

Breath steams around my mouth as I blow out a big sigh. "You've got a point." I flick my gaze up to the castle, wishing I could climb the stairs to the north tower and cuddle up in front of the fire for the rest of the day.

But Juniper's right. And though my feet are reluctant, I force them to carry me into the castle and straight to Headmistress Moonhart's office.

"COME IN," THE HEADMISTRESS CALLS.

I have my hand held aloft, knuckles poised and ready, but I've not yet knocked.

"Witchcraft," Juniper whispers from my pocket.

I smirk for a second, then wipe it away before I grab the door handle and enter the office.

Unlike the chilly corridors, the headmistress's office is warm. It smells like sage and peppermint tea, and apart from the towers of papers sitting on the desk, the room is impeccably clean.

Barron sits on his perch, and he blinks his big yellow eyes as I close the door behind me.

I've always found his gaze unsettling. Probably because he's the headmistress's eyes and ears around campus.

"Miss Wilder," Headmistress Moonhart says. She sits back from her desk and removes the spectacles from her nose, letting them dangle from the beaded chain around her neck. "Please, sit. To what do I owe the pleasure?"

I sink into the chair in front of her desk—the very one I sat in last semester when she assigned me community service with Cairn. Everything feels so different now compared to then.

"Well," I say slowly, trying to get my thoughts in order, "last semester, you let me take a hiatus from my community service. Which I *really* appreciated, by the way."

Her lips quirk up on one side, but she says nothing.

"And I suppose I just wanted to get a jump on things. Do you know yet what my community service will be for this semester?"

"Classes haven't even started yet," the headmistress says, arching one icy brow at me. "Yet you're already here, eager to be of service?"

There's a hint of amusement in her voice, but I stay focused. "Yes."

"Hmm." She reaches for her cup of tea and gives it a small sip, then casts her gaze out one of her office windows. The sun is still shining, and a few rivulets of snowmelt run down the glass panes. It feels like a lifetime that she spends staring out the window before she turns back to me. "I'll admit, I've not yet determined who best to continue your community service, with Mr. Axton gone . . ."

I think she's watching me for a reaction to his name, and I strive not to give one, though my heart squeezes at the reminder of his absence. When I say nothing, she continues.

"So for now, I'd like you to focus on your studies and on controlling that temper. I don't want to hear any complaints from your professors, or you'll be right back in that chair. Do I make myself quite clear?"

She's giving me a break from community service? Maybe even for good? I'm so glad Juniper encouraged me to come up here. I'll have to take her to a café as a thank-you.

"Quite, Headmistress." I'm fighting hard not to smile.

"Good. Now, if you'll excuse me, I have"—her pale gaze flicks to the piles of papers on her desk—"a significant amount of paperwork to do, and I'd like to be done here before I die."

At her unexpected joke, I let out a laugh. The headmistress smiles in return, then takes another sip of tea and shoos me toward the door with a waggle of her jeweled fingers.

She doesn't have to tell me twice.

I'm across the room and about to open the door when the headmistress says, "And the next time you speak with Cairn, please send my regards. I'd like to know how he's settling in."

Slowly, I glance back over my shoulder, and the headmistress is giving me that knowing pointed-eyebrow look again.

"I can do that," I say softly.

Headmistress Moonhart smiles.

Then I get the hell out of there before she can change her mind.

EPILOGUE
CAIRN

Two Months Later

THE DAYS HAVE BEEN RAINY AND COLD, AND my hooves are caked in mud more often than not. But today, the sky is a clear blue, with no clouds to be seen.

It's going to be a perfect spring day.

I've settled into my new position here at the Columbine Conservatory—at least, as much as is possible after only a few months. I'm not the type of person who adjusts easily to new situations, so it's taken me some time to find my place here, but everyone has been warm and welcoming, and though the work is demanding—I'm outdoors sunup to sundown most days of the week—I thrive on it.

Today, I'm planting a new field of potatoes for the community garden. I created the hills and trenches yesterday, and now I'm lugging around bucketfuls of potatoes, bending to press them six inches into the dirt, then patting soil back around them gently.

The field is quiet save for the calling of crows in the nearby trees and the whisper of the spring breeze, so when I hear footsteps in the distance, it catches my attention.

I plant another potato, tuck it into the soil so it'll stay warm, then straighten and lift one hand to shield my eyes against the morning sun.

There's a figure walking toward me, but the sun is at their back, casting them in shadow.

Milo, maybe? He always makes a point to come say hello whenever he sees me working the fields or tidying the orchards, and surprisingly, I've appreciated the company. But this figure doesn't have his lanky stride, and they're not nearly tall enough to be Milo.

So, who is it?

I've met most—if not all—of the other employees here, but we've got lots of volunteers too, so there are always unfamiliar faces around. And though I'm not *really* in the mood to talk to someone new, I draw myself up and prepare a smile.

But as the figure moves closer, coming into focus, the smile is overtaken by surprise. My heart leaps into my throat, and I drop the basket of potatoes I'm carrying, letting it fall to the rich dark soil with a heavy thump.

Then my hooves are moving before I can stay them. And the closer I get to the little figure, the harder my heart beats in my chest.

Neither of us gets a word out before I'm taking her by the hips and lifting her up, twirling her around in the tilled potato field and making her laugh so loud that the crows start up another ruckus. She's wearing a pack on her back, and her hair is pulled into a messy braid, but a few curls have already escaped, and they frame her freckled cheeks as I set her on her feet and she tips her head back to look at me.

"Wh-what are you doing here?" I ask. "Ostara isn't for another few days."

Lyra shrugs and tips her head at me. "We're on break at Coven Crest, so I thought I'd surprise you." Her smile turns a bit shy. "I hope that's okay . . ."

"Okay?" A laugh slips out of me. Then I take her face in my hands and press a kiss to her mouth. It's been much too long since I last felt her lips on mine, and I linger until I need to draw a breath. When I pull back, I say softly, "It's more than okay."

We've been writing letters since the day I left the academy; I have a pile of correspondence from Lyra tucked away into the drawer in my nightstand. The conservatory set me up with a small dwelling a short walk away from the grounds, and at night, when I'm feeling alone or am struggling to sleep, I light a candle and read Lyra's letters, comfort myself with her quips about her classes and jokes about the professors.

But now here she is, in the flesh. I can see her, smell her, *feel* her.

With a sigh, I lean down and press a kiss to the top of her head, breathing in the slight scent of cinnamon that's clinging to her hair.

Lyra reaches up, and her fingers brush the quartz crystal dangling from a cord around my neck.

"Is this from the fox?" she asks.

I nod. "I hear a crystal gifted is stronger than a crystal bought."

She smiles. "Who told you a silly thing like that?"

Now it's my turn to shrug. "Some crazy fire witch I know."

"Crazy?" she asks, feigning shock. "I'm not the one who finds books on *fungi* fascinating."

The laughter she draws out of me is true and deep. "Fungi *is* fascinating. Perhaps I'll read you a chapter or two."

"Or perhaps," she says, reaching up again, this time to run her fingers over my beard, "we can do something *else* together."

My cheeks flare with heat, and I'm grateful no one else is out here working the field with me.

Lyra smiles at my expense, then pushes up onto her toes, and I bend so she can press a kiss to my cheek.

"What's in the bag?" I ask her.

"Oh, you know." She shrugs out of the pack and lets it fall to the dirt, then rolls her shoulders out. "A few days' worth of clothes, shoes, whatever else I might need."

A smile threatens to pull on my mouth. "A few days' worth of clothes?" One of my brows arches up. "So . . . you're staying?"

"Of course I am." Lyra plants her hands on her hips and tips her head at me. Just then, Juniper pops her head out of the pocket of Lyra's sweater and blinks her glassy eyes at me. "You think I came all this way just to turn back around? Nope. You're stuck with me. At least until my classes start up again."

Now the smile is impossible to hold back. I wouldn't want to be stuck with anyone else. Just her. Lyra Wilder, my little flame.

"Well then"—I pick up her pack and am surprised by its weight—"I suppose we should get you settled in."

Lyra casts a glance toward my discarded basket of potatoes. "What about your work?"

"Oh, we'll be back. Did you bring those gloves I bought you?"

Her eyes sparkle in the morning light. "Of course I did."

"Good. Because we've got an acre of potatoes to plant."

"It's a good thing they're fireproof," she says as she reaches her arms overhead and stretches out her back.

I give her a startled look, and she laughs.

"Just kidding. I won't burn anything down. I *promise*."

With a roll of my eyes, I sling an arm around her shoulders, and she tries to loop her arm around my waist, but it doesn't quite make it all the way around.

"Hey, Cairn?" she asks as we start out of the field and onto one of the little paths that meanders through the conservatory's grounds.

"Hmm?"

She stops walking, forcing me to still my hooves and look down at her. Her eyes search mine, though for what, I'm not sure. Then her lips form the words I've secretly been aching to hear, have dreamt of her saying more times than I can count.

"I love you too."

My heart thunders so hard that my blood roars in my ears. I've thought of this moment, have fantasized about all the things I'll say, but now that I'm here, my mouth goes dry, and my tongue feels twisted into knots.

"I-I . . . Y-you . . ."

The words don't want to come out. My cheeks flame with heat again.

But Lyra is just smiling at me. She presses herself to my side, like she doesn't need me to say a thing at all. Like she knows exactly how I feel in return.

"And I love those vanilla-dandelion lattes too. So . . ." She glances up at me.

Finally, my tongue unwinds itself. I chuckle softly. "Yes, little flame, I'll make you one. I'll make you as many as you want."

She squeezes my waist as we resume walking, then says, "I knew I came here for a reason."

I roll my eyes at her and press a kiss to her head. "All about the lattes, hmm?"

"No," she says softly, casting a glance up at me. Her gaze makes me want to melt into a minotaur-size puddle. "But they're a close second."

The sun warms my face as we walk the winding path together, her boots thudding softly while my hooves thump along, and I feel, perhaps for the first time in a very long time, that everything is going to be okay. That I don't need to fear or worry or hide myself away.

That I can finally bloom.

And it's all thanks to her.

THE END

THANK YOU FOR READING!

Thank you so much for reading *A Witch and Her Minotaur*, the second book in the Coven Crest Academy series.

If you'd like to leave a review of this book (which would be *amazing!*), you can do so by scanning the QR code below. Every review helps, and I truly appreciate it! Thank you.

If you're looking for more cozy spicy romance, make sure to pick up the next book in this fantasy academia series, *A Witch and Her Orc*. You can scan the code below to grab your copy!

EMBERLY WYNDHAM is a writer based out of the snowy mountains of Colorado, where she lives with her husband and their many rescued animals.

To learn more and keep up-to-date with her new and upcoming releases, you can follow her on Instagram @emberlywyndham or sign up for her newsletter by scanning the QR code below.